HIS
ILLEGAL
SELF

HIS ILLEGAL SELF

Peter Carey

ALFRED A. KNOPF   NEW YORK   2008

THIS IS A BORZOI BOOK
PUBLISHED BY ALFRED A. KNOPF

www.aaknopf.com

Published simultaneously in Great Britain by Faber and
Faber Limited, London, and in Australia by Random
House Australia, Sydney.

Knopf, Borzoi Books, and the colophon are registered
trademarks of Random House, Inc.

Library of Congress Cataloging-in-Publication Data
Carey, Peter, date.
His illegal self / by Peter Carey. — 1st U.S. ed.
p. cm.
"This is a Borzoi Book."
ISBN 978-0-307-26372-8 (alk. paper)
1. Mothers and sons—Fiction.   2. Radicals—Fiction.
3. Queensland—Fiction.   I. Title.
PR9619.3.C36H57   2008
823'.914–dc22   2007042862

Manufactured in the United States of America
Published February 8, 2008
Second Printing, February 2008

For Bel

HIS
ILLEGAL
SELF

1

There were no photographs of the boy's father in the house upstate. He had been persona non grata since Christmas 1964, six months before the boy was born. There were plenty of pictures of his mom. There she was with short blond hair, her eyes so white against her tan. And that was her also, with black hair, not even a sister to the blonde girl, although maybe they shared a kind of bright attention.

She was an actress like her grandma, it was said. She could change herself into anyone. The boy had no reason to disbelieve this, not having seen his mother since the age of two. She was the prodigal daughter, the damaged saint, like the icon that Grandpa once brought back from Athens—shining silver, musky incense—although no one had ever told the boy how his mother smelled.

Then, when the boy was almost eight, a woman stepped out of the elevator into the apartment on East Sixty-second Street and he recognized her straightaway. No one had told him to expect it.

That was pretty typical of growing up with Grandma Selkirk. You were some kind of lovely insect, expected to know things through your feelers, by the kaleidoscope patterns in the others' eyes. No one would dream of saying, Here is your mother returned to you. Instead his grandma told him to put on his sweater. She collected her purse, found her keys and then all three of them walked down to Bloomingdale's as if it were a deli. This was normal life. Across Park, down Lex. The boy stood close beside the splendid stranger with the lumpy khaki pack strapped onto her back. That was her blood, he could hear it now, pounding in his ears. He had imagined her a wound-up spring, light, bright, blonde, like Grandma in full whir. She was completely different; she was just the same. By the time they were in Bloomingdale's she was arguing about his name.

What did you just call Che? she asked the grandma.

His name, replied Grandma Selkirk, ruffling the boy's darkening summer hair. That's what I called him. She gave the mother a bright white smile. The boy thought, Oh, oh!

It sounded like Jay, the mother said.

The grandma turned sharply to the shopgirl who was busy staring at the hippie mother.

Let me try the Artemis.

Grandma Selkirk was what they call an Upper East Side woman—cheekbones, tailored gray hair—but that was not what she called herself. I am the last bohemian, she liked to say, to the boy, particularly, meaning that no one told her what to do, at least not since Pa Selkirk had thrown the Buddha out the window and gone to live with the Poison Dwarf.

Grandpa had done a whole heap of other things besides, like giving up his board seat, like going spiritual. When Grandpa moved out, Grandma moved out too. The Park Avenue apartment was hers, always had been, but now they used it maybe once a month. Instead they spent their time on Kenoza Lake near Jeffersonville, New York, a town of 400 where "no one" lived. Grandma made raku pots and rowed a heavy clinker boat. The boy hardly saw his grandpa after that, except sometimes there were postcards with very small handwriting. Buster Selkirk could fit a whole ball game on a single card.

For these last five years it had been just Grandma and the boy together and she threaded the squirming live bait to hook the largemouth bass and, also, called him Jay instead of Che. There were no kids to play with. There were no pets because Grandma was allergic. But in fall there were Cox's pippins, wild storms, bare feet, warm mud and the crushed-glass stars spilling across the cooling sky. You can't learn these things anywhere, the grandma said. She said she planned to bring him up Victorian. It was better than "all this."

He was christened Che, right?

Grandma's wrist was pale and smooth as a flounder's belly. The sunny side of her arm was brown but she had dabbed the perfume on the white side—blue blood, that's what he thought, looking at the veins.

Christened? His father is a Jew, the grandma said. This fragrance is too old for her, she told the Bloomingdale's woman who raised a cautious eyebrow at the mother. The mother shrugged as if to say, What are you going to do? Too floral, Grandma Selkirk said without doubting she would know.

So it's Jay?

Grandma spun around and the boy's stomach gave a squishy sort of lurch. Why are you arguing with me? she whispered. Are you emotionally tone-deaf?

The salesgirl pursed her lips in violent sympathy.

Give me the Chanel, said Grandma Selkirk.

While the salesgirl wrapped the perfume, Grandma Selkirk wrote a check. Then she took her pale kid gloves from the glass countertop. The boy watched as she drew them onto each finger, thick as eel skin. He could taste it in his mouth.

You want me to call him Che in Bloomingdale's, his grandma hissed, finally presenting the gift to the mother.

Shush, the mother said.

The grandma raised her eyebrows violently.

Go with the flow, said the mother. The boy petted her on the hip and found her soft, uncorseted.

The flow? The grandma had a bright, fright smile and angry light blue eyes. Go with the *flow!*

Thank you, the girl said, for shopping at Bloomingdale's.

The grandma's attention was all on the mother. Is that what Communists believe? Che, she cried, waving her gloved hand as in charades.

I'm not a Communist. OK?

The boy wanted only peace. He followed up behind, his stomach churning.

Che, Che! Go with the flow! Look at you! Do you think you could make yourself a tiny bit more ridiculous?

The boy considered his illegal mother. He knew who she was although no one would say it outright. He knew her the way he was used to knowing everything important, from hints and whispers, by hearing someone talking on the phone, although this particular event was so much clearer, had been since the minute she blew into the apartment, the way she held him in her arms and squeezed the air from him and kissed his neck. He had thought of her so many nights and here she was, exactly the same, completely different—honey-colored skin and tangled hair in fifteen shades. She had Hindu necklaces, little silver bells around her ankles, an angel sent by God.

Grandma Selkirk plucked at the Hindu beads. What is this? This is what the working class is wearing now?

I am the working class, she said. By definition.

The boy squeezed the grandma's hand but she snatched it free. Where's his father? They keep showing his face on television. Is he going with the flow as well?

The boy burped quietly in his hand. No one could have heard him but Grandma brushed at the air, as if grabbing at a fly. I called him Jay because I was worried for you, she said at last. Maybe it should have been John Doe. God help me, she cried, and the crowds parted before her. Now I understand I was an idiot to worry.

The mother raised her eyebrows at the boy and, finally, reached to take his hand. He was pleased by how it folded around his, soothing, comfortable. She tickled his palm in secret. He smiled up. She smiled down. All around them Grandma raged.

For this, we paid for Harvard. She sighed. Some Rosenbergs.

The boy was deaf, in love.

By now they were out on Lexington Avenue and his grandma was looking for a taxi. The first cab would be theirs, always was. Except that now his hand was inside his true mother's hand and they were marsupials running down into the subway, laughing.

In Bloomingdale's everything had been so white and bright with glistening brass. Now they raced down the steps. He could have flown.

At the turnstiles she released his hand and pushed him under. She slipped off her pack. He was giddy, giggling. She was laughing too. They had entered another planet, and as they pushed down to the platform the ceiling was slimed with alien rust and the floor was flecked and speckled with black gum—so this was the real world that had been crying to him from beneath the grating up on Lex.

They ran together to the local, and his heart was pounding and his stomach was filled with bubbles like an ice-cream float. She took his hand once more and kissed it, stumbling.

The 6 train carried him through the dark, wire skeins unraveling, his entire life changing all at once. He burped again. The cars swayed and screeched, thick teams of brutal cables showing in the windowed dark. And then he was in Grand Central first time ever and they set off underground again, hand in hand, slippery together as newborn goats.

Men lived in cardboard boxes. A blind boy rattled dimes

and quarters in a tin. The S train waited, painted like a warrior, and they jumped together and the doors closed as cruel as traps, chop, chop, chop, and his face was pushed against his mother's jasmine dress. Her hand held the back of his head. He was underground, as Cameron in 5D had predicted. They will come for you, man. They'll break you out of here.

In the tunnels between Times Square and Port Authority a passing freak raised his fist. Right On! he called.

He knew you, right?

She made a face.

He's SDS?

She could not have expected that—he had been studying politics with Cameron.

PL? he asked.

She sort of laughed. Listen to you, she said. Do you know what SDS stands for?

Students for a Democratic Society, he said. PL is Progressive Labor. They're the Maoist fraction. See, you're famous. I know all about you.

I don't think so.

You're sort of like the Weathermen.

I'm what?

I'm pretty sure.

Wrong fraction, baby.

She was teasing him. She shouldn't. He had thought about her every day, forever, lying on the dock beside the lake, where she was burnished, angel sunlight. He knew his daddy was famous too, his face on television, a soldier in the fight. David has changed history.

They waited in line. There was a man with a suitcase tied with bright green rope. He had never been anyplace like this before.

Where are we going?

There was a man whose face was cut by lines like string through Grandma's beeswax. He said, This bus going to Philly, little man.

The boy did not know what Philly was.

Stay here, the mother said, and walked away. He was by himself. He did not like that. The mother was across the hallway talking to a tall thin woman with an unhappy face. He went to see what was happening and she grabbed his arm and squeezed it hard. He cried out. He did not know what he had done.

You hurt me.

Shut up, Jay. She might as well have slapped his legs. She was a stranger, with big dark eyebrows twisted across her face.

You called me Jay, he cried.

Shut up. Just don't talk.

You're not allowed to say shut up.

Her eyes got big as saucers. She dragged him from the ticket line and when she released her hold he was still mad at her. He could have run away but he followed her through a beat-up swing door and into a long passage with white cinder blocks and the smell of pee everywhere and when she came to a doorway marked FACILITY, she turned and squatted in front of him.

You've got to be a big boy, she said.

I'm only seven.

I won't call you Che. Don't you call me anything.

Don't you say shut up.

OK.

Can I call you Mom?

She paused, her mouth open, searching in his eyes for something.

You can call me Dial, she said at last, her color gone all high.

Dial?

Yes.

What sort of name is that?

It's a nickname, baby. Now come along. She held him tight against her and he once more smelled her lovely smell. He was exhausted, a little sick feeling.

What is a nickname?

A secret name people use because they like you.

I like you, Dial. Call me by my nickname too.

I like you, Jay, she said.

They bought the tickets and found the bus and soon they were crawling through the Lincoln Tunnel and out into the terrible misery of the New Jersey Turnpike. It was the first time he actually remembered being with his mother. He carried the Bloomingdale's bag cuddled on his lap, not thinking, just startled and unsettled to be given what he had wanted most of all.

2

He forgot so much, but he remembered this, years later—it was a good seat, an armrest between them which the mother lifted so the boy could rest his face against her upper arm. When she had crammed her big pack between her legs she spelled out a tickly secret word onto his palm, her fingernails a natural seashell pink, her fingers brown.

I know what you wrote, he said.

I don't think so.

He got the stuff from the back pocket of his shorts and found his chewed-up yellow pencil. He rested Cameron's father's business card on his knee and carefully wrote DILE on the back of it. When she had read it he returned everything to its place.

Wow. That's a lot of stuff you carry.

My papers, he said.

I didn't know boys had papers.

The boy could not think what he could say. They sat awhile. He looked up the aisle. He had never been on a Greyhound before and was pretty happy to see the toilet at the back.

You're very tall, Dial, he said at last.

Tall for a girl. Not everybody's cup of tea.

You're my cup of tea, Dial.

She laughed suddenly loudly, putting her lovely hand across her mouth. He wished he could call her Mom.

You have lots of colors, Dial. The boy's ears were burning. He did not know where all these words were coming from. Grandma would have been amazed to hear him talk so much.

The mother took a hank of her hair and pulled it over one eye like a mask, squinting through it, a field of wheat, every seed and stalk a slightly different color. She had a big nose and wide lips. She was very beautiful, everyone had always said so, but this was bigger than they said, better.

I'm a bitzer, she said.

What's a bitzer, Dial?

Suddenly she kissed his cheek.

Bits of this and bits of that.

He was shy again, looked up the aisle. The windshield glass was starred with sunlight.

Dial was searching in the big hiking pack between her legs. She had lots of books down there, he saw them, candy too, some yellow socks.

How will Grandma find me?

The book she now removed had two dogs fighting on its cover, blood was everywhere, she was giving him a Hershey bar. The chocolate was soft and bendy. Thank you, he said. How will she find me, Dial?

She opened her strange book at the beginning. He noted with disapproval that she cracked its spine.

Grandma knew we were going to run away?

Uh-huh, she said, and turned a page.

He tasted the melted chocolate, considering this.

Is the chocolate nice? she asked at last.

Yes, Dial. Thank you. It's my favorite.

She lowered the dog book to her lap. You'll talk to her real soon, she said. We'll phone her.

Where will we go?

You heard—Philly.

Apart from that.

It's a surprise, sweetie. Don't look so worried. It's the best surprise you could ever have.

She went back to her book. He thought, If my grandma had known I was leaving she would have kissed me good-bye. Also—she would have made him take his own suitcase and promise to brush his teeth. So his grandma was against all this. A good sign, so he figured.

What sort of surprise? he asked. He could think of only one surprise he wanted. His heart was going fast again.

A really, really good one, she said, not looking up.

He asked was it a motel but he didn't think it was, not for a second.

Better than that, she said. And turned a page.

He asked was it the beach but he didn't think it was that either. The beach made her lower the book once more. Do you like to swim at Kenoza Lake?

You know about the lake?

Baby, you and I were there together.

No, he said, confused.

At Kenoza Lake.

But at Kenoza Lake he never had a mother. That was the biggest thing about it. It would always be summer, in his memory, the roadsides dense with goldenrod and the women from the village coming to steal the white hydrangeas just like their mothers stole before them. The geese would be heading up to Canada and the Boeings spinning their white contrails across the cold blue sky—loneliness and hope, expanding like paper flowers in water.

It was always summer, always chilled by fall, the mother's absence everywhere in the air, in the maple leaves, for instance, lifting their silver undersides in the breeze which corrugated the surface of Kenoza Lake as his grandmother swam to and fro between the dock and a point in the middle of the lake where she could line up the middle chimney with the blinking amber light up on 52. Later he would wonder more about his missing grandfather and the Poison Dwarf who had once been Grandma's friend, but that would be a different person who would ask those questions, all the old cells having died, been sloughed off, become dust in the New York City air.

He could swim too. He had the shoulders even then, but the lake water was slimy and viscous and it left a clammy feeling on his skin which the sun would not burn off. He never did ask but he was certain it was millions of little dead things and he thought of the wailing signals on the radio and lay on his stomach on the dock and his back became black and his stomach was pale and ghostly as a fish.

Small black ants were almost everywhere. Some he killed for no good reason.

He looked up at Dial. She had huge dark eyes, like an actress on a billboard in Times Square. He would have swum with her any day he could.

Would you like to go to a beach? she asked him now.

But this wasn't what he wanted.

Will we stay in a motel?

She looked at him with wonder. You outrageous little creature, she said. We're just going to a sort of scuzzy house. We'll probably be sleeping on the floor.

Maybe there's TV, he said. None of this was what he really meant. It was his upbringing, to "not say."

A lot better than TV, she said.

That's where the surprise is, Dial? In the scuzzy house?

Yes, Jay.

He was so happy he thought he might be sick. He snuggled into her then, his head resting against her generous breasts, and she stroked his head, the part low on the neck where all the short hairs are.

Maybe I can guess what the surprise is, he said after a while. In the scuzzy house.

You know I won't tell you if you do.

He did not need to say. He knew what it was exactly. Just as Cameron had foretold. His real life was just starting. He was going to see his dad.

3

Except for one single photograph, the boy had never seen his
dad, not even on TV. There had been no television permitted
in Grandma's house on Kenoza Lake, so after he had helped
light the fires in fall the boy picked among the high musty
shelves of paperbacks—some words as plain as pebbles, many
more that held their secrets like the crunchy bodies of wasps
or grasshoppers. He could read some, as he liked to say.
Upstairs there was a proper library with a sliding ladder and
heavy books containing engravings of fish and elk and small
flowers with German names which made him sad. On the big
torn sofas where he peered into these treasures, there was
likely to be an abandoned Kipling or Rider Haggard or
Robert Louis Stevenson which his grandma would continue
with at dusk. In this silky water-stained room with its slatted
squinting views across the lake, there was a big glowing valve
radio which played only static and a wailing oscillating electric
cry, some deep and secret sadness he imagined coming from
beneath the choppy water slapping at the dock below.

Down in the city, at the Belvedere, there was a pink GE
portable TV which always sat on the marble kitchen countertop; once, when he thought his grandma was napping, he

plugged it in. This was the only time she hurt him, twisting his arm and holding his chin so he could not escape her eyes. She spit, she was so crazy—he must not watch TV.

Not ever.

Her given reason was as tangled as old nylon line, snagged with hooks and spinners and white oxidized lead weights, but the true reason he was not allowed to watch was straight and short and he learned it from Gladys the Haitian maid—you don't be getting yourself upset seeing your mommy and daddy in the hands of the po-lees. You never do forget a thing like that.

Cameron Fox was the son of the art dealers in 5D. He had been expelled from Groton on account of the hair he would not cut, maybe something else as well. Grandma paid Cameron to be a babysitter. She had no idea.

It was in Cameron's room the boy saw the poster of Che Guevara and learned who he was and why he had no mother and father. Not even Gladys was going to tell him this stuff. After his mother and the Dobbs Street Cell had robbed the bank in Bronxville, a judge had given Che to the permanent care of his grandma. That's what Cameron said. You got a right to know, man. Cameron was sixteen. He said, Your grandpa threw a Buddha out the D line window. A fucking Buddha, man. He's a cool old guy. I smelled him smoking weed out on the stairs. Do you get to hang out with him?

No chance. No way. The one time they found Grandpa and the Poison Dwarf at Sixty-second Street, the boy and his grandma went to the Carlyle.

Cameron told the boy he was a political prisoner locked up at Kenoza Lake. His grandma made him play ludo which was a game from, like, a century before. Cameron gave him a full-page picture of his father from *Life*. Cameron read him the caption. Beyond your command. His dad was cool looking, with wild fair hair. He held his fingers in a V.

He looks like you, said Cameron Fox. You should get this framed, he said. Your father is a great American.

But the boy left 5D by the Clorox stairs and before he entered his grandma's kitchen he folded up his father very carefully and kept him in his pocket. That was the beginning of his papers more or less.

In the boy's pocket there were clear bits and mysteries. Cameron would sometimes try to explain but then he would stop and say, That's too theoretical right now. Or: You would have to know more words. Cameron was six feet tall with a long straight nose and a long chin and an eye which was just a little to one side. He read to Che from *Steppenwolf* until they both got bored with it, but he would not let him watch TV either. He said television was the devil. They played poker for pennies. Cameron put on Country Joe and the Fish and he sat in ski socks before the electric radiator, spreading the skin condition that he hoped would save him from Vietnam.

The boy looked out for TV but never saw too much. Once or twice they were in a diner with TV but Grandma made them turn it off. She was a force. She said so.

So when Dial and Jay came into the Philadelphia Greyhound station, it was a big deal to see the black-and-white TV, high up in the corner of the waiting room. The 76ers were losing to Chicago. Old men were watching. They groaned. They spit. Goddamn. The boy stared also, waiting for the show to change to maybe Rowan and Martin, some other thing he'd heard of, Say good night, Dick. He was excited when the mother went out to find a telephone.

Don't talk to anyone, she said, OK?

OK, he said. He stared at the blue devil, knowing something wonderful would happen next.

The Bulls fouled three times before the mother came back.

What next? he asked, noticing she had gotten sad. She crouched in front of him.

We'll stay in a hotel, she said. How about that?

You said we were going to a scuzzy house, he said.

Plans have changed, she said, getting all busy with a cigarette.

With room service? He was acting excited, but he was very frightened now, by her smell, by the way she did that thing—kind of hiding her emotions in the smoke.

I can't afford room service, she said, and wasted her cigarette beneath her heel.

In the corner of his eye he could see cartoons. That was nothing to him now.

Are you listening to me, Jay?

There's no one else, he said. He meant, Who else could he listen to, but she understood something else and hugged him to her tightly.

What's wrong?

I like you, Jay. Her eyes had gone all watery.

I like you, Dial, he said, but he did not want to follow her outside into the dark and shadow, beside tall buses pouring their waste into the pizza parlors. When they were walking upstairs he imagined they were going somewhere bad.

What is this?

A hotel, baby.

Not like the motel in Middletown, New York, where they stayed in the snowstorm, not the Carlyle, that's for sure. He was gutted as a largemouth bass. Something had gone wrong.

They had to climb the stairs to find the foyer. The desk was quilted with red leather. Behind it sat a woman hooked up to a tank of gas. She took fifteen dollars in her fat ringed hand—no bath, no playing instruments of any kind. Then they walked along green corridors with long tubes of light above, and the sounds of TVs applauding from the rooms. Dial's face was green in the hallway, then dark and shrunken inside the room. There were lace curtains, a red neon CHECKS CASHED. A single bed with a TV near the ceiling.

Not yet, she said, seeing where his attention was.

You promised.

I promised, yes. We can lie in bed and watch TV, but you must wait until I come back.

Where are you going now?

I have to do some more stuff, about the secret.

Is the secret OK?

Yes, it's OK.

Then can I come?

Baby, if you come it won't be a secret. I won't be long.

She was kneeling. Looking at him. Pale. Way too close.

Just stay here, she said. Don't let anyone inside.

And she kissed and hugged him way too hard.

After the key turned in the lock he stood beneath the television. The screen was dusty, spotted. Someone had run a finger down it.

He sat on the bed and watched the door awhile. The bedspread was pale blue and kind of crinkly, nasty. Once someone walked past. Then they came back the other way. He stayed away from the window but he could see the red wash of the CHECKS CASHED sign.

Dial had left her backpack on a chair. Its mouth was tied up with a piece of cord but you could still see some stuff inside—her book and a box of something small and bright like candy. That was what he went for, naturally, fishing it out with just two fingers. UNO is one of the world's most popular family card games—he read this—with rules easy enough for kids, but challenges and excitement for all ages. He dropped the Uno back inside the pack, thinking she did not know her son.

The TV was beyond his reach.

He dragged across a chair and sat on it, still looking up. He could see the small red button. POWER.

A woman in high heels clattered down the hallways, laughing, crying maybe. He climbed up on the chair and pushed the button.

He was real close as the picture got called up from the

tube, gathering itself and puffing out until it almost tore his eyes.

He saw the picture, did not understand who was sending it—there he was, him, Che Selkirk, at Kenoza Lake, New York, holding up a largemouth bass and squinting. The sound was roaring. Everything was gold and bleeding orange at the edges. He turned it off, and heard it suck back in the tube.

Something very bad had happened. He did not know what it could be.

4

What had gone wrong was not explained to him. Did the TV cause this or not? All Dial said was—We've got to go.

Tomorrow?

Right now.

When they fled Philly he had still not gotten his surprise or called his grandma. He had never been in an airplane and then he was bouncing around the sky above the earth, living in black air belonging to no place. He had flown to Oakland to a motel which turned out pretty good. He did not know exactly where he was. They did not watch TV but she read him all her book, out loud, the one with the fighting dogs. He thought *The Call of the Wild* must be the best book ever written. Dial never said anything but she had lived at Kenoza Lake and knew he came from a house almost identical to Buck the dog's. The judge's place stood back from the road, half hidden among the trees, through which glimpses could be caught of the wide cool veranda that ran around all four sides. So Jack London wrote.

They ran across the highway to the pizza place and back. They ate so much pizza the whole room smelled of it, and they played Uno together which turned out much better than you would think. He did not mention poker yet, but they played Uno for Days Inn matches.

Dial tried to call Grandma but she did not answer. The boy listened to the phone himself. It rang and rang.

When they were nearly out of cash they went to Seattle and Dial got a heap of money and after that they flew to Sydney, Australia. She told him it was a long way. He asked was the secret still OK. She said it was. He did not mind then. He beat her at poker. Then she taught him solitaire. Plus she had so many little tricks and puzzles in that pack of hers, rings you had to learn to pull apart, another book by Jack London, and all the way to Australia he was happy. He had been busted free by parents, just as Cameron had predicted.

Sydney turned out to be a big city so they got a bus to Brisbane. He got bored with that, they both did. Brisbane was really hot. Dial went looking for a head shop and he assumed it related to his dad but all that happened was they met a fat freak girl and learned that if they went north they would find places not even on a map.

Turn on, tune in, drop out, the fat girl said.

Later Dial said, I never want to hear that hippie shit again. He did not tell her Cameron said that all the time.

But Cameron could not imagine the boy hitchhiking in this world beyond the Clorox stairs—the foreign sky, bruised like cheekbones, heavy rain streaming in a distant fringe. A spooky yellow light shone on the highway and there was a fine hot clay dust, dry on the boy's toes, mud on his now homeless tongue, powder on the needles of *Pinus radiata* plantations.

It was one hundred degrees Fahrenheit more or less. They kept on walking.

Two black lanes north, two lanes south, some foreign grass in the middle. To the east and west were neatly mown verges about thirty feet wide and then there were the dull green walls of the *Pinus radiata* plantations, sliced by yellow fire roads but deathly quiet—not a possum or a snake, not even a hopping carrion crow, could ever live there.

The boy had no idea where on earth he stood. He understood the names of hardly anything, himself included.

In this entire continent he knew only the big-faced, big-boned mother with her bag full of entertainments. She was two long strides ahead—long, long hippie skirt, T-shirt, rubber flip-flops, walking way too fast. What he really knew about her, he could have written on a candy wrapper. She was a radical, but that was as obvious as the exit sign ahead.

The boy spelled out the sign. Caboolture?

A town, she said, it's nothing. She would not slow.

What sort of town?

His strong hair was now disguised, dyed black, cut like a hedge, revealing a band of pale untanned skin around his neck. He rubbed at the crown and squinted up at the sign—CABOOLTURE—dumb black letters on a dumb white board, an ugly redneck sort of thing, he thought.

What sort of town, Dial?

Come on, she said. An Australian town.

He should have asked other stuff, Where is my father, where is Grandma, but sometimes it seemed she was sick of him already.

Morons, she shouted at the passing car. I hope you drown. She was so tall, so pretty with a big farm boy's stride. His cup of tea, his flesh and blood, forever.

No one is going to pick us up here, Dial. They're all going the other way.

Thanks, she said. I hadn't noticed. She was not used to little kids.

The cars on the southbound road were bumper to bumper, their yellow headlights glowing the color of the Pan Am Building at dusk. It was sometime around noon. He wished she could find a place to curl up with jet lag.

We could go to that town, he said, or words like that. Maybe there's a motel. That was what he loved the most, just to be with her cuddling while she read to him, her hair tickling his face.

There's no motel, the mother said.

I bet there is, he said.

She stopped and turned.

What? he demanded. What!

Her hair had so many shifting tones you could never say exactly what it was, but her eyebrows were plain black, and when they pressed down on her eyes, like now, she was a scary witch.

OK, she said, that's enough.

She had done this once in Port Authority. She had scared him then as well.

Around this time, a beat-up 1964 Ford station wagon, its paintwork gone powdery with sun and age, paused at the exit of the Golden Fleece service station on the Brisbane side of Caboolture. The driver revved the engine once and a flood of oil-blue smoke spread slowly across the pump island and dispersed into the scrubby field where two itchy-looking horses stood, their bony haunches directed at the fleeing cars.

Look at the bloody lemmings, said Trevor.

The boy did not know Trevor but he would be familiar soon enough, and for a damn long time after that as well, and he would always connect the name to that particular body—a strong man, sleek as a porpoise, sheathed in a good half-inch-thick coat of fat which seemed to feed his brown taut skin, giving it a healthy fish-oil kind of shine. He had a mashed-up ear, a short haircut, as short as a soldier's, reddish brown, smelling of marijuana, papaya and mango. When Trevor was not naked, and he was naked every chance he got, he wore baggy Indian pajama pants, and when he smiled, like now, at the fleeing tourists, he revealed a jagged tooth.

They reckon destructive winds off Caloundra of two hundred K's, said the driver. This was called John the Rabbitoh but was really Jean Rabiteau, of so-called French extraction. No one knew where he came from but he was a drop-dead handsome man of maybe twenty-five. He had high cheekbones, long black hair, brown eyes and a whippy wide-shouldered narrow-waisted body. He had a broad nasal accent and he smelled of cut grass and radiator hose and two-stroke fuel.

Bang! Trevor made a pistol with his hands which were as broad and stubby as his strong barrel of a body. Bang! Bang! He showed his chipped tooth and shot the drivers one by one.

Turning up the road toward the storm, the Rabbitoh stayed quiet about Trevor's murders. He had his own thoughts involving the damned souls and the wrath of God. He hunched over the steering wheel peering up into the lowering sky and the nasty yellow light around its smudgy skirts.

We'll be back in the valley by the time it hits.

This was a good guess, but it would turn out to be incorrect because, as the Ford passed the Caboolture exit, they saw the mother and the boy trudging north.

It was Trevor who called stop, Trevor who lived in a stockade at the top of a very steep unfriendly road, whose most common expression was "your alarm clock is your key to freedom," who woke every morning at 5 a.m. and hid out in the bush until it was clear the police would not raid him, Trevor, who saw spies and traitors everywhere, said, Pick her up.

By now they were two hundred yards down the road, but John stopped.

Back up.

No need.

Trevor turned and saw Dial running at him, her yellow hair rising in snaky waves, her titties like puppies fighting inside her shirt.

5

Inside the Ford were smells which the boy could not have named or untangled—long wisps of WD-40 and marijuana, floating threads of stuff associated with freaks who made their own repairs, dandelion chains of dust and molecules of automotive plastics which rose up in the moldy heat, 1961, 1964, 1967.

At Kenoza Lake he had gotten accustomed to moldy paper, books with yellow pages, the rotting leaves in late November, the smell of dairy cows across the lane. As he scrambled across the busted sunken boneless backseat of John the Rabbitoh's wagon, he tried to like where he had come. His dad would maybe smell like this exactly, underground.

You OK, baby?

I'm cool, he said.

As the first fat raindrops splatted like jelly against the windshield, the mother pulled him close against her generous breast. She was all he had for now.

Trevor, said the snaggle-toothed passenger, not looking at the boy. His skin was smooth and taut but his edges were all raw and poor, like he had crawled along a drainpipe to arrive here.

Dial, said the mother.

Trevor was now offering drugs and the boy was certain that he was through the doorway which had been waiting for him all his life. His grandma had always fretted about it, being stolen back by revolutionaries. She never spoke directly to the subject, so he had to listen through the wall—his history in whispers, brushing, scratching on the windowpane.

The edge of the storm took the car like a kitten in its mouth. The driver stared into the rearview mirror. Where you heading? he asked the mother who was already dealing from the pack.

She answered, North, which made the boy certain it could not be true. He had three wild cards which were very good. He drew his finger across his throat to tell her he would win.

The lemmings are going south, said Trevor.

What's with that? She matched the discard pile, red on red.

Cyclone, said Trevor. Going to wash Noosa Sound back into the sea. Bang! Bang! Those houses are going to be walking round the sand like crabs.

Beach, he thought. He was down to three cards already. The mother's hand was getting all weighed down.

You're American? Trevor asked her. What we call a cyclone, you call a hurricane.

Uno, cried the boy. Triumphant.

I can't read or write, Trevor announced, frowning at the card. He asked the mother, How far north?

The mother hugged the boy to her and he hid from Trevor's inquiring stare. I don't like to plan, she said.

She did not deal another hand. Instead she held the boy as they traveled through the storm, whispering that she loved him, stroking his head.

When he woke the car had stopped. It was raining on his legs and the mother was not there. Three doors were open shaking violently in the wind. Outside was dark, and the storm came inside the car and lifted the Uno cards and slapped them around the windows.

Dial!

He was alone, illegal, "on the lamb." The rain hurt his legs like needles.

Dial!

He pulled himself into the seat, his bare legs retracted, his back straight, his hands balled into fists. He was way too scared to cry but when the mother finally returned he shouted at her.

Where were you?

Shush, she said, reaching out for him, but he drew away from her bony cold hands. Behind her the bushes slashed and squabbled in the dark.

You left me!

The road is flooded.

Where is the driver? He was scared to hear himself, so loud, like someone else.

Dial was not scared. She paused and narrowed her eyes and pushed back her sodden hair which dripped across his face.

He's coming back, she said evenly. We're all coming back, OK?

OK, he said.

He watched silently as she dug down into her big lumpy khaki bag, deciding that he would not take candy, not even chocolate.

What will happen now, he asked, but he could already see she did not know, had nothing to offer, not even candy, only a big blue sweater which she wrapped around his legs.

6

Not so long ago Dial had been sitting in a pleasant room near Poughkeepsie, New York. She had been dressed in a black cashmere sweater and a simple gray skirt and her Charles Jourdan court shoes had already produced their first expensive blister on her heel. There was, in this particularly cozy office, a Tabriz rug on the floor and a painting, clearly by Roger Fry, on the wall opposite. If it was puzzling that the chair of an English department, whose place of work this was, would own an artwork quite so valuable, then the location of the office, inside the gatehouse of Vassar College, suggested a history that might finally make it all explicable. Dial was a socialist, but snob enough to find this irresistible.

It was an early Monday afternoon in mid-October. All the crap with the selection committee, the so-called P&B, was finally done. The Pound scholar, who had been the committee's first choice, had been nice enough to go to Yale instead. The Austen professor had been sucked up to, the prickly dean had been pacified and now there was nothing left to do but enjoy this milky tea, and maybe elicit the story of how this steel-blue Roger Fry had come to this American wall where it managed to look so dull and erotic all at once. There was a sleepy log fire in the grate and Dial could look down at the rolled lawns which, in spite of the efforts of the gardeners— three in sight just then—were littered with the tweedy colors of the fall. Dial experienced a delicious sense of possession you could never get from a state-owned park.

As the faculty had observed all day, the vermilions of an East Coast fall, the "red peak," was just one weekend away. This was not an excitement she had ever felt in Dorchester where the yellowing leaves on the highway dividers suggested death by poisoning and triggered angry memories of too-thin coats, chilly ankle-high drafts blowing down the hallway of her childhood home, her "study."

Dial's companion settled back into her teal wingback chair and predicted the red peak once again. This was Patricia Abercrombie, a Chaucerian of fifty, lumpy, round faced with piano legs and a pasty sad sort of face with deep vertical lines in her upper lip. To Dial there seemed to be something missing, a lack of some element of character that made her appear out of focus or underwater. Indeed, if Dial was now insincere in the surprise she showed about the coming red peak, it was mainly in the hope that if she could only demonstrate enough interest, enough goodwill, she might penetrate the Abercrombie bark and somehow touch the living wood.

Patricia Abercrombie, being thirty years a Vassar girl, and far sharper than she appeared, retreated from all this shallow brightness.

I believe, she said at last, raising her pale red eyebrows as she lifted her cup. I believe we have a friend in common.

Oh? said Dial, to whom this seemed beyond the bounds of possibility.

Susan Selkirk, said the chair.

Now it was Dial who had her heartwood touched, not pleasantly.

You know of whom I speak?

Yes, I was at school with her.

The chair's eyes clearly registered this for what it was, a

cowardly attempt to deny a friendship. Susan was our son's friend, she said softly. But she was our orphan baby, really.

Oh.

I think she's terribly lonely, the chair said.

Of course, said Dial, hearing a sort of moo in her false sympathy.

That's the other side of everything, said the chair, holding her gaze. Very sad and very lonely. Poor girl.

Patricia Abercrombie broke away to write something on the corner of her *New York Times.* Dial watched with perfect numbness, having gone through the entire selection process assuming that this aspect of her history was unknown and would, had it been unearthed, have immediately disqualified her. She watched as the chair tore a small strip from the *Times.* Dial knew what it was going to be. It was impossible, but it would be Susan's phone number.

On the other side of the world she would recall the weird mixture of fear and satisfaction she had felt as she took that paper in her hand. Patricia Abercrombie *smiled* at her. This time Dial did not notice the lines on her lip—but the glint in her green eyes. God, she thought, who in the fuck are you?

Nothing more was said about the piece of paper, and soon she walked with Patricia Abercrombie across the grass where she was "delivered" with her secret blistered heel into the care of the dean.

Whatever conspiracy had been enacted was not acknowledged. There was not so much as an extra squeeze in their farewell handshakes and it would not be until, years later, reading *Vassar Girls,* that she had any inkling of the eccentric power she had brushed against so casually.

And what will you do now? the Dean asked her, when Patricia Abercrombie had gone, and her social security card had been copied and her health plan had been selected.

I think there's a train to the city at two.

No, I mean until the spring semester.

You know, she said, and in that second she was vain

enough to feel her youth, her beauty, her whole possibility. You know, she said, I have not the least idea.

What luxury, said the Dean who had previously been her greatest obstacle. How lovely.

And that afternoon, at Poughkeepsie railway station, Dial, whose real name was Anna Xenos, redeemed what had once been her father's backpack and lugged it to the bathroom and kicked off her shoes and changed out of what seemed to her to be a rather specious sort of drag. Sitting on the toilet, she repacked so that her interview clothes were on the very bottom. She changed into tights, a camisole, not so much for warmth as protection against the abrasions of a long Nepalese dress patched together from reds and browns and tiny mirrors. She had carried a Harvard book bag to the interview, worn casually as Cliffy girls did that year, over the shoulder and on the back. Now she fitted the bag into the pouch where her father had once carried shotgun cartridges, and, still sitting on the toilet, pulled on a loose-fitting pair of fur-lined boots. Her blister thus soothed, she steadied herself with one hand and undid her hair and fluffed it out not minding, no matter how often she said the opposite, that she did, indeed, look kind of wild.

She was on the 2 platform just as the train from Albany came in, and when she boarded she found a telephone waiting, directly opposite her. If not for this she might never have called Susan Selkirk. But she was high on life, on possibility, and she was on the phone before she even took a seat . . . 215? Philly? She wasn't sure. It took six of her quarters. Ridiculous. Like phoning a rock star or a famous author whom your aunt had known, something you only did because you could, because you were not nobody.

Hello, Susan. It's Dial.

Give me your number, said someone, not Susan. We'll call you back.

There was a number, too. She gave it, not unhappy to see a few quarters returned.

She waited for the famous felon as if she were herself some kind of actor in a film, resting her head against the glass, watching the power lines dance like sheet music across the reflection of her extraordinary dress. She was about to talk to America's most-wanted woman. She was going to MoMA before it closed this afternoon. She was staying with her friend Madeleine on West Fourteenth Street. That's all she knew about her future. She had no lover, no father or mother, no home but Boston whose "rapcha" and "capcha" occasionally burst the surface of her speech. She watched the power lines rising and falling beside the Hudson and thought, Remember this moment, how beautiful and strange the world is.

When the phone rang, she saw her hair reflected in the sky. Hello.

Well, said that piercing girlie voice, if it's not the "bvains."

Hi, she said not at all offended by the "bvains." Rather pleased.

Far out, cried Susan. Dial had forgotten how she sounded, the shrill pitch.

What a *coincidence,* Susan said. Listen I'm going on vacation, you dig. I was just wondering where you are?

Dial could see the conductors walking through the car. The conductor could see her. But she could see Susan Selkirk in the *Boston Globe,* photographed from the ceiling of the Bronxville Chase Manhattan. What might or might not have been a revolver was in her hand. That was what had happened to SDS. Students for a *Democratic* Society?

No shit, said Susan. I was just talking to my mom about you. I mean, like, now.

Your mom remembered me?

She'd rather remember you than me. But listen, I sort of was wanting to say hi to my guy.

Which guy?

He was your guy too.

On the telephone, blasting through Croton-on-Hudson,

Dial blushed, pulling her hair by the roots, looking at her staring face in the glass.

The baby, Susan Selkirk said. For Christ's sake. I mean my son.

Right.

Call back, Susan Selkirk said suddenly. Tonight. Can you do that for me? Please, please. This is not cool, not now.

I'm going out to see *The Godfather* with Madeleine.

You're seeing the fucking *Godfather.*

Sure. Why not?

There was a silence and Dial didn't rush to fill it.

Sure, said Susan, why the fuck not!

Another silence.

I need this favor, Susan said at last. If not for me, then for the Movement.

Dial was a sucker. Susan knew she was a sucker. She wandered back down through the car, hefting her awkward heavy pack, laughing incredulously at herself, at Susan Selkirk who could still issue commands like the revolution was a family business. For the Movement! Please.

She tucked the phone number in her purse and let her mood be made by bigger things, by the great luxury of time, a fall day with sunshine, and the Hudson still as glass. If Susan Selkirk affected her at all, it was only to highlight the richness of her new life which was intensifying daily—Vassar, MoMA, Manhattan, all the possibilities suggested by this gorgeous ride beside the Hudson with the sun pushing down above the golden Palisades.

By the time the train dipped underground at 125th Street, she had forgotten Susan Selkirk. And it was only very late that night, on calculating her expenses and counting the remaining money in her purse, that she found the scrap of paper. When she called it was not because of any deep friendship for Susan. But she had all the time in the world, so she made an arrangement to meet her near Clark Street in Brooklyn.

Susan, quite typically, sent two strangers to interrogate her and again she was too curious to be decently offended.

Later all she would remember was their teeth, big and long on one, small and square on the other, but both young women's mouths were full of perfectly straight teeth, clear signs of class that contradicted their dowdy clothes which were a sort of depressed portrait of the unhappy working class. Their hair had been cut gracelessly with kitchen scissors and they had about them a severe judgmental quality that made Dial feel too tall, too pretty, too frivolous for their company.

You know the kid, right? Her son?

Once I did. Freshman year.

She wants to see her son.

Susan does?

We don't use names. OK.

The one with the long teeth was tall and skinny. Her dowdy little sweater was gray cashmere. She lit a cigarette and smoked it with both hands pushed in the pockets of her thrift store coat.

OK, said Dial. It did not help her that she noticed the privileged teeth, the expensive sweater. Neither undercut the moral authority she had been raised to respect. She never could be far enough left for Susan, SDS, herself. She thought the student left were fantasists, yet when the Maoists told her she would be shot after the revolution she was inclined to believe it was true.

She's going on vacation, dig?

Dial understood that *vacation* was code for something else but she was staring at the girl's stringy blond hair, wondering if there was something in that un-made-up face, something under those pressing dark eyebrows, that might give Dial human entry.

It's dangerous, the girl said, looking over her shoulder at a skinny beat-up plane tree as if its shivery branches might reveal a bug. The grandmother will let you take him.

Mrs. Selkirk has no idea who I am.

Yes, she does. If you meet with her at eleven, you take the kid back by noon. Done. That's all we're asking. You will have done your little bit.

Little bit, thought Dial. You patronizing little bitch. Do you actually know Phoebe Selkirk? she asked the short one. Have you met her?

Listen, Susan is begging you. You know, like *begging*, man.

Dial thought, You said her name, moron. Plus where does all this "man" shit come from.

Oh sure, she said.

You know why the old lady trusts you? You want to know? You want to just stand there being sarcastic?

Dial shrugged. But of course she wished to know.

You never talked to the *Post*.

And that, of course, was completely true. Not just the *Post* but the *News*, the *Globe*, even the *Times*. And that was why she would call Grandma Selkirk, because the old lady, at least, had seen the steel at Dial's core, that although she could not stand Phoebe Selkirk's Upper East Side ass, she would never betray her trust. That was who she was.

Dial dropped a dime in Brooklyn Heights, and the phone rang on Park Avenue. Hello, she said, this is Anna Xenos.

Yes, I am recording this.

The Selkirks were like animals in the zoo. How amazing she should know them at all.

Yes. This is Anna. Hi.

Did they give you the address of my apartment?

I know your apartment, Mrs. Selkirk. Remember I worked for you.

When you get to my age everyone has worked for you.

What is it you want me to do?

They've told you.

Yes, broadly, Dial said, thinking, Oh please don't piss me off too much.

Very well, the old lady said. Would you please come to me tomorrow at 10:45. You must bring him back in sixty minutes.

And that's it, right? She thought, *Must.*

Will you be asking for a fee?

Oh please listen to yourself, she said. And returned the phone to the care of the Puritans. She could so easily not do this. She stood above the gritty artery of the BQE wondering why, of all the extraordinary things she could do in New York, she would waste her time this way.

Well, there was the boy, but who would remember that she carried the weight of his squirming life from May until September 1966—cruel ear infections long ago, jagged teeth like shards of quartz attacking from inside, high fevers, cold baths, all the smells of cloves, shit, jasmine oil she mixed with Johnson & Johnson so he always smelled like a newly anointed prince. She had thought she loved him then.

You'll go with her to Bloomingdale's, the tall one said, refusing to lean companionably across the rail. She wants to buy Susan a gift. You accompany her while she purchases it. Then you take the gift and you take the 6 train to Grand Central, then the shuttle, then walk through the passage to Port Authority. Susan will meet you both there.

The number I called was in Philly.

Yes. That's right.

I'm from Boston. I don't know Port Authority.

Just walk, Dial. OK? We'll be watching you.

Dial was mostly thinking, Wait till I tell Madeleine this. Madeleine was a Long Island Jew with a Communist father. Who else would understand these fucked-up feelings swelling in her breast right now, her scorn for the cashmere sweater, the guilty certainty that these joyless bank robbers were on the right side of the war.

If not for me, then for the Movement, Susan Selkirk had said.

Every time it got her, every goddamn time.

7

There was nothing in the Belvedere's lobby she recognized from her long-ago visit—neither the loud checkerboard of marble tiles, nor the huge faux-Grecian vase. It had been May 1966, six years ago, a time when her speech was still thick with Boston. Today she remembered only what disappointing uses the Selkirk money had been put to—frumpy sofas and matching rosewood end tables. True, there had been a de Kooning on the living room wall, but she had been way too nervous to stare at it. The apartment generally suggested that there had not been a new idea in furniture design this century.

She walked from the doorman to the elevator operator, arguing, with her big backpack and her stride, her perfect right to be there.

The elevator man regarded her tits with what she thought of as her father's dark DP eyes.

Efharisto, she said.

You're welcome, the displaced person said, transferring his attention to the lights.

As the elevator opened into the apartment she both met and remembered the incongruous smell of burned toast. The very small, very ordinary kitchen was partially visible in the hallway to the left. The Park Avenue sky was straight ahead, and the sun, at that time of morning, was so bright that it took her a moment to see the little creature, a glowing nimbus surrounding him, like a startled fox in a morning meadow.

Hello, she said. Is that you?

To her immense surprise he propelled himself toward her, and she, unprepared for six years of solid growth, was winded by the heft of him, the breadth of his chest, the weight of his bones, his dense needy secret life.

You can't possibly remember me, she cried, delighted, slipping free of her backpack.

The boy did not reply, just hugged her like a terrific little animal, grinding his chin against her leg.

Phoebe Selkirk had perhaps been there all the while, but it took a moment for Dial to become aware of her.

The visitor made an unsuccessful attempt to separate from her admirer.

Well—the older woman extended a hand—it appears we once again have the right person for the job.

She had become old, and Dial, imagining she could feel the skeleton in her grip, released the hand abruptly and smiled too eagerly.

Phoebe Selkirk seemed less confident, but she was of course still beautiful, with high cheekbones and strong steely gray hair which easily held the superficially simple cut—high on the nape, the long strong hair sweeping toward her perhaps overly determined jaw.

Now! she said, and at this single command, the boy released his hold and, without looking back at Dial, ran down the hallway.

Dial found herself saying how very pleased she was to come, realizing, with some astonishment, that she was perfectly sincere.

The boy appeared again around the back of the bookshelf. The blue one? He smiled at her.

With the zip, his grandmother said. That one.

As he disappeared again the old lady extracted a brown paper bag from the bookshelf and pushed it hard at Dial.

Take, take, Mrs. Selkirk ordered, quickly.

Inside the bag Dial saw books, a card game, chocolate bars. Quick, take it.

When Dial hesitated Mrs. Selkirk kneeled before the visitor's backpack and unbuckled it.

She'll be late, she said, thrusting everything inside. She was never on time. He'll need entertaining.

Dial raised an eyebrow at her.

Yes, the old lady acknowledged the reprimand. I'm a bully.

Is this OK? the boy called.

The sweater, a Cambridge blue, managed to produce an echoing blue among the interstices of his velvety gray eyes.

You have lovely hair, Dial said, then felt foolish for saying something so fond.

But he raised his chin at her as if inviting her to touch.

The grandmother did not exactly smile, but there was that slight wavering of the lips and she combed her brown hands roughly through her own hair. Dial thought, It's your hair he has. Good genes. The blue sweater was similarly privileged, the dense slightly greasy textures of New Zealand, the memory of many acres contained within its knit.

Well, shall we go? said Mrs. Selkirk brightly, holding out her hand toward the boy and, at the same time, touching Dial lightly upon the elbow. In this and other small ways, Phoebe Selkirk showed herself to be well disposed toward Dial but it was impossible not to see, in the elevator, in the lobby, that she was suffering in some way. There was a sadness as she touched the boy on the shoulder, on his head, turned back the sleeve of his sweater from his wrists.

This "play date," she said, rolling her eyes at the term, is meant to be from twelve to one.

Yes, I know.

She'll be late, so don't get agitated.

They said twelve.

Trust me, she'll be late. Just be back by two. Two-thirty even, that's fine. I wish she would just come here, you know. She could have. Nothing would have happened. You tell her that. Hurry, these WALK signs only last a second.

Dial was surprised to find herself wanting to display sympathy but she felt too indelicate to offer it, too coarse, like a rough mud doll beside something fine.

She could have come to the apartment, Mrs. Selkirk continued, a little winded by her sprint across Park. The staff would die before they gave her up. They've known her all her life.

This seemed a rather reckless notion, but Dial did not comment directly. She's your daughter, she said, pleased that this could mean almost anything.

Alas, she is, said Mrs. Selkirk. Her father's daughter too.

At Lex, the old lady had called the boy Jay for the first time. Dial had no issue with this. In fact she was all for it. She had always thought Che a ridiculous name, an indication of everything that was wrong with the so-called Movement. If you go carrying pictures of Chairman Mao, you ain't going to make it with anyone anyhow. But she was uncertain she had heard correctly. The next time she heard Che and when she asked the question about his name, in Bloomingdale's, she did it quite innocently. Such were the barbs she triggered. It was as if she'd accidentally brushed a poison jellyfish.

Dial was no longer a dirt poor scholarship girl. She did not have to take this shit. She was a Vassar professor, not that this old cow would know, or think to ask. Anna Xenos had her own temper issues and she would have enjoyed walking away, had it not been for this lovely little boy who presumably did not need more torture in his life. Dial looked at him with pity, observed his anxious hand stroking his grandma's arm while the idiot bought Chanel. Dial would have been hard-pressed to imagine a purchase more perverse or willful—Chanel for a woman who named her child Che and her parents Class Enemies.

With the wrapped gift clasped in her hands she looked directly into Dial's eyes. For a moment she faltered, looking down at her gift, maybe seeing just what she had done. Then she shoved it violently at the messenger.

You want me to call him Che in Bloomingdale's.

Dial thought, This woman has been driven mad by grief.

At the door, she suddenly felt her arm snatched.

Just go, Phoebe Selkirk hissed, go now. If anything happens to him, I'll kill you.

And with that Dial took the boy's hand and ran, laughing hysterically. Jesus, she thought, as the backpack slammed against her spine. Jesus Christ, what would it be like to have Susan Selkirk as your daughter, a child who would burn down everything you owned, not least this perfect little boy with his perfect little boy legs, falling socks, banged-up shin and expensive sweater made from merino sheep, the face, the father's face, dear Jesus.

He looked at her adoringly, little glances, smiles. She thought how glorious it was to be loved, she, Dial, who was not loved by anyone. She felt herself just absorb this little boy, his small damp hand dissolving in her own.

Walking out of breath along the passageway from Times Square to Port Authority a fellow freak came at them, smiling, long ringlets, badges across his denim jacket. He raised his hand to salute her.

Was this a creep?

When he slapped her hand she felt the slip of paper. How ridiculous was this.

He was PL? the boy asked.

Listen to you, she said. PL!

You're famous. I know all about you.

No, no, not at all. I think you forgot me absolutely.

She looked at the little creature. Darling parrot. What could he know of PL, fucking Maoists with cashmere sweaters, shouting men, the thirty-second orgasm.

She uncurled the paper in her hand.

What is it, Dial?

Directions, baby.

For what?

She looked at his lifted eager face, realizing he had no idea what was about to happen. No one had told him a thing. These people with their fucking children, thrown here, dragged there, stolen by judges, given to grandmothers, holding her hand. It was not up to her to start his education. She did what she was told, found gate 10. A line had started to form and through the dark glass she could see a bus, the driver eating from a crumpled mess of silver foil.

When's the bus get in, she asked no one in particular.

Don't know nothing about no bus get in. This was a black man with his face cut by creases. He must have been seventy and the brand of the trumpet was marked clearly on his lips.

Where are we going, Dial?

This bus going to *Philly*, little man.

Dial retreated across the busy corridor, and here she and the boy squatted, watching gates 9, 10, 11 through the moving forest of legs. The line at 10 grew longer. She was waiting, as predicted. She wanted to give him the chocolate, but who knew how long they would be here. And he seemed perfectly content, his little body pressed against her thigh.

Do you have any idea what we're waiting for?

He ducked his head and looked down at his shoes. It's very interesting, he said.

She was still smiling when she recognized, at the end of the line, curved shoulders inside a London Fog. It was the sort of coat you find on Howard Street, folded beside power cords and shoes on the pavement.

Stay here, she told the boy.

The ugly sister of the revolution was waiting for her, thrusting an envelope at her as she arrived.

Here.

As Dial took the envelope, she felt the boy's hand pulling

on her dress. Across the hallway was her backpack, her purse, her Vassar letter, everything inside. She seized the boy's shoulder. Stay here, she said fiercely. Do not move. By the time she was back the ugly sister had gone and the boy was offended with her.

Jay, she said, her heart beating, you mustn't leave the bag. That's my purse.

You hurt me, he said.

Shit, she thought.

She was looking at two round-trip tickets to Philadelphia.

Shut up, Jay, she said.

You called me Jay, he cried.

Shut up. Just don't talk now.

You're not allowed to say shut up.

She was not going to fucking Philadelphia.

Come here. She dragged him from the ticket line and into a narrow passage off the concourse. It stank. Smelled like someone was living here.

The kid was acting up. She was trying to read the tickets. She was so stressed she almost overlooked the faint pencil in a childish hand. *Change of plan. Mrs. Selkirk expects you to go to Ph and be back tonight. You will be reimbursed for expenses.* There was a Philadelphia phone number.

So she was to go to Philly. Like that. Well fuck them. Rich people. She was going to have dinner with Madeleine tonight.

The passengers were boarding. She checked the tickets again. They would not be back at Port Authority until almost midnight. Is that how you treat your child, you spoiled rich cow.

You cannot be a baby, she told the boy, squatting down in front of him so he would see she was serious. You've got to be a big boy.

I'm only seven, he said. His lip was trembling. You're not allowed to say shut up.

OK. I'm sorry.

Because you're not meant to.

OK. You're right. She offered him her hand and he took it.

Will you call me Che? he asked as she stood.

Sure. Che. It's a deal. But still he hesitated.

What?

Can I call you Mom?

8

A tree fell in Australia. The hippie car entered its crown, like a brick being forced into a shoe. Branches banged and broke beneath the tires and you could feel them spring up like busted bones or spikes and scrape beneath your bare feet on the floor.

Stop! the mother cried.

The boy grasped the front seat and peered over the driver's rancid-butter shoulder. Leaves spun against the windshield like in a car wash, pouring rain. Then a jolt. He bit the seat and tasted blood. He saw a mighty branch, arched, white, bones showing through a skirt of leaves.

Flying buttress, said the Rabbitoh, the one with long black hair.

The mother was pressed against the boy, all tied up with worry. He could feel the heavy weight of the tree, pushing and groaning on the roof like a boat tied against a pier. The air was roaring, carrying inside its throat a clearer harder hammering. He wished they could go home.

Trevor lit a joint, and as its flame ran halfway up its length, the boy saw him twist in his seat and offer it to the mother but her arms uncoiled from around her chest and she struck at it. She shouldn't have.

You're getting high!

Sparks rushed from her hand which she whacked against the seat. A second later she took the boy's hand and rubbed it as if he had gotten on fire as well. She should be careful.

Trevor quietly repaired his injured drugs. The boy could not tell if he was angry or not. He did not say a word but made a humming sound like Jed Schitcher who sold deer meat in the fall. Jed Schitcher's name was on the packets in Grandma's freezer but now the boy was thinking of Jed's skinning knife, him breathing through his mouth, the steaming blue-white stomach never seen by eyes before.

I've got a kid here, the mother said.

Hello kid, said Trevor. You're with feral hippies, Trevor said. How does that feel, kid? His voice went high as he held the smoke.

The boy did not like being teased.

A branch dropped on the roof and the mother sort of squeaked.

Number one rule, Trevor said, never pick up SMs.

The boy did not know what SM meant, only that it must be rude to his mother or himself.

You mean single mother, right? Dial asked.

Trevor picked his teeth.

Just take us to a shelter, OK?

This *is* a shelter, said Trevor. There isn't a better shelter than this.

Please, the mother said. I know it is a drag for you. I'm sorry.

I think you should take us to the town, said the boy.

That made a great big hole of silence in the car. The boy waited with his heart banging in his ears. Then the engine started and Dial squeezed his hand real hard. The car scraped back out into the road. In a short time they got to the little township of Yandina where nothing lived but violent dark.

Leaves and branches everywhere, the street looked skinned, rippling like melted tin.

No shelter here, babe, said Trevor.

But then they found a bright light burning.

There you are, said Trevor. Star of fucking Bethlehem.

The Rabbitoh poked the yellow headlights into the drive of the Yandina Caravan Park. You want to kill your kid, go right ahead.

We're fine, the boy said. Thank you very much.

He felt the mother hesitating. Then he understood what she was seeing through the windshield—a grandma and grandpa with bare legs and black raincoats, poor people, mooring their shuddering trailer to the toilet block. The grandpa had varicose veins. He also had a long blue nylon rope—weightless, glistening, threading through the storm.

A sheet of yellow paper slapped the windshield and when it departed there appeared one more man—red face, one-hundred-ten-volt blue eyes, long white hair stretching up into the night.

The mother lowered her window and the storm rushed in like a tomcat, occupying the backseat and spraying the inside of the windshield.

Five dollars for the lot of youse, the man shouted. Room for all. I've got a nice clean Globe Trotter.

The boy began gathering the Uno cards but the mother dragged him out before he got done. Here, she told the man, here's five.

Trevor and the Rabbitoh fled like cowards, suddenly reversing onto the highway, and the stinging gravel was cruel on his bare legs. The boy and his mother ran toward a trailer home shivering on its blocks.

Then the generator failed, so the boy would recall when he only lived inside the memory of a man.

Under hypnotism on East Seventy-sixth Street he would once more see the spooky-eyed proprietor lighting two propane lights which roared like jets at forty thousand feet. At that moment he was recognized, he was certain, and he stared straight back. Years later he understood—he had wanted to get caught. After the hypnosis he drank Armagnac in the Carlyle, flirting mildly with the waitress. You look familiar, she said.

In a minute the pair of them were up the ladder beneath the dented metal and the mother held him to her in the rocking bed.

It's better here, Dial, he said. We're doing fine.

I'm proud of you, she said. You spoke up for us.

His usual sleeping thoughts were of his mother coming to rescue him. Now he had her, he was safe and inside the heaving chest of storm; he went to sleep and when he was tipped out it was hours later and he was falling to the earth.

9

Throughout the night the trailer was punched and hammered so unpredictably, with such force, it seemed this thing might really kill them. There was nothing for Dail to do but hold the boy, listen to the adenoidal whispers of his sleep, while her legs ached with all the terror she had banned from her embrace.

There were some calmer stretches, but each return of violence seemed more drunken. The trailer began to lift and drop and the noise was soon so loud that the physical world lost all cohesion, and Dial found herself clinging to the axles of a ghost train. She could not let go, could not make it stop. She lay rigid in the bed, whispering to the boy—prayers, thoughts, wishes, things she hoped would worm their way like pretty threads into his sleeping brain.

There was no moon, no lightning that she could see. When she was tipped over it was into a sea of ink, her body wrapped around the sleeping child.

Her head cracked. She saw stars. She thought, Comic strip.

It's OK, baby, it's OK, babe. She was not knocked out but she could feel the ceiling with her backbone, sliding along the ground, grinding across stones as the trailer moved along the earth while she remained rigid, anticipating some horror, a stabbing blade, a hoe turned lethal in the night.

Baby. Che.

He did not answer and she thought, He's dead.

What happened, Mom?

Shush, she said, feeling the terror of that word even in the middle of this other fear. Hush. It's just the storm.

Are we OK?

Shush, she ordered.

Then came a noise without meaning, like a giant Mexican tin crow flapping its wings against the walls. She thought, What does it matter who his mother is? We are being torn apart.

We're OK, baby, it'll finish soon.

Then he was very quiet.

Che?

He was asleep.

Their blankets had fallen with them and she wrapped him tight, keeping her ear near his mouth so she could know he was alive. She tried to feel his pulse but he tugged his arm free in irritation and slept with his nose down and his bottom in the air.

Perhaps he was in a coma—Manslaughter, she thought. They were rocketed and buffeted, wheels in the air, soft belly offered to the sky until, finally, there came a time when the movement was not much worse than being in a dinghy moored too tightly for the chop. Her sleep was cut with something white and sharp, a knife of light went clear through her lids. She opened her eyes, saw the furry velvet shapes and then the lightning. Not lightning. She thought oxyacetylene. A rescue team. She carefully untangled herself from the boy, leaving him with his arms thrown wide, his lips gone violet-brown.

Sitting on the ceiling she could see through the top half of the door, showers of exploding sparks rising into the rain, a dancing snake of power line on a Kombi van. Figures dressed in trash bags stood before this wild machine while the water lapped at their feet, electric worms wriggling inside the river's molten plastic-looking heart.

Dial found her backpack, then realized it was directly beneath a leak. So what, she thought. They were both alive. Her scarf was dripping wet, but the passports were OK inside their plastic sleeves. In the bottom she found some papers, a soggy mess of railway timetables and directions to Vassar, also her letter of appointment. It was nothing. Easily get another, but she sat cross-legged in the intermittent gloom and extracted the envelope and very carefully peeled the four tips apart so that the letter itself was exposed, sodden and vulnerable but blessedly whole. It meant nothing, but she held it in two hands, as if fearful she would burst its secret yolk. Carefully she placed it flat on the aluminum ceiling that was now her floor. Then, using her wet scarf, she began to smooth it flat, and as she squeezed out the final bubble the paper tore in half. Fuck it. She balled it in her fist and squeezed it, wringing the water into her lap. Fuck it fuck it fuck it fuck it. The fucking professor gave her Susan's number, but no one made her call it. She did not even like the Selkirks. Vassar should take her back, fuck them, fuck it. She did not even know that she was crying. But he did, the boy.

Are you OK? he whispered.

She had no choice. She had to be OK. She came back to bed and held him.

Are you crying, Dial?

I'm fine, baby. I didn't sleep much, that's all.

Why are you crying?

It's nothing, baby, something that happened a long time ago.

10

What had happened long ago was she had been a total fool. That was a long time ago and very recent. She believed people, always had—for instance, the handwriting on the ticket. *Change of plan. Mrs. Selkirk expects you back tonight.* The worst was—she believed it because the hand was so dogged, so dull, so lacking in imagination. She was such a snob she did not see the lie. And so she had let herself be their instrument, be used to steal the child.

He was a sweet boy, in many ways, but he was not hers. And this was definitely not her life.

The Philly Greyhound station had been a scuzzy place and it was with serious reluctance that she had left him in the waiting room alone. The telephone was just outside the door, by the restrooms, by the back door to the pizza parlor. She did not yet know she had been manipulated. She was still being a good girl and a snob all at once. She phoned the Philadelphia number written on her ticket. The line was busy. As the coin returned a strung-out woman, very white with scared blond hair and puffy eyes, came through from the pizza parlor. They locked eyes before Dial turned away.

Here you are, honey.

The woman was holding up a string of pearls. One of her nails was missing. Make me an offer, baby. I'll give you a good price.

The number was busy. She shook her head at the pearls. The woman had a red line running up her leg from her sneaker to her knee. She hunched over her purse and removed four quarters and realized she was being misunderstood.

She deposited the quarters and listened to the phone ringing on Park Avenue. The woman was close behind her. She could smell stale bread and antiseptic.

The phone was picked up.

Hello.

There was a noise, like ice cubes rattling. Hello. It was a man. In the background there was an interfering woman.

Who is it? the man asked, perhaps obediently. Dial heard a three-martini lunch traveling through the dusk from Park.

Anna Xenos.

Anna Zeno, the man said. Idiot, she thought, as he placed his hand across the phone.

There was some kind of shuffling, a fast fierce expletive. She noted with relief that the pearl woman had retreated to the bathroom door where she appeared to be wrapping the necklace in newspaper.

Where are you? Phoebe Selkirk exploded in her ear.

In Philadelphia, of course.

There was a long silence.

You have my boy.

Of course.

Another long silence and when she spoke again her voice had hit another register. What do you want? asked Mrs. Selkirk.

What do I want? said Dial. She should have said, They gave me a ticket and a phone number. The number does not answer. What should I do? But she was watching a very strange sick woman slide past, her eyes on Dial, her nylon jacket brushing noisily against the wall.

What do you want, damn you.

Mrs. Selkirk, do not speak to me like that. I'm not your servant anymore.

You were not to leave New York. You were to have him back here. Where are you? Tell me now.

I am trying to dial the damn number I was given. That's what I am trying to do. I have some drug addict pestering me and your grandson is by himself, all right. Here I am. Now *you* tell me what I am to do.

This produced the most extraordinary outburst of crying which Dial was not prepared for. Again the man and Mrs. Selkirk argued. Again the hand went across the receiver.

Hello, he said.

Will you please kindly tell me what I am to do.

You may as well know, young missy, we know who you are and this call has been traced.

The woman with the pearls was standing now, at the entrance to the waiting room. Dial thought, Don't go in there, but she did, sliding, not perfectly in control.

Do you have any idea who you are dealing with, the man said, made stupid by his slur.

I'll call you back, Dial said.

She rushed back to the waiting room door where she could see the boy had taken out his papers and was laying them out beside him on the seat. Above his head a silent television displayed a picture of Susan Selkirk: PHILLY BOMB BLAST. 2 DEAD.

The woman with the pearls was at her shoulder, her eyes also on the set.

What happened? Dial whispered.

Crazy bitch blew herself up.

Here?

Up near Temple. Fool.

When?

She shook her head, meaning Who could say. She held out

her newspaper parcel as if a deal had been concluded. Caught in the weird focus of her baleful gaze, Dial opened her change purse and gave her three singles.

God bless you, said the woman, and thrust the paper into Dial's hand.

You've got blood poisoning, Dial said.

The woman started, then raised her upper lip to laugh.

Your leg, Dial said.

The woman shook her head and began to laugh uncontrollably, staggering a little as she made her way out to the street.

Dial untangled the newspaper and was not at all surprised to find it empty.

Who was that, the boy asked when she returned.

Susan Selkirk was making bombs! She wanted me to bring her child to a bomb factory.

I've got to call New York, she said.

She balled up the newspaper and thrust it in the trash. When she looked up her yearbook picture was on television. She thought, They think I'm blown to pieces. The boy was still sorting out his papers. She snatched one of his papers up. What's that? she asked, forcing him to look.

D-i-l-e, he said, holding up her card.

The boy's picture was on the screen right now.

I know, she said. I really dig your papers. Her heart was pounding. Her eyes were everywhere, on the card, the screen, the woman in the street who was now walking toward a man with a suitcase.

The news finished. She said, I won't be a moment, baby. Are you OK?

He looked up. What a strange contained creature he was, folding up his papers so they were mostly the size of a cigarette pack, stacking them carefully on top of one another. I'm fine. He smiled at her, holding up his left hand to show his splayed fingers and his rubber bands. I'm cool, he said.

At the Belvedere, they had seen the news, or not. They

knew Susan Selkirk was dead, perhaps. The phone was answered by a new man, colder, clearer, with a Brooklyn accent. Could it have been the cops so fast?

Hi ya, Anna. What's up?

She had not even said her name.

I was instructed to come here to Philadelphia, she told whoever it was. I was just doing what I was asked to do by the family.

Anna, Mrs. Selkirk put the child in your care for two hours.

Would a cop say that? Wouldn't he know it would scare her? In her mind's eye she could see the bus ticket, the hand-writing. She understood: Susan Selkirk had used her to steal her child.

So, the man said, and of course he was a cop. So, what are your plans now, Anna?

I'm coming back on the bus, she said, thinking she had a Massachusetts state bursary check—two thousand dollars—in her purse.

Uh-huh. Back to the city. What time, Anna?

Oh, I'll be on the next one, she said. Up the road there was a snaky red neon: CHECKS CASHED.

So you're near the bus station now, the man said.

She could see the wash of police light on the shining hall-way floor.

See you then, she said. She hung up.

What next? the boy asked when she returned to him. He was already binding his rubber bands around his papers as she crouched in front of him. Was it weird for one so young to be so neat? She could see the street over his shoulder. The woman with the pearls was sitting on the hood of a police car.

We'll stay in a hotel, she said. How about that?

You said we were going to a scuzzy house, he said, but he smiled at her again, his eyes so wide and trusting she wanted to tell him not to be like that.

Plans have changed, she said. She did not say, Your mommy screwed us both.

When he had his papers in their proper place she led him down toward the washrooms, out through the pizza parlor, out into another street. She had no idea where she was, or where they were going, but when they came to a hotel she knew this had to be the one. The stairs smelled like the woman with blood poisoning, of disinfectant and the thing the disinfectant was there to hide. She paid out her own money. She took the key which was wired to a huge link of chain and she led him along the hallway past numbered doors each one of which she expected contained someone vile or sad.

There were no shadows in their room.

Where are you going now? he asked and she hugged him too hard, and then acted casual, checking her purse for the Massachusetts money. All she knew was she was in trouble. She had been tricked. The only witness who could save her had just killed herself with her messy habits. Crumbelina, Dial had called her, secretly of course. Crumbelina had smeared butter across the countertops in Somerville. She could not make a bed, let alone a revolution.

She was sorry she had to abandon this boy. She kissed him and locked herself out. She was the Alice May Twitchell Fellow. She was an assistant professor at Vassar College. So this could not be true, that she was apparently a fugitive, fleeing down a creepy hallway in Philadelphia.

11

The mother and the boy were adrift, together in a trailer, with her Harvard book bag hugged between them, and the boy pretended that the prowling storm was just boat spray on Kenoza Lake, in his face and on his feet, and the mother was warm and foggy and he held her tight, his lips against her arm no matter what. He slept and when he woke the light was gray as East River mist and the trailer was fluttering but no longer rocking. Water dripped beside him, pooling in the bright green lake of rug.

How could he have been happy? It was in almost every sense impossible. He had been torn from his soil, thrown through the sky. In spite of which he remembered, vividly, years later—a brief period of deep tranquillity.

The door was in the ceiling, opening to a pale gray sky. He was washed clean of worry, restored.

Then a rooster crowed. Then someone tried to start a chain saw. And then the kitten came, and the kitten was in no way calm.

At first the boy did not even recognize it as a creature with a heart, but something sprung and needled, metal, plastic, a scratchy noise that had to bring itself to him to be identified, a tiny rib cage with drowned rat fur and wild green eyes and it came along the top of the kitchen drawers on which he and Dial were lying and the boy saw all its fright and made a purring noise himself and opened his mouth, O.

Poor kitty. How did you get here?

He took off his T-shirt and wrapped it around the kitty—pink mouth asking, green eyes blaming, sharp teeth threatening revenge.

Dial gave over her cardigan for the cat to travel in, gray with blue stripes, one pocket big enough for a book, the other for a kitten. Thus the boy carried him to the upside-down door with the glass in its bottom panel. See that? Wild trees had been stripped bare, a power line had fallen, showers of yellow sparklers in the rain. The straights not really doing anything but standing with their arms folded against the roaring brown river which was now lapping around the edge of the toilets.

He's lucky he found us, Dial.

Who?

Buck.

Buck?

Dial never knew this, but the boy nearly named the cat Kipling, for the Cat That Walked by Himself, for Grandma, for the red-and-gold book upstairs, for the smell of paper one hundred years of age. Instead he named him Buck, for the dog in Jack London's book—He had been suddenly jerked from the heart of civilization and flung into the heart of things primordial.

What's primordial, Dial.

She bit her lip. You crazy little thing, she said. Primordial. What is it.

Wild things, she had said, the law of the wild.

It's a good name for him, he said.

12

All her life Anna Xenos would think of that moment, on the phone in the Greyhound station, when she might have explained herself to whomever she was speaking to. Yet each of the thousands of times she walked that particular road she arrived at the same point where there was no road at all—she crashed and burned before Philly, at Vassar, in the chair's office, when she had gotten high on knowing Susan Selkirk, when she took the phone number, when she looked down at the groundsmen and the fall leaves and thought she belonged there. That was her fatal flaw and it was deep as a septic crack in the heel of her foot, a dirty little crevice that went right down to her bone. When she telephoned Susan Selkirk she was her mother's daughter, bringing home her employer's silver, relishing her connection with the famous.

Hello, Bvains, said Susan Selkirk, the patronizing bitch.

How does it feel?

A complete unknown, walking barefoot up the middle of an empty highway toward Yandina, Queensland, Australia, with a rich boy in one hand and a cat in her damn pocket and all her worldly assets gathered around her person. The black-top was empty, littered with leaves and twigs, a branch or two, but mostly smooth and weirdly slappy in the rain. If there was a way out of this, she did not see it and she once again regretted not leaving him in that hotel room. That might seem cruel to pet lovers and sentimentalists, but he would be with his grandma now, safe in bed on the other side of the world.

She was from Southie. This township was not like anything she understood. There was no convenience store or deli that she could recognize, just a cutesy post office, small regular cottages with hedges and peeling paint. There was a bar which was like the fishermen's bars along the Delaware at Callicoon, staring redneck windows, dirty glass protecting the sexual bravado of morons.

Dial, look.

The boy had found a bottle full of milk and was already poking his dirty fingernail at its foil top.

Stop it.

She snatched it from him. Her heart was beating way too fast, this sudden terror of transgression.

Where'd you get that?

On the stoop.

Baby, she said, this is a very redneck place. Do you understand? We do not steal. We don't want to get arrested.

He looked at her, all bruised and blaming.

We can get in *so* much trouble, she insisted.

For drinking milk? He dared to raise his eyebrows.

Yes, for drinking goddamned milk. She would not be a mother. All her life she watched the Irish girls, a new crop each season, their bellies pushing at their jeans.

You shouldn't yell, he said.

Oh please! She replaced the single bottle on the weathered single step and, without holding out her hand for him, walked diagonally across the deserted street to the post office, a small clapboard building with a raised white painted veranda. He came rushing behind her and she felt a ridiculous and savage pleasure in her victory.

Should we get cat food, Dial?

Against all her inclinations, she laughed, and kissed him.

No, he said. Really. As if he could not accept such intimacy. Should we? he asked.

She raised an eyebrow.

There was no one around except a peculiar woman with a duck-leg walk who emerged from the street alongside the bar, but that was about one hundred yards farther down.

Buck is hungry, the boy said, but Dial did not have her contact lenses and was trying to resolve what she was seeing, not a woman at all. Maybe the hippie. The skirt was a sarong. His strange breasts soon revealed themselves as trousers, stuffed like sausages, hanging around his neck. She had never seen Trevor walk before, but this was how he did it—a sort of heterosexual sashay.

Dial removed her cardigan and gave it to the boy, the protesting kitten swinging loudly to and fro.

You can pet him until we find him food.

She watched Trevor getting closer. She thought, My armpits stink.

Where did you come from? she asked.

They had not parted on good terms, but this morning it seemed they had a history. He replied with a smile, hidden like chewing tobacco, tucked inside the corner of his mouth.

Hello boy, the hippie said, removing the lumpy trousers from around his neck. Hello cat.

Away from the dreadful car, he was different, his eyes wider, less stoned probably, and he gave off a surprising aura of good health. The raindrops stood on his bare brown skin as if it was a well-oiled coat or healthy vegetable. From his unknotted trouser legs he produced a large papaya, a hand of tiny bananas, the stems still oozing a pale white sap, a huge green zucchini, another papaya, this one with a bright green patch, and a purple eggplant, all of them wet and lustrous.

Plus, he said.

A bottle of milk.

The boy caught Dial's eye and she rubbed his head

roughly as if to acknowledge that she would let him win that round. It was with some distinct pleasure that she observed him watch Trevor remove the silver foil. He cocked his head attentively as the hippie dipped his square-tipped finger into the milk and offered it to the kitten's open sharp-toothed mouth.

Give's your hand, he said to the boy, in that musical accent they had. She watched with approval as he dipped the boy's finger in the wildly creamy milk, guiding it to the kitten's desperate tongue. She liked him then, more than she had imagined possible.

Trevor led the way up the veranda steps. He was not tall, indeed two inches shorter than Dial, but she was relieved that he had a real physical authority as he squatted, pouring milk directly into his cupped hand.

Our trailer tipped over, the boy said.

You bet, he said. Of course.

Trevor hopped about the floor, found a wooden-handled clasp knife in his trousers and drew its blade around the papaya which opened like a book—a color plate *Carica papaya*. Trevor scooped the black seeds in one swift movement and held them dripping in his fist.

I hurt my arm, the boy said. I fell out of my bed.

Eat food, the man instructed.

Trevor threw the seeds over the rail.

Just put your face in it, he told the boy, giving the other half to Dial. He did not look at her but as she took the dripping fruit she felt some double entendre which she did not like at all. It made her hesitate, but at the same time she found herself thinking about her appearance, that her hair was oily and flat on her head. My nose is huge, she thought, before she gave in to the papaya. But when this was finished there was nothing else, no plan, no strategy, and when the postmaster arrived to open shop she saw how he looked down on her, her face wet with papaya, her great Greek nose sticking in the air.

13

The boy ate six small bananas, maybe eight, and his belly was tight as a drum. There was a water tap down the steps and when he washed his hands he saw the black seeds shining in the dirt. He dug them up and washed them too, setting them on the concrete sidewalk. When he had ten of them he turned them over to dry their undersides and then he put them in his back pocket with his stuff. There were also little creepy bugs with lots of legs.

Back on the veranda he poured more milk for Buck, who sniffed it and then walked away, preferring the hem of Dial's long hippie dress. In the Best Western in Seattle the boy had watched Dial sew up that very hem, purple with blue-green waxy thread. That had been in the days after Bloomingdale's, but they had moved on to *White Fang* already. He had a passport. His hair had been buzzed and dyed and he believed his mother's hem was now everything, not only to her, but to him as well. At customs he thought he heard its contents shiver. Most likely it was beyond adult hearing, but now Buck definitely heard something, like a deck of whispery cards being dealt, perhaps, or two green leaves sliding face-to-face. His gray-striped ears pricked up. He stepped delicately out across the post office veranda floor. He batted once at the hem, but Dial's hand swept down like God's from heaven, circling his pet life and his organs.

Buck peed. The boy poured him milk so he would know he loved him just the same, but the cat cocked his head, and watched it drip away.

Buck, Buck, Buck. He grabbed. Buck feinted left and then leaped on the hem.

Now Dial grabbed. Then Buck squawked. Dial unhooked his claws, and held him out toward the boy, who tucked the fierce little creature inside the cardigan and tied him in a friendly knot.

Take him for a walk.

He took Buck down the steps and showed him the seeds and washed two for him. He taught him to count. Buck tried to kill the bugs and then got puzzled and then he went back up the steps and the boy washed some more seeds and lined them up, about thirty, before he was ordered to take Buck away again.

Where can I go?

He meant, Don't send me away from you.

There's a very interesting war memorial, Trevor said.

I'm OK here, the boy said.

Go, called Dial.

He dropped Buck in the cardigan and slung the cardigan around his neck. At the far end of the street, in front of the Wild West bar, he could see a lonely statue ringed by long green grass. In the old chapel near 116th Street he had seen white marble slabs with the names of Columbia students who had died in the Civil War. His grandma took him. She said, These children want to make another civil war.

She had meant his mom and dad. He was old enough to know she should not talk to him like this.

They never think they'll die, she said, her voice getting

that catch to it, a sort of flutter she saved for stuff like this. She didn't know how bad this felt. She didn't know he listened to her breathing in the night.

I know, he said—to stop her being bohemian, to make her quiet.

As the boy came down the post office steps he had to jump over the Rabbitoh arranging his long brown legs.

The sky was gray and thick and furry. Steam rose from the blacktop. When he arrived at the memorial he saw a small bronze lizard cross the soldier's dead blind eyes.

Yellow lights arrived flashing like a police car—a truck. The driver stared at him and raised a finger from the wheel. It was a local wave, but the boy did not know what sort of sign it was. He was not worried very much but he hurried back to the post office where Buck got free and jumped up to the railing. He was about eight inches long, all pink mouth and spiky hair.

Dial laughed at him so Buck flew through the air. His barbed-hook claws found the lovely purple hem, and when Dial jumped to her feet, he still hung there. No one imagined how confused he felt. Trevor was leaning back resting on one elbow but he hardly had to reach to get one hand around his milky middle. As he yanked, Buck screamed.

Let go, you silly bugger.

The claws were caught. Trevor pulled harder. The dress ripped. A flood of green hundred-dollar bills sliced through the gray cyclonic air.

The mother's speckly eyes flicked up and down the street, then toward the dark open door of the post office. She lifted a single bill from between her long straight toes.

Trevor kneeled and unhooked the claws from the torn hem and then gave the cat to the boy.

Scram, he said.

The boy's throat was dry. He moved closer to Dial, next to, and behind.

The Rabbitoh came forward across the floor like a squatting monkey in a dance, his long hands harvesting the spilled bills which he stacked and shuffled as he neared.

Don't sweat it, he said. It's cool. He passed his loot to the mother without expression. She protected the remainder of the injured velvet in one hand.

If you knew us, said Trevor, you wouldn't look like that.

How *do* I look, the mother asked.

Like you just shat yourself, said Trevor.

Dial threw her head back and laughed all wrong, like a fat kid on the first day at school.

The boy could not see her face, only the bright light in the eyes of both the men.

14

As Trevor slipped his trousers on, he never took his eyes off
the mother.

You better come for a walk, he said.

Dial did not move.

Little chat, Trevor insisted, his mouth opening on the left
side.

The boy watched everything, his throat gone very dry.

The mother held up the broken hem, meaning the
hundred-dollar bills would fall out if she stood. This money
was their life and death; she had made that very clear when
they received it from his father's friends. With money you
could pay the pigs, buy a room with a bath, a real hotel. If
someone might hurt you, then you gave them something
folded. It was just like Grandma paid the janitor, the super,
Eduardo, an envelope every Christmas. Do you think they
really like you?

Can't walk, suggested Trevor.

Uh-huh. Dial's cheeks were pink as bubble gum.

The boy thought, Give him the money. Make him go away.
He wished they had found his dad in Sydney but the squat
they went to was filled with junkies who did not know his

name. He wished his dad would drive into the street, right now.

Trevor called, Hey, Rabbitoh.

Jean Rabiteau was once more seated on the post office steps, cleaning his fingernails with a silver clasp knife. The knife seemed sharp. He was paying a worrying amount of attention to such a simple job.

Want to get the vehicle, mate?

The Rabbitoh uncoiled himself. When he was upright he removed his hat, flicked his glossy black hair out of his eyes. He replaced the hat so the brim was low and hid his thoughts from view. Then he wandered off down toward the Wild West bar, not hurrying, but prancy in bare feet.

John and me, Trevor said, we can take care of your items.

The boy thought, Just pay him. Make them go away.

At least there are two of us, said Trevor.

Dial laughed but her hand was wet and slippery.

Trevor raised a pale eyebrow and showed an old scar line hinged across its middle.

No one's making you do nothing, he said at last. He paused to watch the sun slice across the mother's great long legs. We can drive you to the bank in Nambour, he said. The big town with the sugar mill.

It was an ugly town; the boy had seen the cruel black stacks, the freight cars of sugarcane rolling through the thunder, a bad dream on the dark side of the earth.

Nambour, Trevor said. You saw it yesterday.

As he spoke, the Ford slid in, pinching its bumper hard along the curb. The Rabbitoh's elbow was stuck out the window, but what the boy noticed most was a quick flash of silver in his hidden hand.

You can go back to Nambour, Trevor said. If you so desire, babe. We'll drop you there right now.

The mother looked over her shoulder where the sad-eyed postmaster was sorting out the mail. She said, Can we discuss this somewhere less public?

The boy preferred the postmaster to watch over them, but Trevor took the mother's hand and led her away from him, down the steps. She held out her hem like a bridesmaid at his cousin Branford's wedding.

The car's floor was awash with bad black water from the storm. The boy held Buck inside his woolly pouch. The pair of them, cat and boy, looked down together as the water surged and sloshed. As they accelerated up the highway five soggy Uno cards sailed out from under the front seat. Buck struggled, then went still.

Trevor's arm lay along the top of his seat like a squeezing snake. They left the highway, drove past five small houses. Then the blacktop ended, and Trevor twisted himself to look back at Dial whose feet were tucked beneath her hibiscus skirt.

You could just fix up the hem, he said. Do you have a needle?

Dial kind of stared him down.

Do you?

Dial did not budge.

Or you can just get out, Trevor said suddenly. He jerked away. I don't give a fuck, he said. But he did give some kind of fuck because he spun around again. If you go to the bank in Nambour, he said, they'll call the cops before you leave. Christ, get over yourself.

The boy's stomach tasted like the inside of a tuna can.

Please, Trevor said, and showed his ragged teeth, you have no fucking idea of where you are or who I am, so don't be fucking sarcastic. You're American. You wouldn't know if you were up yourself.

The car slowed, then stopped. No one spoke. They should have left the car right then.

I'm sorry, Dial said.

In response the car began to creep between the walls of bush, and the Uno cards went under the seat and only three returned, two reds, a yellow.

What's happening? the boy asked. No one heard him anymore.

The car left the dirt road for something worse, a kind of track which wound up a ridge, along a hillside rutted with deep tire marks.

The mother gripped the top of the seat in front. What's going on here?

He thought, Just give them money, Dial.

Buck twisted and complained. Trevor told him to shut his mouth. The car smashed against the cutting and an acacia poked in Dial's open window and left a long line of blood from eye to mouth. They were on a downhill slalom on a long shining streak of yellow mud—plunging, sick and slick, John swinging on the useless wheel, the boy now feeling throw-up in his throat.

There was one last bump and something heavy crashed on the metal floor. They came to rest at a flat place where people had driven in a circle.

What's this? the mother asked.

The bank, said Trevor.

The boy thought maybe he would not vomit. He heard crows, saw burned-out cars, a lot of sorry-looking charcoal, bust-up fires.

We'll leave you to count, Trevor said.

The boy's stomach was a football of bad old air. He stayed with the mother as she slid the money from her hem.

Will you give it to them?

What do you think?

But what will happen to us then?

She put her arms around him and kissed him on his neck. Being squiffy in the stomach, he pulled away.

I don't have time for this, she said.

She soon gave the hippies money. First she laid it on the hot hood of the wagon. Then Trevor counted. Then John. It was eighteen thousand one hundred American.

The boy said, I have to be sick.

All right, Dial said, where is the safe?

Trevor nodded backward at the woods.

Do we have to walk far?

Leave it to Beaver, said Trevor. The boy watched while he slipped between the saplings, hipless, no butt in his pajama pants. Then he followed, his stomach heaving as he ran.

15

He vomited in the lantana and across his feet. He held the kitty to one side and threw up along a kind of path—severed stems, cut branches, banana and papaya. Stuff from his stomach, stuff he never even ate, spread across the blackberries.

He had nothing to wipe himself with except the cardigan. He spat. There was a sea of ferns beyond the brambles, like fish bones, covering a wide saddle. He broke off some of these to clean himself as well as he could.

Vomiting was ugly, shameful, mixed up with his feelings about soggy Uno cards and seeds. He told the cat he was sorry for the smell. The trees were wide apart here. They had twisted gray corded bark. Different birds were high up in their khaki canopies but there was another noise, like water, maybe wind.

He stroked the kitten's bony head but even the tips of his fingers seemed fouled and filthy. He could hear a river, or it was the wind high in the trees, or the two, mixed up together.

He could smell damp. He knew damp. Maple woods in summer, rotting things, black mud. He went farther along the left side of the saddle, not far. Here was the edge of a rough red riverbank, no question. A big tree had fallen, its clay- and pebble-crusted roots naked in the air like dried-out innards. The trunk, which made a bridge between the flood bank and the low bank, was about as big across as a man is tall and he soon found a place, just below the disturbed earth, where you could jump down onto its broad back, like the back of an elephant or a slippery seal, and he walked along it, with the kitten now meowing softly, down to the place where the timber splintered and smashed and speared into the earth. The smell of damp was rich with rot.

Steel pincers pierced his skin.

He screamed.

He jumped to the soft ground. He hurt his foot. He dropped the cat. He ripped at his shirt.

Stay still, said Trevor, who came from nowhere, a nasty-looking groundhog, completely naked, covered in mud and dirt. Stay still.

The boy shrieked in fear.

Trevor took the boy's shirt off over his head. The pain went on and on without reason.

Got it, Trevor said.

And held a shining ant, two inches long, a stinking, angry, black, plastic-coated, dying Australian thing.

Bull ant, he said.

The boy stayed frozen, vomity, ashamed, his pain still pulsing, while Trevor walked down among the wide tall grass toward Buck, who was drinking something. Trevor found water too, enough to wash some mud from his own body. He shook himself like a dog. Then he grabbed the cat, held it locked inside his arm.

Did you come looking to see where my stash is hid? He had pale blue eyes, hard as broken bathroom tile.

The kitten was afraid, his mouth as wide and pink as dentistry.

No, sir.

Trevor returned the cat and then put both his hands on the

boy's square bare shoulders. He did not squeeze or hurt, but it was a hard and heavy weight without forgiveness.

You wouldn't want to see.

I want to wash.

You understand it would be a bad thing to see?

I threw up, the boy said. I need to wash the stuff off.

Once, not so long before, he had pooped himself. He had been hosed down in public by a nasty man in boots.

Come here, said Trevor.

The boy was relieved to feel his hand held gently.

See, Trevor said.

The boy looked down into the ground—it was the damp he had smelled, a smeary rainbow, thick clumps of brown grass.

Snakes.

He could see no snakes. All he saw was water.

There. What do you reckon that is?

He thought, A bone?

It's not a good idea to come looking for my stash. You understand me.

At that moment the boy saw the actual stash, in the fallen tree. On the underside there was a splintered rotten place where there was blue plastic showing clear as day.

You understand? Trevor's eyes were cold enough to hurt.

Yes, sir.

Don't call me sir, Trevor said.

The boy washed his arms and legs and down his front. He did not stare at where the money was.

You OK now?

Yes thank you.

You don't come back here without me, OK. The voice was not unkind.

From the corner of his eye the boy could see the flag of blue plastic. It was so clear, like underpants showing through an unzipped pair of shorts.

Always look at the ground, Trevor said, as they headed up the saddle.

The boy did what he was told.

Where's your father?

What?

Where's your dad? Trevor mocked the boy's shrug. What does that mean?

I don't know, sir, he said, his heart like a washing machine inside his ears. He thought his dad might be in Sydney but no one knew his name.

Trevor took the boy's chin and tilted it so there was no escaping the interrogation.

The boy's blood was swooshing and thumping in his ears. He met Trevor's cold gaze and let himself be seen in all his everything.

That's right, Trevor said as he released him. That's right.

The boy understood his secret had been touched. There had been a conversation of some sort.

16

She had gone through Sydney and Brisbane on chocolate bars and Coca-Cola, trusting the force of her will and energy to reach the other side. It was what she was used to doing, and of course there had been more to it than Hershey bars. In the aftermath of Susan Selkirk's death she had trusted Harvard men to save her. She knew famous people, Dave Rubbo, Bernadine Dohrn, Mike Waltzer, Susan Selkirk obviously. On the run with Che she had trusted the Movement, most particularly that Harvard representative of Students for a Democratic Society whose silky penis she had once loved holding between her lips. It was he, with his large hand resting very lightly on her forearm, who had persuaded her that they would be safe and cared for in Australia.

We've got people there, he said.

What crap that turned out to be.

It was the Movement which had provided the passports, so she was given to understand, although what the Movement was by 1972 depended on whom you were talking to. Some like Waltzer were now campaigning for the Democrats; Bernadine Dohrn and the others had formed the Weather Underground. Susan Selkirk had belonged to a faction that had threatened to shoot Mike Waltzer. Instead she'd gone underground and blown herself sky-high.

Dave Rubbo said he was in an alliance with the Black Panthers. He showed Dial an AK47 and gave her air tickets from San Francisco to Honolulu to Sydney, Australia. He scared her. She took the bundles of dollars not understanding the transaction. She bought nuts and candy and comics for the flight. She had no guidebook, no Australian currency. She had no idea of what Australia even *was*. She would not have imagined a tomato would grow in Australia, or a cucumber. She could not have named a single work of Australian literature or music. Why would she? It was only temporary. She persisted with this all the way up to Yandina, through the storm, the stolen money. It was only when Trevor and the boy ran into the bush, when she was left alone to face the bulge in Jean Rabiteau's pants, she knew she had fallen into a pit she would not get out of easily.

She picked up a sturdy broken branch, maybe four feet long.

Are you on the Pill?

The branch was seared by fire, black as velvet in her hands. Looking at the Rabbitoh's excited eyes, she thought, He has no idea what I could do to him.

The Rabbitoh stepped forward and she knew that this had always been her destination. She had a father with bullet wounds in both his hands; she should have trusted that.

Cool down, babe.

She saw his fragile collarbone, felt the heat of tropical sunshine on her back, heard the flies attempting to crawl into her ears.

She swung at him and he stepped back, stumbling. This moment had been waiting all her life. This was always going to happen but who could have known? Who could have told her? When, in 1957, she huddled in the doorway of the Girls' Latin School, waiting for the janitor to arrive for work, it was this that was on the other side of that bright green door, not the silverware her mother wished for her. Fish fork, salad fork, dinner fork. The fish fork is shorter, with broader tines to pick out bones. The salad fork is shorter than the dinner fork, and has one tine on the left side that is thicker than the others. This way you can cut the lettuce without a knife. She had no time for silverware. She would crack his fucking collarbone if need be. She could not imagine what came next. In New York she could not imagine Philly. In Philly she could not have imagined Seattle. In Seattle she could not have imagined the Australian Builders Labourers Federation where she had brought the boy and her request for help. She sat beneath the neon wondering who controlled the Australian garment industry, who decided on these Chinese zippers down the front of the maroons and dirty greens. Albania, she thought, must be like this.

But she was cute. She smiled at them. I'm sorry, this particular young man said. He was big and plain with worryingly short hair. They had gone to sit in a coffeehouse in Harris Street, Ultimo. Che was pouring sugar into his Coca-Cola. The young man talked to her earnestly, gazing somewhere above her shoulder.

This is not something we can involve ourselves with. He spoke like this, politely, dully. To Dial he sounded English and when he cupped his hands around his teacup she saw him like someone in a film who would say guv'nor.

He was just so completely *straight*. He was blunt, with conscript's hair.

You know who Dave Rubbo *is*, right. And she was not wrong to expect he would. Those boys had gone a long way since Somerville, gone from playing politics, to being the revolution. She was here because there was an alliance, Dave had said so. This Australian dork was meant to be the vanguard, but he waved all this away.

The executive will not support this, Dial. It's not like you've dodged the draft and we have to hide you.

Draft for what, she asked, watching Che's Coke bubble up

and spill across the table. She found the young man glaring at her directly.

What?

You're joking! he said, wiping up the Coke himself.

Australia is in Vietnam?

His cheeks were red, his eyes blue and cold.

Right? She tried to catch herself. Vietnam.

But he was already standing, an earnest lanky boy, raw jawed, with heavy workman's boots and a tartan shirt. It's a shame, he said, you never learn more about the countries that you fuck with.

But he had misunderstood who she was. I'm in SDS, she said. Dave Rubbo's friend.

He stood with his big hands grasping the back of the chair, looking down at her, the dress, the golden hair she had washed that morning. He laughed through his nose. Good luck, mate, he said to Che.

Thank you, said the boy.

It was not until Bog Onion Road that she could no longer ignore the extent of Dave Rubbo's deceit, but by then she had other creeps to deal with.

When Trevor came back into the clearing, she threw the lump of wood down at the Rabbitoh's feet and walked toward the boy. His hand was sticky but she held it tight.

Where are we going?

There was always a way forward. She dragged the boy, resisting, toward the road.

Oh come *on*. The Rabbitoh was slinking after her, his hands outspread. Don't be so uptight.

We'll drive you, Trevor said. He had to raise his voice because they were already well up the first hill. Do you want a receipt?

Receipt for a fucking robbery, she thought. But she had money left, whosever money it was. She would damn well need it too, and all she knew was she must buy a map, find out where she was. She must go where no one knew about this treasure, this currency that she could not change.

Her name was Anna Xenos. Xenos meant displaced person, stranger, a man who arrived on the island of Zákinthos years before the birth of Christ.

Trevor called, Don't you want to know where I live? His was a full-chested shout, filling the steep valley of peeling trees.

She paused a moment, looking down the track at the two men.

You should get his address, the boy said quietly.

If she had been nicer she would have answered him but she had too many battles raging inside her head. She was imagining their bodies, her's and Che's, found decaying in woods.

What about our money, Dial? Shouldn't we get his address?

Shut up, she said. OK?

She left him to trudge up the track behind her huge hard fury.

Can you, she demanded, just for once, not have an opinion? You're seven, for Christ's sake.

She waited for him to tell her he was almost eight. He didn't. They walked some more, a little slower.

He knows my daddy, he said.

He stopped then and he stood before her, his arms straight by his side, so armored against her that his little gray eyes had become pinholes in his face.

No, she said. He does not.

I think he does, Dial. I'm pretty certain.

She thought, You'll go mad with this, not knowing who you are.

He knows *about* my daddy then, he said. He shoved his hands into his tight little pockets and stared up at her, a dreadful rigid smile upon his face.

No, babe.

He can tell my daddy where we are.

Sweetie, do not do this to yourself.

She had not meant to be harsh but now his chin began to wobble and he would have broken down if he had not heard the Ford laboring up the hill toward them. She pulled the boy off the track, with his face against her stomach, but as the car came to a stop beside them, he slipped free.

Come on, called Trevor, his thick arm lay in the open window. Get in.

No thanks, she said, but the boy was already at the car.

Nothing's going to happen, Trevor said. He's sorry. He nodded toward the driver. He's a creep.

I'm meant to be a Christian, said the Rabbitoh, his eyes shining like an animal's in the darkness of its hide.

Please, Dial, can we?

She opened the door and she and the boy sat close together with the kitten in its cardigan between.

Say you're sorry, Trevor said. She was not displeased by his authority, the bulldog body, the thick neck.

The Rabbitoh then apologized and she watched him fold himself across the steering wheel. She thought of the pleasures of submission, a topic she knew more about than she was ready to admit.

Shush, she said to the Rabbitoh, as if he were a child to be forgiven, not some shit with a very nasty knife and a sense of sexual entitlement.

Trevor turned in his seat and held her eyes. John has written you a receipt, he said slowly. You don't want it, OK, but can I give it to his nibs? It's got my postal address? he asked the driver.

It has, he said.

Trevor gave the piece of paper to the boy, who seemed to read it, but it was unclear how much of this was a performance. He certainly folded it extremely carefully before undoing his rubber bands to accommodate it with his stuff.

Abandoned on the highway they watched the Ford turn toward the back road and leave its blue exhaust lying on the blacktop. They were left alone in the shadeless heat, buffeted by the big trucks, dirt swirling up beside them.

Can we just stop going places, Dial?

Soon, she said.

17

To be honest, he had liked it best in Oakland, when they were just together in the motel, eating pizza, playing cards. She read to him then, like for hours at a time and in the night as well. He was as happy as he could ever remember, to have her to himself finally, at last, and the prospect of his father, that electric cloud of surprise hanging over him like vapor from an open bathroom door. She sat cross-legged on the bed and put her skirt in her lap. She had a big mouth and she kissed him lots, her breath all soft and ashen.

Can we stop going places, Dial.

He saw how she paused and listened to him properly, her eyes resting seriously upon his.

Soon, she said. First we have to go to Nambour, baby.

Maybe we don't need to, Dial.

He had carefully retrieved his sodden Uno cards from the backseat of the car and now she gently took possession, kneeled by the highway and fitted them in the outside pocket of her backpack.

He watched her, thinking it must hurt her knees.

We need to go to Nambour now, she said.

What if we get caught?

Her mouth turned down. She didn't know he saw that, the way the whole of her lower face could lose its bones.

What if they take you away from me, he said.

She did not even look at him, but lifted her pack to her shoulders and combed with her fingers at her hair.

What if I could get our money back, Dial?

Shush.

Because I know where it is.

Her hand got caught in a big tangle and she jerked at it, making a face. It had to hurt.

You're a dear brave boy, she said at last, but you better forget whatever it is you saw.

Why?

Because I said so.

She rubbed his head but the nice mood was spoiled.

It's cool, Dial, he said, trying to get it back again.

Shush, she said.

We'll go with the flow.

That should make her smile. It didn't. She started walking with her thumb held out and he was left to carry Buck under the burning sun, along the rutted gravel edges and through the choking dust beside the Bruce Highway, where they finally caught a ride with the manager of a cactus farm who dropped them by the high school.

There were trees by the school but everything else had been chopped down in Nambour long ago, so there was no shade remaining. They itched and hurt, the mother and the boy. They were unwashed, unloved, ripped, "feral" to the local eye. The mother had one infected bite on her calf. She had ten thousand dollars inside her hem, she whispered. This remaining money was secured by a piece of fuse wire provided by the cactus farmer.

He started to think about a motel. Didn't need to be fancy. They would have to do this now.

They came to a car dealership with big glass windows and he stood beside her and he could feel what she was thinking, that she would try and buy a new car with the American dollars. He wished she wouldn't. She opened the door and walked inside. The air-conditioning was very nice but that was all.

They think we're cockroaches, she whispered as they returned to the street. Fuck them, she said, her blackened cut-up hand once more around the boy's shoulders.

Yes, Dial, said the boy. Fuck them, Dial. Soon they could go to a motel and she would read to him. There was one on the main street. It had air-conditioning and color TV he was pretty certain.

Instead they went to a Laundromat. There was a hippie girl emptying dirty clothes from a trash bag. They looked at her.

Then they found an arcade where the sweet rotten sugar smell of Nambour was overcome by patchouli oil and spoiled bananas.

Are we looking for hippies, Dial?

She would not say.

Maybe they sell books here?

But it was a health food store. Above the bulk dried beans, beside the pile of empty molasses cans, was a notice board with ads for massage and meditation and moon dances. Also: four colored photographs of two log huts with cute shingle roofs. These she looked at.

What is it, Dial?

She read, silently, frowning and wrinkling up her nose.

Who lives there?

It's a place for sale.

Let's just stay in a motel.

Shush. Listen. It is fourteen acres on the edge of rain forest, she said. There is water from a spring. There are five hundred fruit trees and an established vegetable garden. See, there's the papaya, like Trevor bought you.

Can we stay in a motel please?

And coffee bushes, she said, and persimmons and lemons and limes and three different varieties of bananas including lady fingers.

What are lady fingers?

She did not know but would not admit it.

It's in the jungle, isn't it?

She fitted her arm around his shoulder and set to stroking him again.

Do you know what bull ants are, he asked.

She was deaf as a dog with a good smell. There's so much information here, she said. Everything but a phone number.

There is no phone, said the woman behind the counter. She had a nice face, like the girl in the Beach Boys poster Cameron had stuck up on his wall. "Good Vibrations" was the single most important song of the last ten years. He knew that.

You're American? She had long blond hair and faded blue eyes and shiny suntanned skin.

Buenos Aires, said Dial. South America.

Yeah? The girl frowned. So how do youse like the Sunshine Coast?

We were interested in this place at Yandina.

No, the boy thought, please.

Yand-eena.

We're interested in it.

No town water. The girl shook her head and smiled. She did not like them, and the boy was pleased. No electricity, she said, sort of singsong. No TV.

Where is this property, Dial asked.

This property, the girl said, mocking the way Dial talked, is out at Remus Creek Road.

Come on, Dial, the boy said, I want to go.

But Dial folded her arms. Where is that exactly?

The girl shrugged. She took a spotty apple from a plastic bowl and rubbed it on her stomach. You go to Yandina post office, she said at last. People hang out there. Ask them.

She placed the apple daintily in front of her and then selected a second from the same plastic bowl. That your cat in your pocket, she asked.

That's exactly what it is.

The girl put her head to one side and appeared to admire the apples. Then she took a knife and began to carefully slice the first.

She said, I doubt they're into cats out there.

The boy was pleased to hear this.

What would anyone have against a kitten, Dial asked the girl, hauling out the sleeping Buck and kissing him on the nose.

Well there are what we call *Australian* birds. And the cats kill the birds. The girl looked up, unsmiling. People don't like that.

Well, said Dial, stroking Buck's head, he is an Australian cat, so I guess he lives here too.

The girl kept slicing and finally they left the store.

We'll find another house, the boy said. Better even.

They hate Americans, said Dial.

They'd like you if they knew who you were.

We don't want them to know, do we?

I guess we're underground, Dial?

Do you like that?

Cameron said you would come and take me underground. So I sort of knew. We'll find a regular house, he said, thinking it must be somewhere on a regular road where his dad would find them. They would need a telephone for sure.

They were walking through the hazy heat up toward the motel. The air was drunk with sugar and soon they were at the highway and the trucks and vans were raging, loud and foul, their tarpaulins flapping like sails on a foundering yacht. Then came a Peugeot blowing smoke, clouds of it as thick as thunder, a Peugeot 203. It was about the one car model that he knew but he was really annoyed to see Dial thumb it down.

What about the motel?

Shush, she said.

Why, Dial, why? he said, still running after her, the opposite direction he wished to go.

But she was already in the car by then.

The Peugeot driver was a freak, long faced, long toothed, straggle bearded. He had narrow bony shoulders and real thin hairy arms like Cameron's.

As they slid into the front there was a rush of air like flapping canvas—a rooster, wings about six feet wide, rising in the air from the shade of the backseat.

Christ! said Dial.

My chooks! The driver swatted over his shoulder, even as he drove away, as the boy got down among the dust and crumpled newspapers, catching the kitty's tail as it fled beneath the seat. He got scratched for this, right down his arm, but when he squeezed back up between the mother's legs, he had Buck safely by his scruff.

Adam, said the driver, peering too closely at him.

Dial, said the mother.

The boy was mad about the motel. He did not say anything.

And where might we two be off to? The driver had a patchy black beard and very heavy eyebrows which rose as he peered at the boy.

Dial said, We need to get to Remus Creek Road.

The boy groaned out loud.

Shush, said Dial. We have to do this first.

Adam was sitting very, very close to the wheel. He cradled it against his chest, and his peeling nose was now stretching toward the glass.

What's that? He pointed, screwing up his face at a big gas station with palm trees for sale. He was a total dork, but he peered directly at the boy who felt he had to answer.

You mean the trees?

Is it Ampol?

The boy could not understand the way Australians spoke, words like ground beef in their mouths. He did not like them generally.

The brand, the freak cried, the bloody brand.

Esso, said Dial.

Right, the freak said, of course. We're fine now, he said, but obviously he could not see. Tell me when you see the caravan park, he said. Who are you visiting at Remus Creek?

We saw a place for sale.

Ah-hah, said Adam and beamed at each of them in turn. He should watch the road.

Fourteen acres, said Adam. Five hundred fruit trees.

That's it.

What's that?

It's a kitten.

Is that the caravan park?

Can't you see? the boy asked. He didn't care that it was rude.

The driver had stopped in the middle of the highway, opposite a tractor yard. A semitrailer passed them on the inside, its siren blaring, the trailer snaking, huge clouds of dust drifting into the sky.

Little more, said Dial.

And then they swerved through the dust and did not die and the rooster rose and the tailpipe thumped and they were clattering along a corrugated track and the car was filled with dust and feathers.

The boy was not going where this freak was going.

I think we've got some problem with the cat, he said.

Dial elbowed him, hard. It hurt.

Adam peered right and left—How could there be a problem with a cat?

Some girl at the health food shop.

Adam made a farting noise. Health food. Oh mate. *Mate!* Molasses merchants. Pesticides, he said. Insecticides. They are putting genes from bloody jellyfish in sugarcane. That's health food.

That's where we saw the place for sale.

Ah yes, said Adam, well there you are. There you are.

Indeed, he continued, careening down a steep rutted hill and splashing across a narrow ford.

You don't want to worry about a thing, he said.

They were now on a softer road, almost sandy. The road was flat, winding between tall forest trees with shining bone-white trunks.

Do you know the place? Dial asked. Can you drop us some-where near.

Near, said Adam, swinging the car violently to the right, fishtailing up a steep clay driveway. Five hundred fruit trees, he said, pulling on the brake.

Let the kitty go, he said. It's free range here. One hundred percent organic.

18

It was awful. They could not live here, ever. As they entered the larger of the two huts and saw the small black flies crawling across the chairs and tables and the balls of gray fluff gathered between the wide cracks of the floorboards, he saw Dial's startled gaze fall on the sick yellow tar paper. She would never buy this place.

She would be happier locked in jail. Really. It could not be worse than to be hidden away here in the leaky rain. There was a grimy kitchen sink on the back wall and the counter was piled high with pots and pans and paint cans and here, in the grim light of a small lead-light window, little Adam finally found a kettle and then he turned the spigot on a strange thin brass tap. There was a small trickle, then nothing.

Ah, he said, no water.

Even better, thought the boy.

Adam was about five foot five and the mother five foot ten. She had been looking down on him politely but now that there was no water she gently closed her eyes. She unloaded the kitten on the floor and walked out to the narrow deck where she sat cross-legged, her eyelids lowered.

His dad would never find him here.

Buck was another thing entirely. He did not know what he wished to eat the most. He stalked a silver butterfly across a low wooden table and then leaped into a sea of cushions, each one filled with tiny mirrors. These he swatted at awhile.

Adam crossed to the front wall, cups rattling as he went. He poked his peeling nose among the clutter of the workbench—a tangle of plastic irrigation pipe, a chain-saw engine, a length of guttering and so many other tools, a hammer, screwdrivers, a machete, numbers of brown paper bags which would later turn out to hold roofing screws.

Ah! He held up a pair of opera glasses.

The boy's grandpa also had opera glasses. His grandma had been very sad when he took both pairs to his Love Nest.

Adam bared his long teeth. Come on, he said, then raised his eyebrows. Tour.

Dial did not come in from the veranda so the boy had to be polite. He followed Adam outside. He asked, Are there many stinging ants?

See that lantana, above the oranges? Adam squatted in the mud and pointed up the hill. You would want to stay away from there.

The boy planned to stay away from everything.

Adam said, Always look inside your shoes before you put them on.

But the hippie had no shoes himself. He looked mad and homeless, with big long feet and toes like fingers. The boy followed his exact steps over the warm soft ground, around the so-called veggie garden, a jungle, wild passion-fruit vines growing up its chicken-wire fence. From the big corner post they took a thin path, grass seeds tickling the boy's bare knees like biting things with eyes and legs.

We put the goats in here, said Adam, sometimes. It was obvious he could not see what he was talking about. It was only after they had crossed the spooky shady ground of the banana plantation and had slid down a steep embankment that he raised the binoculars to his eyes.

This is the best part of the land, he said at last. The boy felt sorry for him, to be so poor he thought that the place was good.

Adam squatted and brought his instrument to bear on a bunch of insect wire tied to the pipe's end in a sort of muddy hole.

Dig, said Adam, the water table has gone down.

Hearing "water table" the boy imagined something jewel-like and impossible, but he squatted beside the starved thin man and they both dug with their bare hands, scraping out the cacky mud and flinging it onto the dark floor of the banana grove and after a while they came to dirty water.

This is good water, said the man, peering at the yellow slime.

He found a rusty paint can and told the boy to pour yellow water from the can into the pipe while he himself lay with his bare stomach on the ground and held his ear against the pipe and then, at a certain moment, he got up. Then he pushed the pipe beneath the water, and bound back the insect wire.

There, he said. Could you do that by yourself?

The boy knew he never would. I guess, he said.

Good man, said Adam.

On the way back to the hut Adam showed him the wild tomato vines which were threaded like precious veins among the grass.

There's always something to eat, Adam said as he picked the tomatoes, tiny like the ones in Zabar's.

You could hide here forever, he said, looking thoughtfully at the boy.

All around them were what are called cabbage moths, their wings catching the last of the day's sunshine, and above the moths were the bananas, their ripped-up leaves moving like fingers, and below was the inky green of rain forest where arm-thick vines wound around trees with skins like elephants. Beyond the hut, behind the car, the lonely darkness was bleeding along the course of Remus Creek and washing up into the muggy hills.

When they returned to the hut, it was time for the hurricane lamps and there, in the yellow wash of kerosene light, the man filled a kettle with dirty water and then he set to work removing the stalks from the tomatoes. The boy guessed Dial was still out on the deck and the boy was feeling kind of sad, sorry for Adam, who was trapped in a place no one else would ever want. He stayed to be companionable and watched the tomatoes turn into a sauce, dissolving in the slow spitting circles of themselves.

The kitten was asleep, curled up like a dead caterpillar on the cushions. A bat entered through the front door, circled once, and disappeared. The boy wondered when they would be able to leave.

19

She lay on the mudflats between nightmares and the ropy unknown day. A magpie sang. In November, the creepy Rabbitoh had told her, the magpies pecked your head and made blood pour down your face. Some country she'd been sent to.

Dial, the boy said.

She was sleeping in a nest of pillows and musty rugs beneath a ceiling of worrisome water-stained wood. She did not want to wake and deal with what she'd done. It was too hot already.

Dial.

Her skin was itchy, her hair still dirty. She had slept with her head wedged into the tight dark angle where the ceiling met the loft.

Dial!

He needed too damn much too often. She hid her face in her hands, playing peekaboo but also hiding from his breath. She must buy him a damned toothbrush.

Dial, when can we leave?

She opened her arms to him and he buried himself in the warm cave beside her neck. Whatever had happened to him you could feel he had been loved. No matter what a cow his grandma was she had cuddled him and kissed him. He had told Dial the names of the puddings Grandma had cooked: queen, sticky toffee, pineapple upside down, unbelievably Victorian.

When can we leave, he said now, but she could not deal with that. She could feel his immense fragility but what could she do? This place might be their only hope. It was in the middle of the outback, as she understood it, with no phone and no mail delivery. They were off the grid. How else could she use the money to make them safe.

No matter what happens, Dial, can we? Leave?

She looked at his small determined face, his frown, the searching intelligence in those gray eyes.

He's *worried*, she said, mocking Adam, not so much to change the subject, as to begin leading the boy toward the matter that he really must address. They were not going to start drifting.

He has to *confer* with someone, she said, and rolled her eyes.

Can we stay in a motel? Can we?

The dope is *worried* the pigs will grab him for having U.S. dollars.

Finally, she saw him understand. It made his body rigid. You're trying to *buy* it!

Baby, you said you wanted to stop going places.

He jerked away from her. She hardly saw him go, but heard him on the ladder, half falling, landing heavily. As she rose from her blankets the flies rose too and she felt one crawl along her bare arm. She slapped herself.

Che? I'm trying to look after you. She pulled on some underpants so she could decently descend the ladder. The rungs were thin. They hurt her feet.

All I have is U.S. dollars. I don't have a lot of choices.

He did not answer.

She said, It's useless to them, you heard that. We're rich, but the money's worth nothing.

She took his hand. He snatched it back. Come on, she said. She was pleading with him, really, to understand what had happened to her life.

Come on, she said, show me all the stuff you found yesterday.

He kept his hand to himself but he led her out into the long wet grass and took an obvious sulky pleasure showing her to the so-called bathroom, a rusty four-gallon can inside a square wooden box.

Come on, she said. The place itself is sort of pretty. Let's look in the other hut.

And it would have been pretty, in photographs, the varied greens, the log-clad huts with their low sagging verandas. Inside the second hut they found shirts and trousers hanging from four-inch nails. A netted bed faced two windows. Between the windows was a door which opened onto a low dark veranda where bats hung like broken rags.

It's a real jungle, she said. It looked poisonous to her.

There's another hut down there, she said. Do you want to check it count?

You said *ount,* he said.

No I didn't. She laughed but she hated people doing that to her, pointing out the moments when Boston surfaced. He had done this to her at Australian customs, the little WASP, announcing she was saying *mayan* instead of mine. Well, he would have more foreign stuff than that to deal with.

This was going to be his home, not just the acres, or the two huts, but this small third hut down in the darkness of the rain forest, creepier than the others, with nothing in it but an empty pickle jar.

Outside, on the stoop, someone had carved a face into a block of stone. It was not exactly sinister, but it suggested superstition, witchcraft and some very lonely lost life reduced to a hidden corner of the earth.

What does *conferring* mean? The boy pushed the stone over so its face was hidden.

He's chickenshit.

You should not use curse words, you know.

He was hugely upset. She was hugely upset herself but she was the adult and could not show it.

What's the matter, baby?

You shouldn't curse.

Shut up, she thought. She brought him out of the forest, emerging just below the deck of one big leaky shaky hut, beside a bush with shiny leaves and bright red berries which she said was coffee. She wasn't even sure that this was true.

Go on, she said, peel one. You'll see.

Inside the red skin was a white, moist seed, slippery and somehow wrong. The boy was peeling a second bean when she heard an engine and saw the dirty blue-oil smoke, then the car itself. When the motor was turned off it continued knocking and coughing. She was expecting Adam, not Trevor. Now both of them walked through the grass toward them, Trevor staring at the boy a little too intently for her taste.

Hello boy, he said, shirtless, oily, hipless in the sun.

Hello Trevor.

She saw how the boy lifted his chin, allowing himself to be silently interrogated.

She said, Fancy seeing you here.

Trevor chewed his smile in the corner of his mouth. Well, *someone* has to change your money.

Of course, she thought.

The boy also understood. His howl came out of nowhere, like something teased and taunted in a cage. He charged at Trevor like a mad thing. He punched him in his hard hairless stomach and between the legs.

Che! she screamed at him, but Trevor had lifted him up and away and he was still hitting and scratching in the air.

When he was still, Trevor put him back on the ground and the boy looked hatefully at Dial, waiting for her to do something. When he understood she would do nothing, he slashed at the coffee bush and tore a handful of leaves and then he ran through the long dewy grass, leaping with fright at something on the way, continuing through the dense tangle of lantana which would doubtless rip his skin.

I'm sorry, she said to Trevor, but she was frightened now, of everything she'd done. I better go and talk to him, she said.

No, said Trevor, he'll be fine. You have to talk to me.

And she obeyed. She walked with them up the traitor's path, thinking of the boy, knowing exactly where he was, what he felt, inside the empty shed with the pickle bottle, curled up on the filthy floor, growing cooler, slowly more ashamed.

20

Was she really going to buy these mad vines and raging wild lantana, palm trees, chaos, coffee. She might as well have bought an elephant—but you could not hide inside an elephant and you could certainly hide here. That was its single virtue, to place her up a dirt track at the asshole of the earth.

The boy did not like it here, but he could not decide his fate. She was the adult. She followed the two men inside the hut, completely unclear about everything, whether she should buy or walk away, whether they were here to rob or help her. Surely she could defeat them if she had to—one man who could not see and a second man who could not read.

She sat cross-legged in the hut and watched, through a lead-light window, a tiny yellow bird, hovering. It was exquisite, beyond use or understanding.

Adam "located" the tea and "organized" the kettle and Trevor rubbed papaya salve onto the long thin cut that the boy's toenail had made on his hairless barrel chest. He was a mole, vole, pit bull, otter, seal, just not her type, although he didn't understand that yet. They all sat on the cushions and Adam poured the tea, smiling at some out-of-focus fact that was his alone to know. He was emaciated as an Indian ascetic, as unrelated to any life she knew as the yellow hummingbird outside the window.

So! she said. Because she wished to appear definite.

So? said Trevor. Was he mocking her?

So, we're here to talk business, I assume. She was a child playing with money, not her money, but thousands, almost countless.

So, you want to live an *Alternative Lifestyle,* said Trevor.

He *was* mocking her, but she was way tougher than he was. Another thing he did not understand.

So, Dial, you know there are problems.

She heard him say *vere* for there and *pwblems* for problems. She had a degree from Harvard. He couldn't speak or spell. She raised an eyebrow.

You pay Adam foreign money, what can he do with it?

You quite like my foreign money. I see you everywhere these days.

Trevor exhaled, as if offended. But of course he was a criminal, one of the shifty classes her younger brother found so admirable.

All right, he said, now listen.

I'm listening.

No, you are being twitchy and sarcastic. You don't know who I am. You think I am a creep. You don't understand what I have given up to come here.

What have you given up?

There you go, he said, that's what I mean. I was in the middle of building a new gate.

Well she had been about to take a job at Vassar. A gate, she said. Mocking him.

A stockade, said Adam, sucking up. A bloody stockade, Dial, he pleaded.

There was some weird unworldly singsong in their voices, like elves, she thought.

I had six strong men all lined up to work with me, said

Trevor, and now they've gone away. Thank you, Trevor, he said. That was nice of you, Trevor.

Meanwhile the disgusting little flies crawled across the surface of the table. She covered her skin with her dress and she could feel the weight of her remaining money—all there was now between her and Sing Sing. She could not ask him if he had already robbed her.

He said, Do you know how much an American dollar is worth?

He said "worf."

Australia has a dollar of its own, Dial. You're in Australia now. An Australian dollar, he said, is worth more than an American dollar.

Oh God, she thought. This is like the health food store. They hate us. We didn't even know they fucking existed and they've been down here hating us. What did we ever do to them?

I bet that just seems *wrong* to you, he said. You know every country has a telephone code. You know what America's is?

It was 1, of course. She got the point. She said, Why don't we just cut to the chase. You're saying I would have to pay Adam more than we agreed. Is that it?

It's number one, he said. God bless America.

You're jacking up the price.

No.

Just say it, man. Like to my fucking face.

But Trevor wouldn't fight. He produced a pouch of Drum tobacco and got busy with a cigarette. He looked hurt and offended and why wouldn't he if he was what he said he was. But if he was cheating her he would act the same.

I don't understand you, babe. Why would you want to piss me off.

He engaged her eyes directly. Way too invasive. She couldn't hold them long.

Who else is going to help you?

She looked away, as if impatient, but really fearful of being wrong.

Maybe you shouldn't buy Adam's place, he said. You don't look like a farm girl to me.

Well, it was not her money. It was all she had.

Just give me a figure, she said. Just do it.

Six thousand Australian dollars is six thousand six hundred American dollars, Trevor said. He said "fowsand."

Ten percent of that is six hundred and sixty-six.

And he continued but she could not hold the numbers still. She was a Harvard graduate but she could not even do the math. He meanwhile, the autodidact, was spinning numbers in the air.

All right, she thought, I'm doing it.

She pulled out the fuse wire and ripped off her hem. She counted out the money, showing the full length of her gorgeous leg and pushing out currency like cookie dough onto their filthy table.

The boy was going to hate her—tough!

Trevor grinned—the broken teeth, the injured ear.

Excuse me, she said.

She was a fool, a total fool. She felt the wet on her cheeks before she understood that she was crying. Trevor called after her, but she fled the hut, walking briskly. As soon as her feet were on the earth the tears arrived in floods. Then she ran, along the path up to the bananas and down the hill to the spring and from there to the rain forest where she ran to hide inside the shed.

The boy was standing. Diane Arbus. Clenched jaw. Holding out his arm to show his insect bites. All across the floor were bits of paper, not a single one torn straight, some white, some folded over and over, and also little stones and seeds and a pack of playing cards that had gone missing from her bag.

Mommy.

The dark strength of the misunderstanding squeezed her

gut. She felt his body hard against her, so familiar, so foreign. As she held him she looked down at his magpie nest. There was a picture of Dave Rubbo which brought her heart into her throat, and a torn pack of impatiens seeds which was somehow almost worse.

We'll get used to it, he said.

You're a brave boy, she said. He squatted over his stuff and gathered it together. He knocked over the jar. It rolled all the way across the floor and fell into the forest with a small fat thump.

Floor's not level, she said, her voice all thick with snot.

Will I have my surprise? he asked.

Surprise? She laughed, self-mocking, desperate.

When we went to Philly, you know.

What a shitty time you've had, poor baby.

The boy clocked the ruined velvet hem tied around her waist.

How can my dad ever find us now, he said.

Suddenly, it was time for truth.

Your dad doesn't want to find us, baby. You know that. Once she had said the words they settled in her gut like a large gray river rock, little bugs crawling out beneath.

No, he said, gathering himself into himself again. He wants us. He wants me. She could see the tendons in his neck, the tightness of his little jaw.

You remember, baby. In Seattle.

No, he cried.

She thought, I cannot do this, not now. He's too frail.

Shush, she said.

She had heard the cat, that's all. It was a straw. She grasped at it.

Shush. Listen.

She got him to crawl, reluctantly, by her side until they were at the doorway like a pair of andirons waiting for a fire.

21

There was no kitty. The ground dropped away below them, and there, in the broken shadows amid the speckled light that gave the forest floor a spotted skin, was a fat, stumpy-tailed bird with emerald along its back, turquoise on the shoulders, a red rump, a lovely blue beneath its wings. All its sudden beauty made him sad. He wished that it was dead.

Did I talk to my dad in Seattle, he asked.

She shrugged, exhausted.

I didn't, he said. I never saw my dad. What do you mean that he won't come here?

Throughout all this, the bird was part of some dumb dream. It picked up a snail shell and hit it against a rock. For a moment a beam of sunlight got it. A minute later it was gone, swallowed by the wild lantana.

Where was my dad?

On the lawn, with the hose.

That was my dad? No.

As they came out of the rain forest, the boy did not know what he felt. He saw Adam arrive on foot. He was a loser. He had a wad of money, too bright to be worth anything.

That was my dad? With the hose?

The mother would not answer. He saw how she looked around the land as if she had just woken up. She rubbed her sweaty nose with the back of her hand, squinting up the hill behind the dark huts where the sun caught the wild trees. Smooth trunks burst out of the shadow, waxy white, at the same time shining green, and it was absolutely clear, even to a boy, that the mother could not take care of him. She had no idea of where she was or what she'd taken on.

22

His best memory of Seattle was an ice-cream sundae. They had just flown from Oakland. They had taken a taxi. They sat together at the counter and listened to the Jefferson Airplane, chocolate fudge pooling in ice cream.

She said: Are you happy, babe?

He did not understand he was going to be robbed of his father. So he was very happy. There were posters on the wall. He said, They're really trippy.

And she laughed, and laid her hand across his back.

After the sundae, Dial was pretty much cleaned out. So they walked down the Ave to the unisex, hand in hand. She told the unisexer she was good for it. He said OK. That was Joel, a freak with no shirt and long curling black hair and a big Jewish nose.

The mother told him how the boy must be fixed up.

Oh man, he said, don't make me do this, Dial. He had a whiny New York voice and the boy liked him without knowing why.

I'm good for it, Dial said. She winked at the boy.

The boy felt his hair lifted with the end of a comb and dropped back against his neck.

Don't make me cut this, babe.

Don't shit me, man. You know what's going down. You know who this is?

Hey, Che?

Hi.

You've got great hair, Che. It's real pretty. You sure you want me to cut it off?

The boy wanted it so much he could not speak.

What do *you* think, man, the mother said.

Joel wiped the boy's face and sat him on a box.

As the tickling clippers approached his ear, the boy waited with his eyes scrunched up.

Yeah, right, said the barber. You don't mind, kid? Times are tough for you.

I'm OK, he said. He opened his eyes to see the mother walk out on the Ave and close the glass door behind her. He was excited by almost everything that had happened to him, the hotel, the airplane, the sundae, but particularly this high hard buzz against his neck. He was being liberated, as Cameron had said. They will break you out, man. Your life will start for real. Dial was so cool. Men turned their heads as they passed her. Now one walked backward smiling. Dial rolled a cigarette—long fingers, swift pink lick. By the time she had smoked it all his childhood was on the floor.

The barber spun the chair and the boy saw he had become a redneck kid from Jeffersonville. He was a cicada underground.

Dial came back to do inspection. She touched his cheek and winked at him. Give the man some color, she said.

Oh, babe! He's just a kid, Dial.

Black.

The barber raised an eyebrow and it seemed as if he would suggest a different shade, but a moment later he came back with some stuff mixed in a bowl.

Organic, it ain't.

The boy felt the cold chemicals sucking on his scalp and he wasn't scared about this or anything. This was his destiny as he had been told. He was on TV now. He was going to have to be with his dad, his mom, where he belonged. One of these days you're going to rise up singing.

While the dye took, he looked at a comic book, soft and furry pages, stroked by so many hands. In the Batcave Bruce Wayne showed all the different Batman costumes including a pure white costume to make him invisible in the snow. It was the first comic he had ever seen, a hard dark thrill that made his eyes narrow. By the time he finished it he had become a *completely* new person, ink-black hair, two years older easy. The unisexer closed his shop and drove them to the underground which turned out to be a house whose porch had got filled with old carpet and boxes of books that had been rained on and melted like chocolate in the heat. This too excited him—the books—as if nothing that had mattered before would matter now. It was in a street of colored clapboard houses and kids playing stickball and greasers working on their cars.

If his father was there he should have been told.

He and Dial walked straight into an empty hallway where no one ever swept, and then passed into a large high room from which all of normal life had been removed. No one even smiled, not the fierce bearded men, not the women who had not washed enough. The boy had a good eye, an *excellent* eye, which had been proven at the Guggenheim. He had not been told anything but he guessed this was *underground.* He looked out for his handsome dad, their leader, staying close to Dial as she moved around the room, through the echoes, across the opinions, sharp like rocks and broken bricks. When anyone looked at him, he smiled, figuring his father would smile back at him if he was here. But no one smiled, which would be weird even on the main street of Jeffersonville, New York.

The whole house was stressed and angry, with him, it seemed. They were stressed he was on TV. They were stressed Dial was on TV. They should not have come here because it was a secret place. They did not mince their words, as Grandma said. They spoke their minds.

While he held Dial's skirt balled up inside his fist, they began to beat on her. Dial was on an ego trip. Why was she telling jokes? Had the Vietnamese won? Had the pigs left the ghettos?

This was the opposite of everything he had expected from Cameron. Behind a bad-smelling sofa he discovered a slippery bright green sleeping bag and into this he crawled, wedging himself as far under the sofa as he was able. He wished he could go to the bathroom. They beat on her and beat on her. She was a petit bourgeois adventurist. And she brings this fucking brat here, now. She just went and did it. She thinks the revolution is a part-time job.

The boy needed a poop.

What was Dial going to do with the kid now? Did she plan to give him to the pigs?

He could not poop. He was very hot inside the bag.

He heard Dial crying. She was a giant among them and they dared to make her cry.

She screamed at them that they were heartless bastards. Maybe they were talking about the boy. He was scared they would off him.

A man said to leave her alone and that was when he pooped. It snaked out of him and settled in his underpants, hot and stinking, and he put his head inside the bag and pulled the string closed so no one else would know.

Dial said, Do not shoot the messenger.

The boy began to cry and he was still crying when they pulled him from his bag and carried him through the room and out onto the front lawn where a big man with hair across his face and head pulled off his soiled clothes and made him stand facing the wall while he hosed him down. The water was warm at first because the hose had been lying in the sun but then it turned cold and hard and it hurt his skin and only when Dial came running, screaming, from the house, did the man stop.

Fuck you, she said.

He would remember nothing of the man except his watery gray eyes. He rubbed Che's head. He held out his hand to Dial but she turned her back and soaped the boy down gently and he watched with his arms folded and then stamped his foot and walked a circle on the grass and came back one more time to watch.

All around was gentle summer, the cars on the street, the green grass, the ice-cream truck playing "Greensleeves."

The man was holding a big blue towel, not to the boy, to Dial.

I'm sorry, Dial said to him. I guess I've fucked this up.

She wrapped the towel around the boy and then she really cried, great loud gulps of air and snot and the man put his hands around her from behind.

The man said, Don't worry, baby.

His eyes were kind, and wet. His own son was maybe eight inches from his own skin. Later the boy thought there was likely a code the father must live by so no matter how his heart was hurting he could not speak to his son, not even touch his hand, just live his secret itchy life enclosed in hair.

In a humid garden on the other side of the planet earth, his child was lost to him, and he to the child. Clouds of insects were illuminated by the disappearing sun. The boy was an assistant to a starving hippie. The boy had had the air sucked out of him. He was lackluster, without hope. When asked to help he cut the stalk of a big orange pumpkin, but only halfway through. He pulled up two onions and picked one eggplant.

His dad would have introduced himself if he could have foreseen this unhappiness.

Back in the hut, his gut a sloshy sump of misery, the boy watched the skinny hippie "locate" the "spuds" and grease a crusted black roasting pan and fill it with chopped pumpkin and potatoes and onions. He saw how he hung the hurricane lamps beneath the sleeping platform and another in the middle of the doorway to the deck and another off the wall, its usual place because you could see the long thin streak of carbon rising on the yellow tar paper. The boy would live worse than trailer trash. There would be no light switches in his life.

Adam lit a mosquito coil and they had to gather close around it. He had been the owner but now he was free of it. He rolled a joint from three papers and the smoke from the coil was like incense, musty as burning cow poop which he said it was.

The dark came down and the air stayed hot and thick and after a while you could smell the vegetables roasting and the boy lay with his head on the mother's lap. They were tender with each other but he had a secret buzzing anger quiet inside him, a vibration in his chest that got bigger all the time. She should have told him that was his dad.

He heard a meow and there Buck stood. His anger grew some more. In the cat's mouth was a dead creature almost half his size.

Jesus, said Adam.

Buck dropped the dead thing, and showed the boy his wet pink mouth.

On the floor a pitta bird gave up its lifelong secret—the blue beneath its crumpled wing. The boy was crying. His dad was mad at him. Everything in his whole life was crushed and dead and beside this the fact that the pitta was protected, or that humans could only see that blue in flight or death—none of this could mean a thing.

He kicked Buck, lifted him like a football that did not land until the open door.

23

You saw the cat, Dial said to Adam. You fucking petted it, man. You had it on your fucking lap. You can't take my money and then say cats are against the rules. So give me my money back, if that's how it is. Deal is over.

Adam was all hunched up and twisted like a pipe cleaner on the windowsill. I'm into cats, he said, peering sideways at his lawyer, begging him to come and save his life.

The lawyer's name was Phil Warriner. He was tall with surfer's shoulders. He had a big dumb paisley tie, long peaked collar, bushy sideburns, a droopy black mustache.

I'm into cats as well, Phil Warriner said.

Then give the money back, Dial said, almost high on relief. She didn't want to live there anyway. Your client knew about the cat from the beginning, she said.

Then she waited for the lawyer, watching him stroke his mustache like a fool. She could not imagine how this man had ended up in this crappy little office with felt tiles on the floor. All those years in law school and then spend your life in fucking *Nambour*, staring through the window at the Woolworth's loading dock.

The problem isn't cats, he said. It's birds.

Dial turned to Adam, who was hugging himself and rocking. When we got in your car, Dial insisted, when you picked us up. You had a rooster, Adam. We had a cat.

The lawyer took a yellow legal pad and drew a line down the middle.

The question is, babe, Phil Warriner said, do you plan to honor your commitment to the Crystal Community.

She let the *babe* go by. She said, No, no, don't start that. I don't have an obligation to anyone. Adam is the one with the obligation. He didn't tell the truth.

As she spoke the boy, who had been standing hard behind her all this while, lifted Buck from his cardigan pocket and pushed his face into his fur. So now he was kissing his cat. Great. Last night he was kicking it.

The lawyer rolled a thin straight cigarette. We're going to transfer Adam's shares to your name, he said to Dial. That's what we are gathered here to do.

But you can't do it, see, said Dial. She was smiling at him now.

Oh? He tucked the ends in with a red match and lit up, holding in the smoke too long.

There's a rule against the cat.

There is no rule, said the lawyer. They're hippies, jeez.

I've been in communes before, Mr. Warriner. They're full of fucking rules, believe me.

Phil, said the lawyer.

We're *Australian* hippies, Adam pleaded. It's different here.

Dial groaned. The boy was pushing the cat's face into her neck. The kitten licked. Stop it! she cried.

You buy shares, Dial. You get your own land, your own house. It's yours. Tell her, Phil. She can do what she likes, man. Anyway, she paid.

Phil smiled down at his desktop. Dial thought, Are you

patronizing me? She watched the lawyer as he brushed the crumbs of tobacco from his desk to his lap, from his lap onto the floor.

You'll discover, he said, still looking down, that there are not many rules on Remus Creek Road and what rules exist have all been broken many times before. And then he smiled at her, his eyes crinkled. She thought, He's hitting on me.

You're meant to be the lawyer.

I'm an organic lawyer. He grinned, his cigarette jammed in the corner of his mouth.

I can't buy this land, she said.

Look. Phil Warriner arranged his hands in his crotch. You already paid Jimmy Seeds the purchase price.

Jimmy Seeds?

Adam. Same thing.

Same thing? Really. Well once this *person here* had my money he told me I could not have the cat. That's a deal breaker, said Dial.

There are all sorts of families, Adam said. We know that, man. We're against the patriarchy, man.

You are *what*!

The cat is part of your family. The cat has to live there too.

What Jimmy means, said the lawyer, is that you're not meant to have a cat, but no one's going to stop you. They'll just say, That's Dial, she's into cats. She's cool.

So what did you mean, saying I was going to have to do something about that cat?

I was stoned, man, jeez.

So we can have a cat.

Yes, said Adam. Y-e-s.

The mother turned to the boy and sighed.

The boy imagined he was being asked to decide. It would be years before he saw this made no sense. He always remembered the way her brows came down, all black and witchy. He had to answer did he love the cat. Would he live in the outback with no toilet or light switches, where no one would see him ever? It was not fair. He looked out to the lane. A sheet of newspaper was fluttering back and forth, blown by the hot wind. Then a truck arrived and he looked back into the room, avoiding people, staring at a photograph on the wall. It was the color of dead families, long ago.

You know Bo Diddley? the lawyer asked suddenly, unhooking the frame and handing it to the boy. We hung out together in Sydney.

The mother took the picture from the boy and returned it to the lawyer's desk.

Well? she asked the boy.

She was blaming him, but what had he done? He was sorry he kicked the cat. He loved the cat. Not more than he loved his daddy though. It was not fair with everybody looking at him. He was just a little boy.

In any case, Phil Warriner said, picking up a folder, you seem to have made a verbal contract. He upended the folder and watched its contents spill across the desk.

Pull up your chair, he said to the mother.

As she read the document, the boy could hear the paper on the loading dock flapping like something wrecked and broken in a trap.

The mother asked, Who is James Adamek?

That's me, said Adam.

The lawyer pushed a drugstore Bic toward the mother.

The boy watched as she studied the clear plastic pen and then the filing cabinet and the picture of Bo Diddley and the spill of documents now lying in the dusty sunshine. She asked, Where did you go to school?

Phil Warriner laughed.

This is all legal? You're telling me?

Warriner picked up the document and read it quickly once again. He flicked Dial's passport open, read it, checked her face, closed it shut.

Just sign it, Anna, he said. You know what I mean?

24

The deceitful hippie was on a bus to far northern Queensland and she was left with fourteen acres and a piece of paper that said I give my car to Dial. Beside the Bruce Highway at Nambour, in the spewy waving exhaust fumes of the bus, the boy asked her, Can we go to a motel now?

Can we go to a *motel*!

But then she saw that frown-fold by his nose, the shifting secret eyes.

Oh Christ, she thought, what have I done? This had been an unblemished boy and the most remarkable thing about him had not been his handsome father's face but his perfect trust, the way he put his hand in hers and sat beside her on the bus, so close, resting his cheek against her arm. His eyes had been limpid, gray, in some lights, a lovely sulfur blue. His hair had been tousled, curly. It was hard not to touch him all the time. And here he was, his soul all curled up and fearful of attack.

Can we, Dial?

She looked into his eyes and wondered if an equal and opposite rage was burning in that perfect little head.

Can we? Please.

She was already tense about how they would get back to Remus Creek Road. She had no license, could not drive a stick shift.

Can we?

He hung off her finger with his fist, marsupial. How can he have endured all this? In the car she found a crumpled oil-stained map.

Here, she said, what's this?

Is it the sea, Dial? He pushed closer to her, and brushed his cheek against her arm.

We're really near the beach, she said. It was the first time she understood where she had taken him. Would you like that, baby? She lay her hand on his head, the engine of his soul contained within her palm.

And stay in a motel!

Why not! She was not broke yet. She had *Huck Finn* inside her bag. They could play poker and eat pizza and swim all day.

OK get down on the floor, she said. She was insane, of course, even now, particularly now. Get down on the floor? The little creature didn't even argue, just curled himself with the kitten, in among the dust and matches on the rubber matting.

Then she drove, best she could. Wrong side of the road.

As for the boy, he did not seem to mind the sneezing dust and deadhead matches, did not seem irritated that she kept moving her hand from the gear stick to his shoulder and back again. The confused scampy cat soon went off to sleep on the back window ledge, but the boy stayed hiding, knowing the mother loved him once again.

Did you really drive to Montana?

That was his real mother he was talking about. I'm not used to this car, she called. I'm sorry.

Did you have a map then?

It's a stick shift, she persisted. I'll get used to it.

Dial?

Yes.

With his stubborn quietness he was forcing her to look at him. She turned briefly, actually frightened of his seriousness.

Are you scared they will arrest me, Dial?

Don't be silly, she said. She was driving way too slow. She could see the cars behind her and she was looking for a place to pull off the road.

We're underground. That's why I'm on the floor?

Don't talk now. I'm concentrating.

You said I had to lie on the floor.

Shush! she said. There was a tractor yard up ahead and she pulled off. She counted seven cars pass by. Did she have to tell him now?

It's safer on the floor, she said. Just generally.

Can I get up if I put on my seat belt?

Sure you can, she said, pulling back onto the road.

This was how you drove my daddy to Montana, right, Dial?

How the fuck did he know all this stuff.

It was an automatic, babe.

It was a rental, Dial. And with a bullet in your arm.

It was as if he was taunting her. In a minute he would want to see the scar.

Look, she said. This is so pretty. They were traveling between walls of green sugarcane. Above the giant grass towered a small wood house on stilts.

It was a .32, right?

The sugarcane gave way to a forest of thin raggy-barked trees, their white trunks like chalk marks drawn on darkness.

Right, Dial?

Cameron told you all this nonsense, she said at last. How old is Cameron?

He's sixteen. He's a Maoist.

Well, she said, the press is full of lies. He should know that.

She was pulling off the road, unable to go on. She could

not look at him. She stopped beside a mess of churned-up gray soil and broken trees, a sad forest, cut off like a knife.

What are we doing?

She almost told him, I'm not your mother, but she got out of the car, pretending to look for something. She could not live like this, day after day. Some barbarian had been through these woods with bulldozers. There was not a flower to pick, nothing but these spooky injured trees with flaking skin like psoriasis. She tugged at the bark, and it came off in a long sheet, like paper.

That was it. She would take that back to him.

Look, she said. Isn't this cool?

He looked at her more than at the bark. Did he know she had gone mad? What is it, Dial?

Australian tree bark, baby. You can write on it.

He turned it over in his hand, frowning. What do you want me to write? he asked at last.

Draw Buck, she said brightly, back behind the wheel.

I'm going to write a word, he said.

Let me see when you're done.

She could feel him laboring beside her, serious, dogged.

Are you done?

He had written ANA.

She thought, I can't stand this. It has two n's, she said.

Are you angry with me again, Dial?

No, baby. I love you.

She kissed the top of his head. You know, some cats really love the beach.

Are you Anna? he asked.

Look, she cried. They had come onto a rise and there was the sea, miles and miles of it with yellow beaches disappearing into the chalky mist.

Beach! he said.

25

Tired and burned and sandy, they coasted down onto the plain to the west of Coolum, and the tops and bottoms of paperbark trees were already drowning in the melancholy night. The sky was still dark green. The headlights were on but the mother had had trouble seeing through the smeary insect glass. Below the sky was nothing but a smudge of road, wormy white trunks showing in the scrub.

The light made the boy homesick for his grandma. In the evenings the pair of them would drive like this, side by side, into Jeffersonville to Ted's Diner. For a while one summer they would take his bike and he could ride around and around the empty parking lot at Peck's.

There were local kids but they were not friends to him. They had short hair and hard squinting eyes and once when he was eating in Ted's Diner they stole his bike. He knew who did it and where they lived so on every trip to town thereafter he walked up into the little backstreets around Pete's Auction Barn and on one of these occasions, just after dusk, he finally saw his bike lying on a little lawn. No question it was his. It had black electrical tape wound around the middle of the crossbar.

He was wheeling it away when the kid came out and asked him what he thought he was doing.

It's my bike.

Bullshit!

Yes it is.

Liar.

The other boy was maybe eight but when he came down onto the lawn Jay dropped the bike and flew at him so hard he knocked him over and he dropped on him with his knees and smashed him with his fists and he did not stop until the kid's father pulled him off.

Christ, what you doing?

He stole my bike.

The father was a tall wiry man with tattoos up his arms and on his neck. He had wild black sideburns and pouchy eyes.

Hey, boy, he said, it's just a goddamned bike.

Yes sir.

The boy had never been hit. He waited for it. Instead the man put his arm around the shoulder of his weeping son and together they walked up onto their porch and the boy saw a woman rush, like a moth fluttering in the light. He cried then, a kind of ugly hiccup.

Back at Ted's he saw his grandmother.

You found it!

He should have told her, I gave it to him good, some stuff like that, but he was ashamed and dirty and did not know what to say. He kept seeing the father, the tenderness in his dull eyes as he put his arm around his son.

Are you awake, said Dial.

I'm OK, he said.

26

The Peugeot coughed one last time and threw itself a yard farther into the deep dark beneath the overhanging acacia and lantana. Ahead there was a home light burning.

He now had *Huck Finn* in one pocket of the cardigan. You don't know about me, without you have read a book by the name of *The Adventures of Tom Sawyer.* The kitty was in the other pocket as he carried him up the path through the deepest pool of dark—between the two huts—and up the steps beside the papaya, and then into the big hut where it would just be them, and blankets, and a book, nothing better to imagine now. There was a weak yellow light inside, not sufficient to break through the murk of ceiling, just enough to show strange faces at the low table.

He stopped in the doorway, not knowing what to do. The mother clamped her arms around his chest and squashed him against her, breathless as a paper bag. He was so tired he could have cried.

They were hippies—who else! Arms and faces in shadow like a boring painting in the Met. There was a dense cloud of bugs around them, some flying, some dying, some bouncing off the lamp. They smelled of dope. The bugs settled on the boy's sweaty nose and a scabby black moth rose suddenly from the table and smacked briefly at the light.

No one said anything.

Can I help you, Dial said. The only one she recognized was the Rabbitoh, one eye hidden by his raven hair.

A woman's arm offered a joint. The lantern caught the green stones on her wrist, the small silver bells. Dial kept her arms around the boy.

We're waiting for Jimmy Seeds, said the woman with the drugs.

Adam is gone, the mother said.

If he's gone, said a man, he'll come back.

Believe me, said Dial, he's not coming back. We just bought this place today. Really, guys. I'm sorry. We have to go to bed. We've had a heavy day.

There were only five people at the table and all they had was a bag of dope and a teapot but they gave off a bad mood more smelly than the smoke.

She's Dial, said the Rabbitoh, in case you didn't know.

I'm Dial, the mother said stubbornly. This is Jay, my son.

Dial? This was a slender man with a handsome shaven face, a head of tousled tangled hair. He had a rubbery upper lip, maybe funny if you were his friend.

We've known Jimmy a long *long* time, Dial.

A dumb stoned laugh. A woman. The boy could see her in the gloom—curling thick black hair and big breasts loose inside her T-shirt.

The mother said, Adam got the bus to Cairns this afternoon.

The boy took out the book and gave it to the mother in case she should forget their plan.

The hippie woman pushed her hair back and shoved her long wide jaw into the light. I don't want to lay some authority rave on you, Dial, she said, but Jimmy Seeds can't actually sell his shares without the new buyer meeting the community.

She lifted up the lantern. Buck squeezed his eyes shut against the glare.

Anyway, you cannot have the cat.

She stood, revealing herself to be a head shorter than Dial. She had a thick waist and sturdy brown legs.

None of this is your fault, she said to Dial.

It's cool, said the Rabbitoh. We just need to sit down and talk it through.

Sure you do, said Dial, giving the book back to the boy.

The boy let Buck slip away. Then, quiet as a shadow swimming in the dark, he climbed the giddy narrow-runged ladder to the loft. There he lay in the middle of the nest and pulled a fistful of tangled rug across his head. He waited for them to leave, blocking out their endless foreign voices.

27

She lay beside him in the blue light listening to the metallic explosions of possum droppings on the roof. With his moon-black lips, he seemed even more a foundling. To continue to deceive him seemed too cruel, but to tell the truth was even worse. In the humid darkness, Dial screwed up her face imagining how it would feel to have the whole foundation pulled from underneath your life. His real mother had been a star child too, so blessed that when you saw her do the simplest thing, pull on a sweater or break into a jog, for instance, you were aware of a perfectly symmetrical being, each foot the same, each blue eye identical, her even white teeth beyond the reach of orthodontics. She came to Radcliffe at sixteen, summa cum laude from Dalton, fluent in three languages. When she returned to the Belvedere at Christmas 1964 this child was in her womb, a fish with gills, a tadpole heart.

It was the sixties, but years before Radcliffe girls were on the Pill and boys slept over Friday nights. This was a teenage pregnancy with fifties shame and shadows, linocut illustrations in a women's magazine.

Did she even know she was pregnant. She confessed nothing, but it did not take a great deal for Phoebe Selkirk to make the diagnosis. It was Christmas morning when things came to a head, the news giving Buster Selkirk all the reason he needed for a vodka. The day sort of went from there, filled with shouting and wailing and the caterer's trays and boxes were abandoned and Susan retreated to a locked bedroom, alone with a tray of garlic mashed potatoes.

By midnight, lying awake listening to her daughter vomiting in the bathroom, Phoebe Selkirk still had no clear idea of who the father was or what her daughter imagined her life would be from here, only that the subject of "tidying up" her "condition" was not acceptable. That suicide had not been threatened seemed an encouraging sign, in the circumstances.

Mrs. Selkirk had until now proclaimed she had too much energy to sit still on an airplane, but on the following day, which she insisted on calling Boxing Day, she took a single Valium and traveled from Idlewild to Boston and from there to Harvard where her father had endowed a library and a chair. She consulted with no one about this trip, neither daughter nor husband, the latter having, in any case, gone off to sleep at the Harvard Club which was half empty for the holiday. She left her daughter sleeping and called in Gladys from vacation to clean up the mess and keep her company. In Quigley House she met with the dean of students and the president and persuaded them that they were capable of dealing with this little "bump," which she thought of as a kind of hiccup but which was not understood that way by the two men. If the father had been a Harvard man there was no curiosity expressed and in the years when she drank her first martini at exactly six o'clock, Mrs. Selkirk would wryly comment on the three wise men come to discuss the virgin birth.

Mrs. Selkirk made no gift immediately, but she did encourage the dean and president to consider what it was that the School of Arts might have on its Christmas wish list. At the time she could not imagine she would ever blame Harvard for anything.

Phoebe Selkirk was, to put it very mildly indeed, curious about who the baby's father was, but each time the question was asked the girl withdrew further, and her room, normally so bright and orderly, took on a dark dank tangle more suitable to an adolescent boy than the girl who had announced, on her twelfth birthday, her plan to be the American ambassador to France.

So you have no plans for marriage? she asked.

The girl's laughter shocked her to such a degree that she began to wonder if schizophrenia more than pregnancy might be the problem.

In a very small way this disaster was a gift for Phoebe Selkirk, energizing her at a time when she was beginning to cause major trouble on the co-op board. While the boy's cartilage was changing into bone, his grandmother found the house two hours from New York City, Kenoza Lake, Sullivan County, a million miles from anyone she knew.

She announced this to her daughter, who did not comment, and to her husband, who smiled and lifted both arms in the air, a very irritating habit that seemed to absolve him of all responsibility for anything, even his art purchases which he always sold too early or too late. He was kind of famous, although she wished he would shut up about it, for "getting out of" Pollock.

Tomorrow, we're going, she said.

Later everyone would hear that Susan had been too young for Radcliffe and so was going to the Sorbonne for a year, a story her mother later amended when she learned the Kelvin and the Goldstein girls would be doing just the same and wanted to share an apartment in the Sixth.

She took the Peugeot and left her husband the ridiculous Alfa Romeo Spider with the midlife-crisis soft top. It was sunny and clear on the Palisades Parkway but once they crossed Bear Mountain the weather changed and they drove the last miles along 17B in freezing rain. On 52 they slid off the road, but it was close enough to walk. All through this the strange creature, her daughter, once talkative and happy, would not speak. She fell on the ice and bloodied up her knees.

You want to kill my baby, she said.

When Che was slow to talk, his grandma said it was because the mother would not speak to her all through her pregnancy.

She was in contact with the father, of course. Of that Phoebe Selkirk was positive, but how that happened she never could quite figure. Books came for the girl, books of an entirely new type, philosophy, economics, books that would never once have interested her. For years and years afterward she would upbraid herself for paying no attention to the poisonous content of the books—Marx, Sartre, Marcuse—when she spent so much time looking through the marginalia attempting to decipher a code. There was no code. They spoke on the telephone, but by the time the first bill came, quarterly in those years, the boy had grown a proper face and all his insides were working as they should. Then the two women drove down to the city and booked into the Gramercy Park Hotel where no one the Selkirks knew would ever stay.

It was from here, at the bottom of Lexington Avenue, that the mother got a cab to take her to Beth Israel where she gave birth to the boy whose name she registered as Che David Selkirk.

The name caused a huge upset at the hospital, but it was the David that really got the grandma going. Much later, when David Rubbo shook his fist at the secretary of state, the grandma recognized him straightaway.

Ha, she cried, that nose.

The mother had not been able to see the father from December 1964 until July 23, 1965, the night the boy was born. He had been discovered around dawn, his head on her milky breast, asleep. He had long fair curly hair, long lashes, a wide brow and a nose with a Roman hump. Beakish, Grandma would say later, which represented a softening of her opinion. It was a New England nose she now decided. The nurses who had already judged the father of a Che revised their opinions when they had seen him. They gathered in a semicircle, and when he woke they brought the baby for him. He was a baby still himself; they blew their noses.

The boy, the mother and the father would not be together again until freshman registration of 1966 when Miss Selkirk and the babysitter—a scholarship girl from Girls' Latin—quietly took a floor of a triple-decker in Somerville, and the mother entered Radcliffe once again.

Dean Gilpin welcomed the returning student and her mother over tea. She left Che behind on that occasion, and although Dean Gilpin did not order her to hide her baby, this was what they meant when they used the word *discretion*.

So Che was kind of hiding from the start of his life. First at Kenoza Lake and then at Somerville and in both these places he was looked after by the girl from Southie.

The dean was preparing for bigger things than babies. There were fifteen thousand hippies living in Haight-Ashbury. The Beatles said they were more popular than Jesus Christ. Dave Rubbo burned his draft card on NBC. Everyone was ready for anything except, as Anna Xenos noted, Harvard "men" still "craved your bod" and clinked their glasses when a girl walked into the dining hall. They thought it was a whole new world, but they were the babies. Harvard was not ready for the first nursing mother to attend Ec 1.

Che also audited Gov 146. It is hard now to imagine how impossible this was. Harvard graduates with unfailing memories will tell you this could not have happened, but there was a picture in the *Crimson* the next day. Volume 23, issue 3. The father was often in the same pages, first because of the draft card, then because he was leader of SDS.

When Robert McNamara came to Harvard in September

of 1966 it was SDS who led the protest. There were extreme left factions in SDS but it was still three years before the famous split that produced the Weathermen. Che's dad did not have a gun in 1966. What he had was a list of ten questions for the secretary of defense.

The crowd was in good order but the Maoists were watching the back of Quincy House and one of them yelled, *Back door.*

The boy would remember none of this, of course. But the crowd broke, sprinting toward the back. The mother was in the front, Che in her arms, her wild hair streaming, the famous "fabulous" Tibetan shawl flying backward. The crowd bucked. The mother tripped. She plunged forward as the black Lincoln sped around the corner. There was so much criticism to come, but everyone who saw her said she fell like an athlete, rolling, landing on her back with the child safe against her stomach as she slid, not toward home base, but under the front bumper of the rocking car. The crowd went dead quiet then. This is known. A flashbulb popped, five times. That is all recorded. The mother lay still, headfirst, beneath the steaming radiator. Then the boy began to cry, and as the mother slowly raised her head, she saw a small man with a Hitler-like mustache. He was Bill Hicks of the *Boston Globe* and he had just taken the most famous photograph of 1966.

The mother's long tanned back was all messed up and bleeding, but no one else was even scratched, certainly not Che. So it did not matter, you would think, his father thought, his mother thought, especially when looked at in the light of all the deaths in Vietnam.

Grandma Selkirk had a different opinion, and Bill Hicks's famous photo made it comparatively easy to have herself appointed the boy's sole guardian. After that, the boy did not see the mother.

The boy got some of this information from Cameron. But mostly what he had were scraps of paper and rubber bands. It

was the babysitter, staring at him in the Queensland moonlight, who could have given him the rest. She kept her silence,
imagining it would not help to know that your mother took
pills to dry up her breast milk, that she had decided to harden
her heart against you.

28

The pussycat was drunk with heat, passed out in his malodorous cardigan pocket, paying no attention to the ten people, just a few feet away, who were trying to agree on the correct way to hold hands and make a circle. That number included two of America's most wanted and eight Australian hippies. The hippies wore khaki shorts, Kmart shirts at $2.95 or $4.25, Kuta Beach sarongs, overalls, Indian pajamas from a head shop in Caloundra. They all sat cross-legged in what was called the Crystal Community Hall although it was no more than a warped and buckled floor, held up on ten-foot-high bloodwood stumps, both a folly and a sacrifice offered to the Queensland rain and sun.

The knotted bundle of cardigan lay inside the circle, just in front of Dial. The boy sat beside her, leaning forward, listening intently, as their neighbors continued to discuss which arm should be uppermost, which palm up, which palm down, in order that a golden ball of energy would pass around the circle.

Dial was generating sufficient irritation to power a golden ball all by herself.

This is all about Buck, she whispered to the boy. Trust me.

He did not turn.

Did you hear me?

He was deaf to her, completely entranced by the mumbo jumbo.

Hold my hand, she demanded. I'll show you.

Instead he copied Trevor and she had to switch her palm around. The defeat felt way bigger than it was.

To the boy she whispered, Don't worry. This is nothing.

Shush, he said.

And he straightened his back in unconscious imitation of the dreadful Rabbitoh who was directly opposite.

Shush? she thought.

Rebecca engaged her, smiling, and Dial noted the teeth and the stressed-out vein in the dark pool of shadow beneath her eye.

Next to Rebecca sat a short-haired woman whose overalls showed the starved bones of her chest, probably not Dial's enemy but who could tell? Next was a wispy-bearded long-nosed man who appeared to be named Chook. Then Trevor whose eyes had become lidded and evasive. She thought, Trevor sleeps with Rebecca. Next to Trevor lay his machete. Next to the machete was pretty Roger who was gay or a dancer or maybe just a superhippie. He had white teeth and beads around his neck. There were also two boys, Sam and Rufus, running around so wildly that Dial was sure they would fall and die. Who would be a mother?

By the time the om was judged complete, Dial was so tense, she had to speak, to get it over.

So, she said, the cat. Buck.

They just looked at her, smiling.

I met with Phil Warriner. He's your lawyer, right?

Fair enough, said Roger. Phil Warriner, sure.

So he says I can have a cat.

She saw Rebecca about to speak and cut her off. Look, she said, do any of you want to buy me out of this? I'll sell right now.

The Crystal Community had no money. Its members stared at her, away from her. A bare-bottomed blond-haired child pissed out from the edge of the floor. The pee went into the wild lantana, a long clean arc of crystal.

The woman with the starving chest said her sister was into cats. The sister was not yet at a stage of development where she could get by without her cat. She said everybody couldn't grow at the same rate. She thought Dial would in time. Then she said, Yes, a fading away kind of sound. Then she said, So.

Roger had cheekbones like ax heads. He said the problem was they couldn't get their shit together. If they just looked at the community hall they would see that was the problem. The cat was just a symptom, Roger said. He thought they should get the people to come up from Nimbin and lay a rave on them about how to start a bakery and a newspaper. If there was indecision about the cat, it was the community, not the cat.

The real problem, said Rebecca, is that we have a rule that there are no cats. Are we going to enforce it or not?

Roger said that was exactly what he meant. Exactly.

The girl with the starving chest said no one wanted to lay a power trip on anyone else. A lot of people were here because they were through with rules.

The conversation continued like water dribbling from a hose.

Listen, Dial said at last.

Roger had been speaking, but he stopped.

The boy felt the silence, as heavy and dusty as the heat.

I'm sorry about the cat, said Dial. I really am. But you know while we're sitting here arguing about this, Nixon is bombing Cambodia and Laos. Do you want to think what that is doing to the birds? I mean, I just came from a country where my friends are dying trying to end this war. So you will forgive me if I say.

Say what, Dial?

Dial shook her head and sighed.

You're really nice people, she said at last. This is a really

beautiful place. I'm pleased you're not planning to blow your-
selves up, or anyone else. She stroked the boy's back. Not
thinking what she was doing.

Do you know where you are, Dial?

Oh please.

Do you know you're living in a police state?

Yeah, yeah, she said. It did not occur to her for a second
that this might be, in many ways, quite true. Certainly the
name Bjelke-Petersen meant nothing to her. She had never
heard of Cedar Bay, helicopter raids and arson committed by
Queensland police. She did not know there was a Queensland
Health Act which permitted police to search her house without a warrant.

Fine, she said.

She slipped her hand into one pocket and produced Buck,
sleek and soft and supple in his sleep, and from the other
pocket she took a small silver bell and a piece of string and
while they all watched she tied the bell around the kitten's
neck and placed him on the floor.

Buck set off around the circle, rubbing himself against feet
and knees.

Only Trevor reached to touch him, to rub his head. When
Buck saw how he was received by the others he put his tail
high in the air and walked down the broad steps and disappeared into the lantana, his bell ringing softly among the
twittering birds.

Dial stood, and her long shadow stretched across the
buckled floor.

Well, she said, we'll see you guys around.

And then she and the boy walked hand in hand down the
stairs and up the rough clay road, through the hot and heavy
air, to their property.

Why is it bad to be American, Dial?

They'll get used to us, she said. And fuck them anyway.

29

His dad's features existed in his mind like a face made by a windblown tree, but he did have one stable picture and this was in his back pocket and sometimes, in the hot afternoons, he went down into the rain forest to look at it in private. There, in the abandoned dusty little hut with the spooky sculptures by its door, he lay on the sneezy floor together with all his papers and rubber bands. Even in this gloomy place the light shone through his father's curly hair. Angel-headed hipster, Cameron said.

Not the man in Seattle. Not the man with the hose. That man had a mustache which lifted and shivered as if disgusted by the life in front of him. He bore no resemblance to the photo on the floor.

The afternoons were slow and thick as ants. From the door of the abandoned shack the boy could see the melancholy clouds above the ridge as they folded and dissolved and changed from old men into pretty girls into weeping women, growing warts, losing teeth, a mess. He thought he liked this, but he didn't. He packed up his papers and secured them one more time with the rubber band. Under the front step he found a rusty tomahawk and he chopped angrily at what they called a wattle tree and watched the black blood come out of the wet white. He hated where he was. He had stolen a clasp knife from Adam's box and now he whittled at a stick, and although he never felt it cut, the knife slipped, maybe twenty times, and sliced up his fingers. Not really blood, just sticky, sour, no real difference from the sweaty heat, everything smudging into everything else.

He stayed in the forest, hiding from Dial in case she wanted him to walk into Yandina once again.

Dial did not like to drive. They had to walk four miles along a dusty road, four miles back. The heat would kill a spider. Hippies did not stop for them. When they got home, Trevor did not visit. All the single mothers could have said how weird that was, but no single women talked to them. They did not like Buck. They'll get used to us, he said.

In the town he had a sneaky traitor's heart and he would stare like a maniac at anyone who glanced his way. Not having been arrested, he trudged back out along Remus Creek Road. It was not home no matter what she called it, but sometimes he saw how it contained the parts of home he would rather have forgotten—the color of sadness, the same light on the moss side of the trees.

They weeded, Dial and he. They slept when the day got too hot. They found wild cherry tomatoes twining through the knee-high grass. The tomatoes burst inside their mouths, hot and wet, like vegetables from outer space. She was kind to him, but teary in the mornings.

The forest around the huts was laced with narrow winding trails, like veins in a creature as yet unnamed. When the boy discovered the first of these he did not mention it to Dial. Sometimes he heard children's voices echoing, clear as hammer blows or saws, but no child appeared to play, nor did he want them to. He was not used to children, having been brought up alone, Victorian.

In the banana groves he found blue plastic bags the same exactly as the one Trevor used to hide his stash. They were tied around the high fruit, to stop birds' pecking, he assumed. The banana tree was high and curved, dying like a sappy weed. He grazed his thighs and bloodied up his knees until he tore the blue bag from the fruit and then, in the grassless, shadowed banana grove, he carefully refolded his papers and tucked them safe inside.

His father would come for him, along the lacework paths. The boy was too timid to walk these paths himself so did not know the one that led to the big old dogleg bend on Remus Creek. If it had not been for Buck, they would have known about the swimming hole. They would have had hippies drifting in for herbal tea all day.

Dial definitely did not want to see any hippies. She would not even ask for help. When the boy found her trying to saw a piece of four-by-four along a pencil line, he said she should ask Trevor or the Rabbitoh to come and help.

Then she cried outright. She wanted to live somewhere pretty but she did not know how. All she was doing was building a shelf to hold the rice and lentils. It stressed her too much. She made sketches early in the morning. She made him shop with her at Day and Grimes, the hardware store, trying to make up her mind about brackets and screws.

The strawberry-nosed men in white coats asked, Can I help you, missus.

No thank you.

She did not get it—neither did the boy, not yet. She was a hippie, therefore she must be shoplifting. Also, the drunk-nosed men were thinking of the naked bottoms of hippie women at the swimming hole. They had been there after work, those good daddies, parking their utes off the fire trail.

At night Buck returned to lie beneath the roaring propane lamp, and the mother and the boy pulled his ticks off one by one. There were cattle ticks, on his back and stomach, and tiny grass ticks which lined up along his ears like babies feeding at their mother's teat. They used tweezers, a little kerosene. How they were together was more fine and tender than this sounds.

Dial read *Huckleberry Finn* out loud and the air was muggy as Jackson, Mississippi, white ants swarming around the hissing lamp, everybody running for their lives.

It was not until the end of the wet season, in early March, that their first visitor came knocking at their open door, not the Rabbitoh, who Dial had been prepared for, but Trevor. He squatted at the table, and his big new belly pushed against the buttons of his Hawaiian shirt; the boy was pleased to see him. He had gotten all bright and shiny, a whole new layer of fat beneath his skin.

I've been away, Trevor said.

You were on vacation?

Most likely Trevor had been in prison.

Yes, he said, his eyes roaming the room until they settled on the shelf.

I know it's not level, Dial said.

Trevor shifted his attention to the curtains and his face split open in what was a real big grin for him.

The mother ran her banged-up hand roughly through her hair. Fuck you, she said. I'm a homeowner now. She did not know whether to be pissed or pleased.

Pretty, Trevor said, not looking at the curtains anymore.

Thank you, said Dial, going pink along her neck.

And what about his nibs here? asked Trevor, not looking at the boy.

Well you can ask him, she said, smiling so much she was embarrassing.

Would he like to come and help me in my garden?

The boy had been pleased to see Trevor, his visit being the first event to break through the endless veil of heat and flies. He certainly did not mean to sneer at him. He was not aware he now curled his lip at him, showed all the pink shiny gums and square white teeth.

Some other time, said Trevor.

Jesus, said Dial later, we don't have to be at war with everybody.

I'm sorry, Dial. I didn't know. But he had that nasty jealous feeling, so he did know after all.

Be interested in his goddamned garden.

The boy was frightened when she yelled at him.

He said, Will you read some more?

30

The road to Trevor Dobbs's hideout was like he had bragged to the boy already—outlaw, very steep, rutted, washed away, potholes, tank traps, killer rocks, one stained black with oil, the death of an auto owned by someone who had no business. It was on a road that didn't want you any more than you wanted it. On the high side of the cutting there was wild bush but no shade at that hour and the dirt was baked hard and comfortless.

There were no threats or skulls or crossbones nailed to tree trunks but at one place there was an abandoned Volvo in a tree. It seemed to have slid down the hill and then skidded backward into space and there it had come to a stop with its back wheels stuck in a burned old wattle. The front wheels had slipped clear off the edge of the road and it clung to the yellow clay road with just inches to spare. Beneath it was nothing but giddiness.

The Volvo had gotten burned, at the time of the accident or later, you couldn't tell; it was black from fire and brown from rust and thin as cigarette paper, like an eaten wasp abandoned in a web. As the boy and the mother approached they heard a rustling sound in its dark throat. Then—loud flapping, or slapping. The boy's hair was too heavy to stand upright, but it pulled at his scalp and filled his neck with fright.

Then a huge black bird—a vulture, he thought, but a turkey actually—flew out the front window, leaving the shell of rust to rock and sway like a dead flower on a brittle black stem.

The boy's heart was in his ears, his legs were aching. He asked, How will he know where to find me?

Who, baby?

My daddy, he said, his throat stinging.

Dial squatted down before him, her too-big eyes watching him as though he were a mouse in a gluetrap, something she did not know how to kill.

Have you been thinking about your daddy?

What did she think he thought? Forever, through the sweaty nights and burning days.

Oh baby, she said, and reached out to hug him. He tugged away and walked on up the hill, feeling the biting gravel sneaking in between his feet and rubber thongs. Every day his skin got hurt or broken.

Che, talk to me.

I'm Jay, he said. He did not have many ways to hurt her.

Jay, we'll tell your daddy where you are.

He feared that was a lie but at the same time he hoped it wasn't.

How?

I'll write a letter.

He was maybe ten feet farther up the hill now, looking down at her at last. When?

Tonight.

Do you love my daddy, he asked.

She lifted her big scratched hands up to her breast. He understood, or thought he did, but he turned and continued up the hill and did not look at her misery until they arrived, finally, on a wide saddle where it seemed the road had led to nothing more than five big drums of diesel fuel.

Where now? he demanded because he was still angry, because she was meant to know.

She pointed and he saw there were many sets of pale tire marks, not following any single course, but all proceeding in the same direction, ending in a bit of gray among the big trees, a sort of nothing that made his mouth go dry. He followed her toward this blur and only when they were very close did he see it was a heavy net which had been thrown like a spiderweb across a building.

Then he could see a high wall punctuated by thick gray timbers, standing upright like trunks of trees, and the space between filled up with yellow clay and on top of the walls he could make out a corrugated iron roof which had been painted black.

He did not want to go in there.

Dial took him by the hand. But she did not know what it was any better than he did.

I don't think this is his, he said, but he allowed himself to be persuaded forward. It was hard to say what they entered, maybe a shed, a barn, a hut, a garage, a fort—all of these in fact—the bones of the construction would eventually turn out to be a hay shed Trevor Dobbs had stolen from Conondale on New Year's Eve; he had unbolted it and carried away the steel trusses and the roof in a "borrowed" truck. He had driven it up the potholed hill and unloaded the shed and had the truck back home before the first day of 1968. Who his accomplices were, he never did say. He made a lair, a compound. Mud brick walls, one foot thick, bulletproof.

The boy had a very strong feeling he would get in trouble just for going in, but the high wooden gate was open and it was either follow Dial or be left behind. He discovered lengths of milled timber leaning against the inside walls, also many narrow sheets of glass on which was printed TELECOM. A small silver trailer home was parked in one corner. In front of it were piles of sand, gravel, sawdust, black stinky stuff the boy would soon know all too well. Half of the floor was concrete and the other half was dirt and where the walls were not yet finished you looked straight onto the vegetables, some of which—the lettuces, for instance—were growing inside.

Dial called Trevor's name.

This is his hideout, the boy whispered.

Shush, she said. He followed her close between the lettuces out into the garden which was dotted with new plantings among the wild pumpkins and zucchinis and eggplants bulging huge and purple from a bed of yellow flowers.

And there was Trevor Dobbs, holding cut greens across his fat and muddy penis.

The boy did not wish to see his penis, not any part of it, and he was relieved to sense that Dial felt pretty much the same.

I brought your assistant, she called. Her voice was very bright and made-up cheerful but her face was coloring and she turned, just like that, and left.

Dial was running away from him. She should not do that. He ran after her, back in among the shadows of the shed, but she was gone. He sat on a pile of bright yellow sand trying not to cry.

After a while he was aware that Trevor had come inside and had gone into the trailer. He tried not looking at him but saw he did not have much bottom and what he had was very muddy. He came out wearing a pair of shorts.

Then Dial appeared again.

Are you OK, she asked the boy.

He would not even look at her.

Trevor was now washing the green stuff under a hose. Water flooded across the floor or perhaps it was the garden.

You can stay, Trevor said to Dial.

She squatted down so she was the boy's height. It was a dumb suck-up thing to do.

What time do you want me to come back?

He was angry she would make him feel so scared. He turned his back on her and walked out into the garden and pretended to look at things.

When?

When I'm done, he said, wanting to hurt her but not wanting her to go.

Then Trevor was coming toward him dragging a sort of sled, a length of rope around his neck.

This is a pallet, said Trevor. Which was wrong. A palette was what Grandma used to paint with, but Trevor could not read or write, he said that once before. Now he tied both ends of the rope to the front wood slats so it was a long sort of harness and then showed the boy how to put it across his chest and pull it. Like a dog.

Trevor did not waste any time in squatting down to talk. He led the boy to a nasty-looking pile of stuff and said that it was a waterweed that he had harvested from Lake Something-or-Other and now he was going to use it as mulch. Do you know what a mulch is?

By now it was clear Dial had left him.

I'm only a kid, he said.

A mulch stops the water escaping from the ground, Trevor said. We put it around the vegetables and it stops the weeds as well. So what you can do to help me is—put as much of this weed on the pallet as you can pull, and then drag it over to those little cauliflowers. Do you know what a cauliflower is?

How long do I have to do this?

As long as you want.

Half an hour, he said.

Then he would go home.

Half an hour is good, said Trevor.

Later the boy saw him down at the bottom of the garden swinging a pick. He had got naked once again, but now the boy was busy with the dark heavy weed all mashed together like hair when the shower got blocked. He patted the matted stuff around the cauliflower seedlings where, to his confusion, his nostrils filled with the dank and distant long wave smell of Kenoza Lake. Then he did cry, secretly, mourning everything he lost, all the cold empty hollows, the marrow stolen from his bones.

31

She could have just left him outside a police station. But she could not leave him anywhere, not even, finally, with Trevor Dobbs. She hated being a good girl, but that was what she had always been, the one who would work the meat grinder late at night, or deliver the sausages up and down I-95. She was a dog on a leash, even now, walking up to the oil drums and then back again to the net and back to the drums. She was tied to this little rich boy. At the same time she knew she could not, would not, permit this to be her life.

She squatted with her back against the trunk of a gum tree, but this caused bits of peeling bark to fall down her back. Then small black ants crawled up her legs so she returned to Trevor's compound.

From the doorway she could clearly see the missing Che Selkirk loading black hairy matter onto a sled and dragging it along a path to a vegetable plot where he pulled the load apart. He was a strange little thing. He had a gorgeous sly shy smile, too much like his father's. She was touched by his seriousness, how he placed the weed on the freshly watered soil. Thinking him safe she finally walked back down the hill. After only a short time she began gardening herself, but the soil dried so quickly and she had no seed. She could not concentrate on anything. Every little while she went back inside to check, but there was no boy, only a heavy viscous emptiness, a blanket of air, inert surfaces from which tiny black flies rose, her furies.

Back in the garden, Buck caught a frog and tormented it until she had to kill it with a spade and the frog cried and then was still and mashed. All small forms of life, in their wiggling squirming resistance, were like the boy.

When it was very hot she lay beneath the mosquito netting and Buck meowed until she picked him up and let him in. Bell or no bell, he had a blue fluffy feather in his mouth.

Dial slept too long. She was running the instant she left the hut, down to the road, up the hill. Raw throated, dry lipped, she slipped through the nets of Trevor's bunker. There they were, sitting outside the trailer, the boy in a big barber's chair, the man on a fruit box. Trevor took a knife and sliced a watermelon which he held out, a huge dripping slab, toward the boy. The murmur of the boy's voice brought a spasm. Did he ever talk so much to her?

She did not know how real mothers did anything, how they could live without being driven mad.

So she crept away a third time, believing that a mother would not wait like a lump of dead fish inside her hut while the valley slowly lost its light. It was almost dark when she finally walked back up the hill and by now she was angry with the boy for tormenting her and with Trevor for not knowing he should send him home by dark, and with herself for being so careless with her life.

Dark caught up with her on the road. Just past the rusty Volvo she was forced to hold her hand out to feel her way in lurching space. After a while she saw a light weaving and shining through the silky pale-trunked trees and at first she was pleased but then the light went out. She waited for it to come on down the road and find her, standing in what she wrongly judged to be the middle of the track.

Then the light was on her, blinding, blue as lightning in her face.

She held up her hands against its brutal flood.

Who is it?

No one spoke, but the light was hard and cold as ice. Once more she was afraid.

Trevor?

Hello Dial, said the boy.

Oh you little bastard, cried the mother. You little shit. Those were her words. Plus she struck out at him, and knocked the flashlight so hard it bounced and rolled into the ravine, twirling and spinning through the bush until it was nothing more than a glowworm in lantana, far, far below, and they had to walk home in dark and bitter silence.

I'm sorry, Dial, the boy said.

That's OK. I'm sorry too. She could feel his frailty, his beating small boy heart.

Did you hurt your hand.

She could not speak, shaking her head in the dark, shamed by him.

In the hut he showed her what he had been carrying on his back, papaya and melon and pumpkin and eggplant. As he lay the gifts across the table she lit the bright hissing propane and saw his sideways smile.

So, she said, as she set to work on dinner. What did you and Trevor talk about?

Nothing much, he said.

Did you have a nice time?

It was OK.

She was dumb enough to be hurt by his reticence. She was smart enough to know that it was dumb. She made a ratatouille but he was asleep before it was ready, his arm thrown sideways off his cushion, his wide red-lipped mouth almost exactly like his father's. He was about a billion dollars filled with buzzing secrets and she told him, quietly, secretly, she loved him, and carried him off to the other hut where it was easier to get him into bed.

32

He said it was OK, but it was not. In truth the sun had been hot beyond belief. It burned clear through his shirt. He had dragged the sled backward and forward on that sawdust path about a hundred times at least, the load bucking and kicking behind him and the rope sawing across his chest and arms, as if it could slice away his feelings like lamb fat off a chop. When all the cauliflowers were mulched he went on to the next bed. How long this took he did not know.

Smoke-oh!

Sir?

We take a break.

The heat made Trevor look like no one the boy had ever seen in his entire life—a mud man, the trunk of a tree, a watermelon with no waist or hips. He smeared his red face with the back of his black hand and inspected the boy's work. He did not say *well done* or *thank you*.

You want to wash?

The boy was not going to get naked here, no way. He said, What?

Trevor pointed to the shower, right out in the open in a kind of pit beneath a concrete tank.

The boy said, I'm OK.

Just the same he followed Trevor out of the sun, under the roof where it smelled of sawdust and dirt and something sweet and drunk like a burrow.

Trevor showered and came back in his sarong, his brown hair wet and doggy short, and he shook himself and sprayed the boy's dusty skin with water drops. The boy would have liked a nice cold glass of milk. He asked for water but was told to use a garden hose which was black and beat-up and taped together. The water came out cold enough, and he let it spill down his legs on purpose and rubbed some on his face and wiped his muddy hands on his shorts.

Trevor asked him did he like watermelon.

I don't mind, he said.

Sit up there. You know what that chair is?

The chair was strange and scary. He shook his head.

Don't they have barbers in New York?

They have most things, he said.

Trevor was staring above his eyes. The boy knew his blond hair showed at the roots of his disguise.

Trevor asked, You don't know what a barber is?

The boy just waited while he got looked at.

No?

Trevor set up a card table and on this he placed a watermelon and a loaf of bread and a bowl of olives. He held up a single olive between his thumb and forefinger and this made the boy think of his grandma and her six o'clock martini. He made the best damned martinis in Sullivan County. She said so.

You know what this is?

It's an olive.

You eat it with the bread and watermelon.

The boy knew that was wrong.

So, said Trevor, with his face pushed deep in the melon like an animal. So Dial's your mummy. What about your dad. Is he in America?

The boy took a big bite of bread and chewed.

I'm an orphan, Trevor said. He wiped his face with the back of his thick arm. You know what an orphan is?

The boy made himself busy with an olive. It was black, not green, and pointy at one end. He spat the pit into his hand.

It means you haven't got a mother or a father. Do you know where I'm from?

The boy took a bite of melon, just to have his mouth full. He should not have been left alone with Trevor.

Trevor fed himself olives from the bottom of his fist. You're a very lucky boy, he said at last.

The watermelon and olive tasted wrong and good, salt and sweet.

You sad at night?

What?

Trevor's eyes were small but they were bright and sort of wet looking. He blew out his olive pits, fierce like spitballs. You sad at night, I said.

The boy stared at him, his throat burning.

Ask me about my father? Trevor demanded.

The boy was frightened now.

I haven't got one, said Trevor. Ask me about my mother?

Don't you have a mother?

Fuck them all, Trevor said. Don't worry. Look at where I am. He pointed with his knife and they looked together at the piles of stuff, the view.

When this is done, son, this will be a fortress. I've got twenty thousand gallons of water in those tanks. I can have a bloody fountain in the middle of my house. I have fresh veggies, good dope. No one can touch me, man, you understand me. No one knows I even exist. They can't see me with satellites. I am totally a fucking orphan. That's the silver lining. Do you understand?

I guess.

So she split up from your dad?

He's coming here, the boy said very quickly, he's coming pretty soon. He's working right now and he can't come till that's done.

What sort of work is that?

I'm not allowed to say.

He's in jail?

What?

He's doing time?

He went to Harvard, said the boy. He knew it was a powerful thing to say.

Trevor clicked his tongue and shook his head.

The boy said, We should probably get back to work now.

You want to do *more?*

I don't mind.

So he was taught how to throw the watermelon peel in the compost and they worked a good while in the hot sun. Then Trevor decided it was enough so the boy had a shower and put his shorts back on while he was wet.

You want to see something good?

I don't know, he said.

Say yes, said Trevor, it's a gift.

As it happened the boy already had a gift, ten dollars he had seen on Trevor's workbench. He slipped the bright blue bill in the pocket with his stuff. Come on, said Trevor, and the boy followed him through the fallen bark, carrying his gift, while the dry sticks exploded like angry fireworks beneath his feet.

Tit for tat you dirty rat, feed you to the old tomcat.

They set off along the saddle which was gentle enough at first but then became steep and rough with broken shale like scales, the spine of some old scabby dragon. Then they came out into sunlight and crossed over into a high flat field with feathery grass and purple seeds which shone like silver. Through the waving blades the boy imagined he could see paler yellow lines like grown-over paths or car tires, but maybe he was wrong. He listened to the swish of the seeds brushing against his skin. His eyes were mostly down, looking out for snakes.

What was he going to be shown? Something relating to his father.

Soon there was a barbed-wire fence. The posts were gray and bearded with pale green lichen. The wire was a chocolate brown except someone had added a few shiny new bits to make a puzzle of loops and levers so that the fence could be opened and closed like a boneless gate. After that the land fell away to a small flat where baby trees were growing, pale yellow flowers and tough old leaves that tore like leather.

Wattle, said the man.

The boy did not want to go any farther but he was afraid to be left behind and he hurried after Trevor until they came to a high sort of knob or wart about the size of a small house, and this was where the man stopped, retying his sarong, and sniffing around him like a dog.

What are we going to do now?

Trevor's eyes were small and very blue and when they turned to look at him they were bright and glassy and the boy was afraid he would get caught for stealing. Without a word Trevor took his hand and led him around the base of the wart, through some snaky-looking grass, then to a pile of dead branches. He held apart the twigs and branches meaning the boy should go in. He did not want to.

Where are we going? His throat was kind of scratchy dry. He did not know what a man would want to show a boy.

Trevor gave him a little push and so he went ahead and found a rough shed covered with the exact same net that guarded Trevor's house except here it was threaded with dead vines and saplings like a trash pile.

The boy thought, She should not have left me alone.

Go on, said Trevor. Nothing's going to bite you.

Inside this shell the boy found a very pretty pale blue car, its axles set on wooden blocks. There was three or four feet between the car and the netting so there was room to admire it properly.

You know what sort of car this is?

No, said the boy, generally relieved.

You like it.

It's cool, Trevor.

It was dark and strange inside the net, not scary, not at all—the car was so silvery, shiny blue, like ice, or a fall sky. You could also smell the cleaning products and see the little starbursts of sunlight—headlight rims inside the wild stick nest.

It's got huge fucking petrol tanks, said Trevor. It used to be a rally car. You can drive seven hundred miles in this without stopping. Trevor made a pistol with his finger. Bang, he said. You want to fire it up?

What?

Start the engine.

Thank you, Trevor.

The door wasn't even locked. The boy climbed up first and slid across behind the wheel.

See the key? Just turn it.

That's all he did and the engine came to life and Trevor showed him how to get down on the floor and push the pedal to make the engine go real loud. It was clean down there, no dust, nothing but a silver coin which he took and put in the pocket with the paper money. After a while he got sick of being on the floor so they took a brick from the backseat and rested it on the pedal.

Got to keep the battery charged. Trevor explained how that worked. He might as well remember this if he was going to be responsible for Adam's shitty Peugeot.

The boy did not say he was going home. He learned about the generator and they both squatted in the bush some distance off watching the exhaust smoke drift out into the sunlight and disappear. Trevor produced tobacco from the waist of his sarong and began to roll a cigarette.

Everyone thinks that the road stops up at my place, Trevor said. You look at a map, that's what it shows. You ask the police, that's what they'll tell you, but none of that is true.

The boy paid attention to the police.

There's an old survey road all the way through here. This is my back door, you understand? I can drive the way we've walked. It's all passable now. There's nothing to stop me coming out on the Bruce Highway just before Eumundi. So when they come for me, Trevor said, I'm out of here. I'm an orphan, dig it. This is why you need to know me. We learn how to look after ourselves.

I'm not an orphan, said the boy. I'm not!

Hey, take it easy. Trevor ruffled his hair.

The boy pulled away. He felt the man's upset, his eyes traveling angrily across his scalp, although maybe this was just his imagination.

I'm not going to hurt you, said the man.

My dad would kill you, said the boy.

He's your dad, said the man. What choice would he have?

33

The boy's skin got dark as tree bark. He walked up the hill barefoot. Dial was left below, not knowing what to do. She was waiting, for what, for nothing. Outside the open windows the world was green, fecund, everything rotting and being born, but she did not know how to garden and she got herself trapped in the hut with its miserable yellow moisture barrier between the rustic clapboard and the inside frame. Inside the hut was worse than the place she had been born in—rickety, cobwebbed, no straight line or corner and everything made poisonous looking by the yellow shiny paper. This was the alternative architecture, its most reliable component manu-factured by Dow Chemical, Monsanto, 3M.

She made herself drive the car. She had to go somewhere, but she set off along Remus Creek Road not knowing where that might be.

In Nambour she drove past the police station twice. She parked half a block away, still uncertain. Her mouth was dry; she felt sick with the smell of automotive plastics. She locked the car with the windows up, her hands trembling as she did so.

She planned to take one step, then another. She had

brought her passport with her. She did not know which way led back to Brisbane.

She came upon a newsagent with a crouching dark veranda and a low doorway. She had planned to ask which way was south but instead she saw the walls were stacked with pulp fiction. She asked if they might have *The Sea-Wolf,* and having politely considered *Sea of Troubles* and *Sea Babes,* she was directed to a dusty lending library in the School of Arts. The library was useless but the librarian had heard there was a wonderful bookstore at Noosa Junction although she had never been there personally.

What an awful place to spend your life.

Heading back to Yandina, she began to drive more slowly as if tempting something to happen to her, slowing in front of bullying gravel trucks, daring them to destroy her. Approaching the turnoff to Remus Creek Road she found she could not do it. She headed another mile, then three. Somewhere near Eumundi she pulled off the road and sat there with the engine running.

She was parked across a rough sort of track leading into the scraggy bush. Through the smeary windshield she could make out piles of sawdust, some stacks of fresh-cut timber held in racks. There were two abandoned cars, an open-walled shed that might have been the mill and a wiry little man, maybe sixty years of age, who now came out to look at her. He wore shorts and an apron which stopped just above his leathery knees.

He stepped back then, to one side, so she might enter.

She waved that she was leaving. He stood back farther.

She thought, Is this it then? Another throw of the dice.

In a moment she was rolling down a bumpy track, splashing and slipping sideways, into the deep wheel ruts. The miller waited, between two mounds of dead gray sawdust, the gateposts of his foreign world. Behind him was a stack of sappy bright yellow planks, a gorgeous slash of yellow.

He had a mouth like a sock puppet and a short stubby clay pipe. He cocked his head at her.

This is a sawmill?

Last time I looked.

It was the yellow that drew her from the car.

That's blackbut, he said, seeing what she was looking at.

She was close enough to smell its rich sappy odor.

You doing fencing? That's fencing.

I want to line a wall, she decided.

Oh no, love, not suitable. It's for fencing, cheap old fencing. It'll shrink like billy-oh.

She was thinking the walls would be golden in the lamplight.

If I nailed it flat, she said, it couldn't shrink.

It'll curl up like bacon.

Well, I could pin it flat.

You're what they call *alternative*?

I guess so.

He cocked a flirty eyebrow. You could use a nail and bend it over, he said, so as it shrinks it might stay flat. You'd make a kind of L with it. You could do that. You'll be up all night with those nails.

That's OK.

He nodded. His mouth was small and the smile was thin. Hoy! he cried.

From the shadows of the big open-sided shed there emerged a middle-aged giant with a belly and naked legs.

Urge, said the sawmiller, get your beautiful body over here.

And then the two men roped the fence palings onto the Peugeot and she paid them twenty dollars and drove home with her purchase slapping and whipping on the roof. She thought of Camus's asthma patient moving peas from one saucepan into another. Beckett, too. More fun to build a wall.

She did not untie the ropes correctly which was why the boy would later see the yellow bruise and blood-black graze which covered her ankle and the upper part of her foot. When the pain abated she loaded up about six splintery planks in her unprotected arms, carrying them directly into the big hut and dropping them untidily onto the clearest patch of floor. Can't go on. Must go on.

Hello, Dial.

Rebecca and a small boy had made themselves at home among the cushions.

Hello, said Dial, her heart beating violently.

Doing a bit of renovation?

Yes.

Lining the inside at last?

Yes, said Dial, or words to that effect.

You know that timber's going to shrink?

Yes I do.

You butt them up against each other you'll have one-inch gaps.

Who the fuck did these people think they were, walking into your apartment, scratching their hairy legs and eating your papaya? Dial did not sit down. She could not. Her behavior would not help her. Well so be it, she thought. She had never lived anywhere there was no conflict.

Soon she noticed a bad smell which she blamed on the hair sticking out beneath Rebecca's plump arms. The visitor's breasts were big and sweaty, staining her gray T-shirt.

So, Rebecca, this is about the cat?

Rebecca nodded toward a flour sack which had been dropped by the door to the deck. You could say that, she said.

Dial thought, My God, the bitch has killed him.

Have a look, said the stinky woman, why don't you?

Why should I?

It's educational.

Dial approached the bag slowly, a sort of unreal buzzing in her head. Flies crawled around her wounded ankle.

The contents slithered onto the floor like what? Flowers. Grass tussocks. Some stinky mulch. Then she understood what she was looking at: small dead birds, some bright, some dull, some filled with ants and possibly—she saw the movement like a living stomach—maggots. *The Godfather*, she thought. The horse's head in bed.

What the hell are you up to, Rebecca? I never did anything to you.

Oh, you're wrong there, Dial.

Rebecca stood up and her staring blond boy-child stood right beside her, its colorless eyes filled with blank dull righteousness.

This is what you did to me, Rebecca said. You bring your cat into the valley. This is what you do. They're sentient beings, she said, nudging a feathered corpse with her big toe.

They're *what*?

In Buddhism, began Rebecca.

I know what *sentient* means.

Rebecca narrowed her eyes. Then you should know that your cat is destroying our environment and you've got a choice. You can get rid of this cat or we will get rid of you.

Rebecca, you know I talked to Phil Warriner.

This is not America, Dial. We don't decide ethical issues with lawyers.

And with that, she departed, walking heavily on her heels, with her boy already left three steps behind and wailing.

Beneath the vermined bodies the yellow planks lay in shadow, crisscrossed like yarrow sticks on the dusty floor.

34

When it got too hot to work the boy washed and climbed up in the big old barber's chair. Enthroned beneath the baking roof, he looked out across the waves of silver bush where the trees, like aliens, swished their dangerous tails.

Trevor would then bring him bread and olives and papaya or watermelon or cantaloupe. One time there was a huge blue bag of mangoes. The mangoes were "visitors," a class of thing that also included the boy and the dull old horse presently flicking the flies away from his bottom with his nervy tail, a sad beast who spent his mornings being led around the pug mill while Trevor shoveled dirt, and the boy, whose job it was to lead the horse, whispered into his jerky ears and fed him carrots with his palm, his fingers nowhere near his wide blunt teeth. The horse was on a secret assignment from a paddock not so far beyond the rally car. In the heat of the dusty afternoon the boy removed the horse's shellback ticks and splat their blood sacs between his fingernails. Sometimes the horse tried to bite him in return.

The boy was full of saintly concern for the sad biting horse but had mostly forgotten about the cat he had required so urgently. When he was with Dial he remembered Buck of course, but right now he was way more interested in another long-dead cat that had got Trevor into trouble when he was an orphan, freshly stolen from his English parents, so he said, and brought to Australia by the priests at the Dr. Barnardo's Homes.

The boy knew he was not old enough to hear the stories Trevor wished to tell him, but that is why he came. Why he was invited probably. The stories were rich and sticky, like blood and sugar, like something that would later make him ill. There had been many cats on the orphan farm. That was in South Australia. The boy did not know where that was, only that it was cold and loveless and the London boys would suffer ringworm, scabies, beatings, in order to "get a love," i.e., to smooth and pet a cat.

The farting scabby boys were just like him. He was told this often although it was not really true. They had climbed into an attic searching for one particular cat. They knew it was there as they had heard it meowing in the night. In the crawl space they scraped their knees, and they banged their heads on rafters, voices breaking, Puss-puss-puss; but what was so secret in the dark was a public event in the dormitory below where Brother Kiernan waited, sitting on an iron bed, already tapping his cane against his boot. The boys would get punished soon enough.

What was the crime? Trevor spat his olive pits out against the trailer. Bang! Bang! Bang! What was the fucking crime?

This dormitory where Brother Kiernan waited with his cane was not so far, Trevor said, from where the boys would have to line up two years later to view him in his coffin. This scene the grown-up man could still see vividly: the bruised purple undersides of the roses along the quartz-white gravel path, the smell of the blood and bone fertilizer, the stink of death. Brother Kiernan's face was wax, his hair all white. The boy Trevor felt the cruel pinch of the shoes he had been forced to wear for this occasion, shoes that had been confiscated when the orphans first landed on Australian soil.

They took every bloody thing, Trevor said.

Have some more bread, he said.

Any little thing we brought from home. Conkers—do you know what a conker is?—rubber bloody bands. They put our shoes and socks and sweaters into beer cartons and wrote our names on there. ERIC HOBBS they wrote and clipped me across the lug hole when I said the name was wrong. They did not give our shoes back until the occasion of Kiernan's funeral and by then our feet were bigger and harder and we had got used to moving smartly across frost, hard-crushed gravel and all the spikes and pricks and bindy-eyes we never knew before. The shoes clamped us hard at Kiernan's funeral but it felt so good to see the bastard dead. Do you know what I mean, he asked, his eyes too bright, too narrowed.

Do you know what I mean? he asked, stabbing the melon as if to do it harm.

The boy was afraid. He asked about the cat.

The orphans had climbed up into the ceiling and gotten caught and then they were given blue chits which meant they had to report to Kiernan's office.

Trevor sliced more watermelon and handed the boy a fist of olives which he was way too tense to eat.

It was a very small room, Trevor said. We knew it well, firstly because we had helped build it. "Man's work with a boy's body" is what they called it. Just off the ship we were divided into gangs to clear brush, dig trenches, lay foundations, gather granite from the quarry, pour barrows full of concrete, burn ourselves with lime. Boys from ten to fourteen. We made the rooms we were beaten in, and worse.

And Brother Kiernan now made good use of our Christian labor, mate. As punishment for entering the attic, he had us strip and walk around him naked in a circle and he lashed at us with that bloody cane.

The boy was frightened. He moved to wash his plate.

Trevor stayed him with a hand against his arm. I'm telling you about the cat, he said. You'll like the cat. It was because of the cat that he beat our legs and bottoms without mercy, a great huge Irishman with an arm as thick as our legs. We carried those bruises and welts and cuts for bloody weeks. They were nothing. It was the terror in our heads. Nothing could compare with that.

Did you find the cat?

I don't know, said Trevor angrily. Don't interrupt.

What sort of cat was it, the boy insisted.

I had blue eyes, said Trevor. That was my curse.

The cat?

Me. I had blue eyes.

You still have blue eyes, said the boy.

Who gives a fuck these days.

Did the cat have blue eyes?

Trevor sucked in his breath as if he would explode and then he let it out again. The priests liked my blue eyes, can you imagine that? Would you say I was a pretty man?

I should go soon.

No, I'm not a pretty man, and I was not a pretty boy, but the brothers took a liking to my eyes and they left me in such despair I tried to beat my eyes out with a rock so they would change their color. You understand why?

The boy shook his head. He knew he could not leave.

Never mind, said Trevor. You didn't want to hear all this. I understand. I'm sorry. He stood and hurled the remaining watermelon out beyond the edge of the garden and the boy saw it split and fly apart, white flesh broken in the bush.

Whatever a priest did was the will of God, he said. I'm sorry.

That's all right, the boy said.

But they prepared me, Trevor said, wiping his mouth with the back of his hand, surveying his achievement—the big water tanks, the mud bricks they had made that morning now baking in the sun—I can survive anything now, Trevor said, and you're lucky you have met me. Do you know why? Because I can teach you stuff she doesn't know.

The boy looked out across the waving trees. Everything was hard and dry, dead leaves, cracking sticks, no mercy. He thought, This does not apply to me. You can teach my dad too, he said. You can teach us both together.

Trevor was staring at him. The boy did not know why. The olives in his hand were mashed. He wished he had not touched them ever.

Sit down, said Trevor when the boy began to move. Listen to me.

As a result he did not get back down the hill until maybe five o'clock. There was still sunlight in the treetops so she might not be angry with him yet. He heard three hammer blows as he came past the Peugeot and soon afterward he found Dial standing on a rickety chair.

Hi, she said, sort of frozen in position.

She was not mad at him but at a plank of wood. She had managed to pin it to a wall stud.

She said, Is it straight?

He did not want to get involved with mechanical. He said, Did you get a book?

Christ, she said. Just tell me. Is it straight?

You said you'd buy a book for tonight.

Well I did not get a book. Is this straight?

The oven was cold and sour with ashes. He unpacked his backpack and lay a pumpkin and an eggplant on the counter-top. In his pocket he had another two Australian dollars and now they were secret in his hand, wet and balled up like a squishy plum.

Dial had a big white scarf wound around her head, three nails sticking out of her teeth, a rusty hammer in her hand. Just tell me is the string hanging straight, so I can put the nail in.

Dial, please, can I do it later?

Just tell me—is it straight?

Suddenly, violently, he wished all this was over.

Che!

Yes, he said, it's straight. This was true—it was straight if you lined it up with the countertop. But also—it was crooked if you lined it up against the window frame.

Do you love my daddy, he asked.

I told you. Hold it steady.

She hadn't told him anything. He took the end of the board and his eyes were burning. She held a nail against the board, a little silver nail. She tapped it in successfully.

There, she said, that wasn't hard.

But of course when she stood back, she must have seen she had a crooked hippie house. The plank could not look straight compared with anything at all. She didn't speak but went to the oven where he could hear her cleaning out the grate. Out among the tall grass he found some little sticks for kindling and brought them back to her.

Sorry, bubba, she said.

It's OK, he said. He thought he meant it at the time.

Dial lit a mosquito coil and carried it out onto the deck where it sent up comic-strip curls of foreign stink which slowly fell among her yellow hair. As the sun left the ridges to their gloomy dark she breathed it in like perfume.

So why did you ask about your daddy?

He shrugged. She still hadn't answered what he asked.

Your face is dirty.

When is my daddy going to come and get me?

She held out her strong brown arms to him but now he was angry and he looked at the plank on the wall and if he had ever felt safe it must have been a long, long time ago. She took her arms back and folded them across her chest and sat with her back against the open doorway, pretending to look at the poor crooked plank.

There's nothing I can do about your daddy, baby. You know that.

Is he in jail?

Not as far as I know.

That wasn't him, he said angrily. You lied.

Sweetie, that's not nice.

I have a right to know the truth.

You have *what*?

I have a right to know the truth.

Is that what you talk about with Trevor.

No. I have a right.

Listen to me, you spoiled little brat, she said. You go away all day long playing games with Trevor. What I have down here is Rebecca.

She's taken care of.

Where did you learn to talk like that—*taken care of*? She is not taken care of. You know what she brought here?

And so she dumped all her fears in front of him.

This is your cat, she said. We have it because you wanted him. Now you take care of him, you hear me?

Or what?

Or we'll have to go again, that's what, she said. Do you want to do that? Do you want to go looking for another place to live?

I want to go home, he cried.

He expected her to reach for him, to fold him to her breast, but instead she ripped her scarf from her head and threw it on the floor.

Oh great, she said, you want me to go to jail. Thank you, baby, thank you so much.

He looked at her and hated her. Her big nose. Her hairy eyebrows. Her stinky sweaty smell.

I can't believe you, she said.

Shut up, he said suddenly. Shut up. His mind was in a rush of temper. As he walked toward the door the cat rose from its hiding place beneath Adam's bench. The boy rushed at him, stamping his feet.

Bloody cat, he cried, and ran outside.

He walked down to the road by himself. There were crows. Later in the gloom he heard Dial calling for him but by then he had found his way beneath the hut where he huddled up between two propane tanks and watched the dark come down.

35

Trevor came padding softly down the hill with his new flashlight, three feet long, two and a half pounds. It had been free of cost to him, thanks to the roomy overalls he wore when shopping.

His feet were bare, hard, the heels and balls buffed like saddle leather or polished concrete. He did not turn the flashlight on—darkness is your friend. The moon had not yet risen when he got through the last bit of guttered track and arrived at the cane toad territory down by the creek. He could hear the frogs as well, and the water passing over the dam Rebecca's kids had made. Through the flooded gums he could see the candles flickering in her hut. She would be lying on the bed he built for her—he had told the boy about that misunderstanding with Rebecca, but the boy did not have a clue.

A little farther was the cutting into Adam's land. It was not difficult to find. The American babe had a huge propane lamp. She was like an oil refinery. The lamp perched on a three-foot yellow pipe screwed directly to the brand-new gas tank and it spilled light out across the uncut grass, the mustard-yellow path leached white, winged insects rising by his knees.

Trevor called out to announce himself but he did not slow

his pace. The boy watched from his hiding place beneath the hut. He saw Dial's feet meet Trevor's in the bright back doorway, two steps above him. She stepped aside and Trevor brushed past her.

Inside the hut Trevor and Dial faced each other.

You can't torture him like this, he said.

Trevor, what *are* you talking about?

Tell him about his father, Dial. She flinched and Trevor thought, She's left him!

He led the way out onto the piddling little deck that weak lazy Adam had constructed, and here he squatted, the heavy flashlight lying across his lap, the ridiculous uproar of the propane lamp behind him.

You know you could see this place from outer space, he said.

I like to read, she said.

I'm word blind, he said. I was whipped for not reading, he said, but my brain can't do it.

The American did not reply and so he waited until she came to him. She would not come completely. She leaned against the doorframe, half in, half out, but her big dark eyes were sort of naked. He thought, She's single.

I'm an orphan, he explained.

Really.

You shouldn't be pissy with me, Dial. I'm one of your neighbors.

Don't start that.

You should be visiting them. You haven't been friendly. They don't know who you are.

If I wanted friends I would have stayed in Boston.

But you are friendly, Trevor said. He meant it too. I've seen you, Dial. You're kind. You're not his mother but you love him.

He hadn't planned to say that. He didn't even know he knew it. They watched each other in surprise. For a moment she was rigid but then she hugged herself and sighed.

I'm an academic, she said. I shouldn't be here.

I know that, he said.

She gestured at the puzzling plank nailed crookedly on the wall. I hate all this shit.

I can see.

I'm from South Boston. Do you know what that is?

It's in America.

I'm the first person in my family to go to college. Can you imagine what it would mean to them if they could see what I've become.

A hippie, like me.

It's *so* much worse than that.

You're not his mother, though, he said. He wished she would sit closer to him.

You don't know that.

His father's dead. Isn't he! He did not know if this was true or not. He tried to read her bitter smile.

He has a right to know, he said.

He has a *right*?

Yes.

Oh really.

Dial, I know what I'm talking about.

You know what? Stop fucking with his head, man. This is much much worse than you can know. He's not you. No one's going to burn his legs with cigarettes.

She had read the scars, that's all. Big deal.

I know, she said, that you think he's just like you. She spoke gently now, and lay a hand upon his knee.

Trevor shrugged.

But this boy comes from Park Avenue. In New York. He's going to go to Harvard and be a fucking corporate lawyer. He's so absolutely not you, Trevor. He's a fucking *prince*.

So he's going back to that, soon, to his real mother?

Did I say that?

Then what?

She rocked forward on her knees and for a crazy moment,

as she lay her hand on his bare shoulder, he thought she was going to kiss him and he felt a brief giddy surge of blood.

Instead she whispered in his ear—I heard something under the hut. He's out there somewhere.

And together they looked out into the skirt of light, at the places where the tree trunks drowned in dark.

Shush, she said, and there was, as if in response, the sound of a feral animal scurrying beneath the deck, and then fast footfalls on the path and then a great thump as the boy arrived inside the hut, like a possum fallen from a tree, eyes ablaze like gas. Buck was tucked compliantly beneath his arm.

The boy did not say a word. When Trevor approached him, he stood his ground.

Dial watched this happen with a kind of bilious feeling in her gut. When Trevor asked for soap and a towel she was pleased to find them for him, and when he escorted the boy outside, she took a sharp knife and began to cut cherry tomatoes in half, for what reason she could not really have said.

God save us all, she thought.

Soon she heard the slapping sound of the shower. It was just a pipe beneath the floor of the other hut, a slab of sloping concrete that let the water flow away into the bush. It was lovely in the afternoon, but at night there were spiders and bugs biting you. When the boy returned his hair was wet and his face was pink and scrubbed. She had chopped perhaps ten tomatoes, and they lay in half with their tiny yellow seeds glistening on the bench.

Trevor asked the boy, Where are your clean clothes?

He pointed up to the loft bed.

Then go get dressed.

The boy's face had some strange soapy glaze, but he obeyed, and Trevor came to the countertop. He removed the knife from her hand and lay a fistful of weed inside her palm. Then, without asking her permission, he began to crack eggs into a bowl. Yesterday's spring onions had not wilted and with this and not much more than a few baby tomatoes he put together three omelets which they ate in silence.

Afterward the boy helped Trevor to wash and dry the dishes. Watching this, Dial tasted green and bitter jealousy rising from her gorge. So now she did not want him taken from her? How fucked was that?

The boy stayed close by Trevor, rubbing his soap-wet hands on his clean shorts.

Trevor turned off the propane lamp. In the sudden quiet the boy heard the panic of a single insect in a web. His own breath was held like a crumpled milk carton in his bony chest.

Trevor sat, his back against the doorframe opposite where Dial was squatting.

You know those boards are going to shrink, he said.

The boy sat too, cross-legged, pink faced, closer to Trevor than to Dial.

They're green, Trevor said.

Oh, really?

The boy saw how the moonlight was caught in the gauze of many little wings, white ants, mosquitoes, moths with black jeweled bodies.

I'm just telling you, Trevor said.

And I appreciate your kindness.

And then no one spoke and it made the boy feel sick and worried like when you watch the Kenoza Lake stars and try to imagine the end of space. You build a brick wall but when you break through, there is still more space. You can scare yourself to death.

The boy said, I'm an orphan, aren't I?

He was pretty scared, to hear himself say that.

He expected Dial would reach out to him then, and he would push her clear away. Dial did not move.

No one spoke some more.

The boy thought, What have I done? Behind him were the shadows of the stupid timber lying on the floor.

Where's my daddy, he asked.

The frogs were singing to one another, things were dying in the night. He could see Dial's hair, the cold fiery edge of it. There was papaya balm on Trevor's leg ulcer. Made him smell like rotten fruit.

Where is my daddy, Dial?

I don't know, she said at last.

You promised you would write to him. You must know.

Not really.

Like that.

In the dark, finally, she reached out to touch his streaming hopeless face.

The air was suddenly filled with parts of him, each bit sharp enough to cut. You liar!

Where is his dad? asked Trevor. He deserves to know.

You, said Dial.

You, she began again, are a cruel and dangerous fool.

Don't you ever call me a fool.

Oh, please. Don't be so precious. He isn't you. He's someone else. You couldn't imagine him if you lived to be a hundred.

Are you his mother then?

The boy got quiet and listened.

What, said Dial.

You heard me, said Trevor, but Dial was already standing and staring behind her into the dark. She brushed past the boy, bumped the lamp. He thought she was going to climb up to the loft but when she came back she was carrying a length of two-by-four and she cracked Trevor across the back with it.

The boy cried out.

Trevor roared, rolled, a mouse, a cockroach.

Dial would not permit him escape. She thudded him twice more, across the ribs. The boy watched the big man curl up like a baby. Then he rolled clear off the deck. Onto the smelly dirt where Adam used to pee.

Dial looked down into the stink, timber in her hand. No one spoke.

Trevor whimpered. She threw the wood on top of him and turned away. When she wiped her nose and stepped toward him, the boy did not know what to do.

Come here, she said, but the boy ran out into the night and down the hill, past the car, and on the dark road below he smelled papaya balm.

Are you there? he whispered.

36

She stacked the wet dishes, crying quietly. There was nowhere to store them in this slum.

Her mother would have died to see her genius in a dump like this. She did die. Anyway. Of Ajax, Mr. Clean, Murphy Oil. Died of the knives and forks of Patricia Van Gunsteren who never knew who her housekeeper was. They had not the least idea, is what Dial thought. No clue. She pulled hardwood splinters from her hand while the propane light hissed in a white fury at the empty hut.

No one has the least idea of who I am. Not that little bratty boy who stole her heart and ran. Not Trevor, not Chook, not Roger, not scrawny chicken Adam. How could these B-list hippies understand that Dial was an SDS goddess. Who could see that? Hardly herself.

In Cambridge she had covered herself with peasant dresses, bits of mirrors, sheep's wool boots as if she were the corrupt princess of Nepal. Harvard babies did not see the contradiction.

They called her Dial because she said dialectic had been invented by Zeno. So they mocked her, idiots. She was the truth teller. She only lied to the boy to keep him from hurt, and for her sin her intestines were pulled from her on a Catherine wheel.

She stole the boy. Is that what she had wanted? She did not think so. Maybe she wanted to make love to his pretty daddy or did she want to hurt the daddy, make him burn in hell, the creep?

She took her own papa to the house in Somerville and dear George walked across the Persian rug in dusty boots. He was five foot four, his greased-back hair standing high up from his head. He did not even notice the baby, baby Che, sweet Jesus in the crib. But he shook pretty Dave Rubbo's hand. You want to know about the revolution, comrade?

George Xenos had bullet wounds in the middle of each palm, his fingers crabbing so he held his knife and fork like a trained bear. He was not ashamed. He would show you, comrades—how he had been forced to place his hands on the pillow of a woman's bed. The fascists shot him with a Mauser. He would tell you the caliber. Not German bastards. Greek bastards. He laughed. Even his missing teeth appeared heroic.

He came to Somerville in September '66, a few weeks before the McNamara visit. There was mud on his boots, clean white socks turned over, his strong short legs shown off in summer shorts.

Comrades, he said, not knowing why they called his daughter Dial. Comrades, he said, choosing not to see the new hair on their boy lips. But he too had had soft boy hair once, sixteen years old, baby fluff, a fighter in the mountains of Macedonia.

Fuck Stalin, he told the leaders of SDS. Fuck Churchill too. By 1945 the comrades had won Greece. They were betrayed first by the British and then the USSR.

You don't have no revolutionary situation, he said. This is America. God bless America, he said, and still they loved him, a workingman from Southie. He could say there was no revolutionary situation in America and they did not stone him.

They drank his ouzo, played knuckles, arm wrestled on the floor.

Papa flirted with Susan and Melinda and the leggy Smith girl who had VD. Two weeks later Mama was dying in St. Vincent's.

He had asked the Harvard comrades to visit his yard, admire his illegal sausage factory. Two days later he sent word not to come.

So they were saved, Susan Selkirk, Mark Dorum, Mike Waltzer, all those people who were later in the newspaper, saved from grappling with the dialectic which was his life.

By the end of 1966 his two sons had run off, one to be a drug dealer in New York City, the other to have sex with a widow in Gloucester, Massachusetts. He was left only with the scholar, and it was she who drove to Southie from Cambridge at night and on weekends and did what her brothers should have, boning the scrag ends, working the grinder, lining up the casings in their sticking dispenser. She could lift the big plastic vats of scrap meat from floor to bench. She could have arm wrestled those Harvard boys flat to the floor.

Who was going to tell them? Not cute Dial. Someone else would have to teach them—do not please be romantic about the working class, no matter what you think of the stigmata on poor Papa's small square hands. For the working people he risked his lovely boy skin in the mountains, but when some Irish fellows tried to renegotiate a price after he had delivered, it was George Xenos who took his wrecker's bar and beat their refrigerator so hard the cockroaches fell in showers from catastrophe.

This is how we renegotiate in Greece.

Get in the truck, he told his daughter. You drive.

She turned up the propane so it roared. On my father's knee I learned it, she thought, weeping, at my mother's breast.

She thought, If you are watching me from outer space, watch this, boys.

She took a fistful of nails and fed some into her mouth and

dropped the remainder in the crumpled paper bag. She picked up the hammer and a long whippy yellow length of paling and she rested this against the wall, on top of the piece she had previously pinned in place.

And then she nailed it in. Straight in. She could build a proper home for him. Are you watching, boys?

Two nails at every stud, one at the top and one at the bottom. And that was pretty much how she continued all that night, working until there was morning mist across the floor and even then she could not stop, not because it looked so fabulous but because she knew she would die of grief if she did not continue, because her eyes stung and her throat closed over and the pain came in huge sweeping waves, during which she could barely stand. She would have him, she would feed him, she would watch him grow. There were lives way worse than that. She knew them personally.

37

No one loved him. He removed his shorts and underpants and folded them carefully. Then he squatted above the pit and looked down across the dammed-up valley full of mist and white-veiled trees. He was gooseflesh, head to toe. The birds were pretty quiet, but he could hear a tap-tap echoing far below.

He did not know how he could ever get back to Kenoza Lake.

When he had wiped himself he poured an ice-cream tub of lime and a second scoop of sawdust into the pit and closed the heavy-hinged lid.

A magpie gargled as he turned to go. Trevor's alarm clock rang as the boy came back beneath the roof.

Trevor? He watched the open mouth and broken foreign teeth. Do you want to wake up?

Trevor showed a bloody crocodile eye, groaned, rolled and revealed his beaten back—black and purple like an old lady's dress. The clock engine unwound. Trevor began to snore.

He would make her buy him a plane ticket. That's what he was thinking when he squatted beside the bed of cauliflowers and drove his arm beneath the mulch. With his cheek pressed flat against the soil, his fingers found his buried blue banana bag.

The sun was striking the trees above the mist, waking up some birds who brought down a loud shower of bark or seeds on the tin roof. By the time he smelled the papaya salve, it was too late.

You cunning little bugger, said Trevor, and kicked at the mulch with his big toe and exposed his secret to the light. He had money in that bag and other stuff as well.

Trevor put his hands on his hips and pushed his nose toward him. What you got?

My dad, the boy said, surprising himself. He lay back on the mulch and drove his arm deep in the bag. He could feel the Uno cards, the poker pack, his ticket to Shea Stadium, a business card, a coin, three bills, a stone, and the folded page from *Life* magazine. He never showed this to anyone but he had to show it to Trevor now.

It's sort of beat up, he said.

Trevor studied the page of *Life*. He could not read. What's the matter with her? he said as he refolded it.

Does she hit you?

I know she's not my mother, the boy said, tears welling up. I know, OK!

You shouldn't eavesdrop, Trevor said.

You're not fair, the boy said. You shouldn't talk about me. You don't know me hardly. He snatched back his father's picture and pushed it down into his shorts, burning with the pleasure of destruction.

Here's a story for you, Trevor said. There was a boy like you had a teacup handle. It was like a little bone, a bit of chicken bone, a wishing bone, the leftovers of a saint put in a wooden box. Reliquary, he said.

The boy did not care for Trevor's stories anymore.

The boy with the teacup handle, said Trevor, told us his

older brother had the matching cup and this was how they would know each other, because the brother would produce the cup and they would join and be made whole.

The boy was hardly listening. He was thinking how to purchase a ticket by himself.

I knew this fellow real well, said Trevor. He went around saying that his brother was ten years older and he was driving from Brisbane to Adelaide with the cup. Are you listening?

Trevor wanted the boy to look at him, but the boy sat with his cheek against his knees staring off into the bush. I'm going to Harvard, he said at last. You can't imagine me. He was crying so hard he could hardly see. He tried to lie down on the dirt but the dirt just bit him back. He stumbled up the path, howling, and took the pallet and dragged it bumping along the path. In his mind he could see the teacup handle, the dried-out bones, the wooden box and the poor smelly orphan boy, dead of death most likely.

You come on home now, Dial said.

She was standing behind him, by the cabbages, an army coat around her shoulders, a hammer in her hand.

Against the current of his anger, the boy ran to her and pushed his face into her stomach and she wrapped the coat around him hard.

Carry me, he said. His face was wet and snotty and he buried himself in her smoke-dust hair as she carted him along the saddle where the oil drums stood, then down the jolting yellow hill. She crushed him so tight it nearly broke him. When he slipped down her body she hoisted him back up. He wrapped his legs around her waist but she did not finally give up his weight until her army coat dropped off her shoulders and fell to the dirt and lay there like a big old dog.

This was by the rusted Volvo, where the turkey lived. The boy had worse things than that to be afraid of now.

She kissed him on his dirty forehead and tried to look him in his eyes but he did not want her seeing what he thought. He grabbed the hammer from her hand and ran at the car, smashing its headlights. This took much longer than you might expect, but she did not try to stop him and when the lights were pretty much destroyed he bashed at the part of the car body that was wedged onto the road. It would not budge.

She watched him with her arms folded, her eyes sort of soft and vague.

He said, We can go get your wood. The wood you hit him with, he said, waiting to see what she would say. He picked up a pebble and threw it at the car. We could put the wood under the car and make it fall.

Sure, she said.

I hate the car, he pressed on. I hate that bird. I'm going to kill it.

To his surprise, she did not tell him he should not kill.

You wait, she said.

What did that mean?

You'll see.

He imagined this meant she was going to show him photographs although when he considered this later he saw she gave him no reason to think anything at all. Grandma Selkirk had many old photographs she kept in shoeboxes, brown and dusty yellow. When the wind was bitter off the lake they would go through the pictures together by the smoky fire. There was an uncle who was crazy about Packards. There was an aunt who lost all her money drinking wine in Paris. This was his true history, in the box. Trevor could have no idea.

What will I see, Dial?

You wait, she said. You'll see.

They set off down the washed-out hill, around the deep gutters made by storms and even deeper holes probably done by the orphan in a rage. There were crowbar marks like stab wounds in the clay.

You wait, she said, trying to make him laugh, but her hand was wet so he knew she was afraid and he was too. As they turned up the cutting into their driveway, the sun got swallowed by the clouds and there was a dull sad cast to everything. Shut your eyes, she said, they were only halfway up the track. His breath caught in his chest as she steered him by the shoulders along the thin clay path between the huts.

Now lift your foot, she said. One more step.

He smelled the sawdust before he opened his eyes and saw the fresh-milled wood nailed onto the walls, the yellow moisture barrier now a secret hidden like a letter in a book.

We'll make it very beautiful, she said, it's the only thing we can do. We'll make a lovely home. Those crooked nails are there to keep the boards flat while they dry. After that we'll cover the space between with other bits of wood.

Battens, he said. He could not live here.

Yes, they call them battens. Then we'll paint with linseed oil. Do you know what that smells like.

No.

Have you been in an artist's studio?

You are not my mother, are you?

They were standing facing each other in the middle of the hut, with the kitchen sort of behind them and the big open door in front, and there was sawdust everywhere around their feet. Dial squatted down, to be his height.

I knew you when you were just born, she said. I bathed you, she said. You were all slippery with soap. I was so scared I'd drop you.

Were you the babysitter, Dial?

She was crying but he did not care. You were only little, she said. You had an expensive knitted jacket your grandma gave you and I burned it with the iron.

The tears frightened him, the strange red twist they gave her face.

That's why you talk funny, he said.

He had meant to be mean, and she walked out on the deck and he heard her blow her nose.

She is my grandma, right.

Yes.

Grandpa is my grandpa.

Yes, of course.

So why did you steal me, he said and saw how he made her wince.

I did *not* steal you. I was taking you to see your mama.

He felt a huge angry power to hurt her, like he could do anything and not be stopped. You stole me, he said. You brought me where no one could find me.

She reached her hand for him, and although he would not let her touch him, he allowed himself to be persuaded to the cushions. She sat beside him. Her eyes were red and deep beside her great big nose. He thought the nose was ugly and he could hurt her any way he liked.

I didn't steal you, she said.

You lied!

He waited for her to reach out her arms and catch him, but she just hugged herself as if her stomach hurt. Her lips were cracked and parted and her brows pushed down.

My mommy's dead, he said.

He watched her shrivel.

Your mommy wanted to see you, but that was against the law.

You nearly got me run over by a car.

Your mommy did that, yes.

You nearly got me killed.

Your mother was underground. Do you know what that means?

SDS, he said. I know. You know I know.

She hesitated as if she was going to say that he was wrong.

Do you remember in Philly, the Greyhound station.

Why?

There were lots of sirens in the street.

No.

I came to take you to your mother but your mother died. I couldn't tell you. It was terrible.

His throat was burning. His mother died. How did she die. He dared not ask. You should have taken me back.

Honey, I would have gone to jail.

He shrugged. He could hardly see.

You don't care if I go to jail?

You shouldn't have stolen me. You should have taken me to my dad.

I did.

No you didn't, he shouted. You shouldn't lie.

Listen to me, you little idiot. Who do you think hosed you down when you pooped your pants. Who did that to you? That was your lovely daddy. I forgave him everything till then. Don't turn on me. My life is totally destroyed by this. I'm a teacher. I'm not meant to be here.

Then go away, he said.

You go away, she said. I'm sick of you.

You want me to go away?

Yes, she said. Go, go now.

And so he did. He headed down the path between the huts, his legs falling forward, just sort of spilling down the hill. He could not go to Trevor's anymore, so he ran the other way along the valley floor and he was still running when he came past the hall.

There were three cars there. The stupid mumbo jumbos were on the platform and they all came to stare at him as he headed down the road, bawling like a mad bad baby in the dust.

38

He listened for the sound of the Peugeot coming to get him back, the wheeze, the whir, the cough. He would have heard it above the pounding blood, the air tearing at his chest. When he arrived at the ford, he stopped and waited more. Had the mumbo jumbos called to him just then he would have gone to them. Their voices would have echoed along the creek like saws or hammers, but nothing came along the water except a brilliant breathless nameless bird—blue back, orange chest, flying about two inches above the ford. His grandma would have known it—she knew the names of every-thing, water strider, Atlas moth. She could show you a dead bee through a magnifying glass. His grandma loved him, stroked his head, was always there, still swimming across the lake, her heart just broke in pieces as Jed Schitcher said.

Past the ford, the road got steep and mean as murderers but he was not going back. Soon enough he was up on the plateau where dirt tracks ran off among the gray spiky grass between the big fire-blackened trees.

When he was hosed down on the lawn in Seattle, the water hit him hard as stones. She was not his mother. She just watched. Her face was way too big. The color of her skin was darker, her smell was dusty, like apricot beneath the jasmine.

He must have walked an hour, he figured, and still it seemed he got no farther. When he heard a car coming from the direction of the redneck town, he was pleased at first but then he climbed up the dry clay bank and squatted in the broken bush. One minute the road was empty, then it was full of brilliant blue—a new auto towing a trailer and a curling tail of pinkish dust.

When the car came around the bend, he lay down on the scratchy dirt, pebbles on his cheek and stomach. The car stopped and waited, hissing quietly to itself, just out of sight, below the cutting. Then it set off crawling, bumping onto a bandit track on the far side of the road. When the engine quit, the quiet was big and still as water on a lake so he clearly heard the magpies and the brown and black and yellow birds the size of wrens.

A door opened, then slammed shut. He could now see the driver—about the distance to first base, not a mumbo jumbo but a redneck with glasses thick as soda bottles and hair oiled flat on his tiny shrunk old head. His neck was thin and did not fill his collar and he poked his nose forward, sort of sniffing. Then he peed real loud, like a creature on a farm.

The rednecks in Sullivan County had plaid shirts and baseball caps with DIESEL something written on the front. This one was not like that. He walked around some. Then he was kneeling on the ground. The boy's hair pulled at his scalp. But then he heard the sound of a saw.

The man worked for about an hour. Once he sat and smoked a cigarette. Once he had a drink of something.

Once he said, Mary.

There were nasty small black ants crawling along the boy's arms. He would have killed them except there was no point. The sun went behind the clouds leaving everything dull dead green, burned black, tarnished silver. The boy stood very carefully and began to make his way through the low worn-out scrub, planning to get behind the ridge, then come back on the road a ways ahead.

Coo-ee! The cry burst out in the silence, a dreadful sound.

The man had his hands up to his glasses, pretending to have binoculars.

Hello young man, he called.

The boy walked quickly, covered with a prickly coat of fright.

You come down here, the man said.

He could hear the man coughing and clambering up the bank to get him. He ran then, until he got down behind the ridge. Trees with dinosaur feathers—wattles—he cut around to the left, trying to be quiet among all the crackling sticks. For a long time he could hear the breathing, but around the bottom of the ridge it got quiet and even the high ocean of gloomy trees was still.

He had been certain of where he was headed but the road was not in its expected place. If he had been born in Australia he would have known to retrace his steps before he died, but he was from New York and there was a long dry rocky gully ahead of him, and at the end of that was a view of cane fields and some high electric pylons.

He was positive he had seen those pylons and that sugar-cane before, and then it came to him what he must do.

39

Dial fell asleep, curled up in bed, alone with her hammer and her molting pillow and the mosquito net pulled like a veil across her bare carpenter's knees. The boy was miles away when she awoke. She had no clue, having slept until that hour of the afternoon when the hot sun fell directly on the corrugated iron, heating it until it pulled angrily against its hippie fastenings. Bang—the roof exploded. Who would have known that bloodless things could cry like this.

Her eyes opened to see Trevor Dobbs standing silently beside the bed. She thought—He has come to tell me the boy is going to live with him. She watched his smile, thinking he had no idea how cruel he was, or what he had destroyed. He seemed dry and cool in all this unrelenting heat, an English apple, mottled but healthy.

A fly had found its way inside the net. When it crawled along her neck, she killed it.

She thought, He has come to collect the boy's clothes.

They want to talk to you, he said.

FBI, she thought. She had been waiting for this.

Trevor pulled aside the mosquito net and she let him take her hand as if she were an invalid. Her mouth was dry as chalk.

They're your neighbors, he said. You've got to talk to them. They can invalidate your sale. He said *in-vwelidate*, softly.

This caused some considerable confusion as Dial began questioning the legal reach of the FBI.

Your *neighbors*. Jeez. Who did you think?

So she agreed to meet with the neighbors, but like a prisoner with her hands clasped behind her back, following the weirdly graceful feral in falling white pajama pants. They went through the long grass, across the road, down to the shaded creek and then beside the shallow runs where Trevor jumped lightly from rock to rock ahead of her. Children had made dams, lines of rocks, memorials that caused her to catch her breath.

The stream was just thirty yards from her hut but she had never walked here before. She never showed this to the boy before she lost him to Trevor Dobbs. There were corners of the mossy damp that made her sad. Of course it was her papa. He would have loved this, a damp, green dappled part. He was from Samos, an island with a green half and a dry half. Peaches on one side, priests on the other. In New England he had found a mossy-smelling home, running through leafy tunnels with his beagles and his gun. They had hunted cottontails together.

Remus Creek was a paradise with ferns of all varieties, palms, creepers with the skin of baby elephants, its water shallow but perfectly clear so that the small pebbles shone red and yellow in among the rippling gray. Poor Papa.

They arrived at a stand of flooded gums, tall thin eucalypts with shiny white-green bark and there in front of them were the foundations for the rotting buckled floor and when she followed Trevor up the wide wooden steps she thought of platforms in the jungle, Aztec, Mayan, sites of sacrifice.

The mumbo jumbos were waiting for her in a semicircle and Trevor went to sit at one end next to Rebecca leaving Dial alone, squinting into the sun.

Rebecca said, We have a rule, and in those four words Dial felt the bilious bitter taste of her dislike.

Dial did not answer but she saw that not even pretty Roger would catch her eye. The girl with the starving chest was playing with her toes.

Rebecca said, You know what I'm talking about, Dial. She looked sideways at Trevor as she spoke. Again Dial thought, She's sleeping with him.

Yes, said Dial, you said you had a rule.

About cats.

Yes, you said that before.

Yes, and you said there was a lawyer who told you not to worry, but he was wrong, Dial. He admits he was wrong, said Rebecca. She held out a letter.

Dial nodded at the letter but went no closer to accepting it. She was thinking, I cannot take this shit. I will not. She was also thinking about the boy who had chosen to live up the hill with Trevor. His clothes would be removed as if he'd died, nothing left behind, not even a plastic toy to break her heart. She thought, I do have to take this. Then she thought, not for the first or last time either—This is where I've ended up.

So what do you want me to do? She tried to smile.

Get rid of the cat.

I take it none of you want him?

Ha-ha, said Rebecca.

No one else spoke, but Rebecca stood and walked off the platform with her great fat ass wobbling inside her cotton pants. In a moment a car door slammed and when Rebecca returned Dial could hear Buck. He arrived up on the platform, a prisoner in a metal cage.

Rebecca held out the cage and Dial took it.

Buck was meowing piteously.

I know you think this is cruel, Rebecca said, but considering he's a murderer . . .

Dial was reading the metal manufacturer's label on the heavy cage. FERAL-TRAPPA. She set it down and opened up the wire door and inside she saw Buck's pink complaining mouth. He stood and sat. His front paw was caught, a sort of mousetrap for a cat.

Feral, she said.

It means wild, said Rebecca. The feral cat is declared as a class two species under the Land Protection Act.

You've crushed his fucking leg. He's not feral. He's my son's cat.

He's not your son, said Rebecca.

Dial looked to Trevor who looked away. She set down the cage and gently lifted the sprung arm of the trap and brought Buck into the light. He cried, and raked his claw down her arm.

You've crushed him. You know this won't mend.

It is a her, said Rebecca.

Dial stood on the platform under the harsh violet sky. The time-warp idiots, she thought. Why don't you fight for something real?

You can't look after that cat, said Rebecca. You can't even look after the kid.

Dial could look after Buck. That was all she knew to do. If you shot a cottontail you often found him wounded, struggling. You picked him up quickly, stilled your heart, stretched his neck. And it was done.

She stood before them. She did it swiftly. In a few seconds Buck was a warm pelt in her bleeding arms.

Go watch Walt Disney, she said to Rebecca.

She turned and walked down off the Aztec platform and passed between the flooded gums, along the shadowed creek with its stones and dams. She was crying then, not loudly. She found a shovel in the garden and carried Buck down into the rain forest and there, before the abandoned hut with the stone gargoyle, she dug down into the soil, chopping through the fresh white wounded roots, laying him in the crumbling black soil and covering him.

She had no prayers, comrade. Dear Papa, that was all.

40

When the boy was four years old, and before that probably as well, Grandma Selkirk would take him to the Guggenheim Museum and order him to run down the spiral ramp which— she said so—was what was intended by the architect, Frank Lord Right. That had been the boy's misunderstanding. Grandma used the name herself whenever possible. How perfect, she said. Frank Lord Right was not building Calvary, she said, did not mean us to trudge upward to our crucifixion. Push UP on the elevator button, his grandma said, then run like the wind.

Three times he got in trouble with the guards apparently— he had no memory of this but he sure recalled Grandma's argu- ment with the tiny black guard after she cupped her hands on the Brancusi head. The guard said, Get back, then Grandma called for someone higher up and in the end she was the only person in New York allowed to touch the head.

It is art, she told the guard, who hated her for being bohemian, she said so.

Afterward she said, That guard could not have imagined that Brancusi was my friend. History would prove this not quite true, but never mind. She touched the boy's own head the same as she touched the Brancusi, fitting her palm around it. She loved him. He felt it there, an almost exact notion of how precious he was to her. She was a smeller too, always sniffing the salt and death in seaweed, the waters of the lake, the crush of dried lavender. Her nose was small and straight. It was her best "instrument," she said so. He would lie with her on the sofa in the big room at Kenoza Lake and she would go to sleep and the boy would sit with his hands on his knees and will her to continue breathing, the perfume of martini in the summer night, forever and ever, world without end.

The boy knew the names of smells, but it was his "visual intelligence" that was thought to be his "gift." This was unmasked one winter Saturday when the Guggenheim had *activities*. The boy could not escape *activities*, and was forced to obey a leaflet containing a tiny section of a Jackson Pollock painting. Grandma said he had to match the little bit of picture with one of the three whole Pollocks on the museum walls.

When he found it pretty easy she looked at him so fiercely he knew he had done something good. You have the Selkirk eye, she said.

During the week she brought back her powdery friends from the English-Speaking Union, to see if they could do the same. They could not match her grandson. Four years old.

None of this had ever helped him in any way that he could understand.

When he saw the power lines and the cane fields and he made his way down the dry gully he had no idea that the Australian bush was crusted, creased, folded on itself, long gray ridges and bright streaky torn bits where the earth had tried to pull itself in half, or that he was like an ant making his way across a Jackson Pollock without a map. He did not know the story of the lost child or the drover's wife and he came down the gully, jumping from broken rock to broken rock, and when he lost sight of the road ahead, he had lots of worries, mostly how he would get back to Kenoza Lake, but it did not enter his head that he might perish here.

He got a thorn in his hand and this broke off inside the flesh and he suffered a scratch on his cheek, but when he entered the lifeless pine forest at the bottom of the gully he walked without hesitation through the creepy quiet toward the dry white road.

Coming out into the sunlight, he understood that he could turn left to reach Yandina, but he turned right and so headed deeper into the bush, trudging along the lonely road which he remembered from the day after the storm. What had been slick and slimy had set hard and the ridge and rut of truck tires were now becoming clouds of dust, like dead souls rising in small whirls and skirmishes.

A little along, set back into the plantation and guarded by a chicken-wire fence, was a small house with a flower garden in the front. It was painted emerald green and the roof was a rusty red. At the beat-up front gate was a fat old woman with a floral apron and dusty-looking stockings on her creased-up legs. Her face was round and kind.

The woman said hello and asked him would he like a glass of water on account of all the dust. They had such a weird way of talking here, like Hobbits maybe.

He said he'd rather have a glass of milk.

Would you like a bicky too?

The boy didn't know a bicky was a cookie so he said no.

He waited at the gate, watching bees crawling around inside the black part of the poppies and when the woman returned he drank the milk.

He thanked her, and said he had to go.

She watched him depart, not saying anything, and after he had walked a bit he began to think she could tell someone which way he went. He was up to no good, as his grandma would have said. So he walked back to the gate where the old woman was standing, still holding his empty glass.

Excuse me, he said, is the town this way?

You were going the wrong way, she said. I knewed it.

He said, Thank you, miss. He walked toward the town until she could not see him anymore and then he cut into the pine forest and walked back along the creepy quiet carpet floor coming around behind her house and only returning to the road when he was beyond her view. He was on his own.

He came down out of the pines at the place where the road split in two. He knew the steep scary track was called Bog Onion. At the bottom was the place with the blue plastic bag.

Leave it to Beaver, he said.

The burned-out cars and the broken-up log fires made it clear which way he had to go and he entered the bush at the exact same place where Trevor had cut his way through with a machete. The slash wounds had gone gray and dead looking, but some were now releasing baby leaves and small pink thorns as soft as the rasp of a cat's tongue.

He pushed his way through the tangle and then into the feathery knee-high sea of fishbone ferns. He headed along the side of the saddle until he found the rough red bank of dirt, the fallen tree with pebble-crusted roots. He took off his T-shirt so he would be able to feel a bull ant's legs upon his back and he kept his eyes down as he walked along the fallen trunk. He jumped as he had jumped before.

He walked into the soak and felt the mud ooze around his feet and he bent and made a little hole with his hands and drank the water which tasted of bark and blackberry and lantana leaf and dirt. He knew what was behind him, in the hollow of the fallen tree which jutted like a cannon from the bank—you could see a tiny, tiny bit of blue, pushed deep inside. He climbed up on the trunk and pushed his head into the dark hole in the sweet yellow rotting wood. He got his fist around the slippery bag and pulled until it popped out, lumpy and much heavier than he had thought. It landed on the soil and lost its breath.

He waited with his hands folded in front of him, his ear

cocked, trying to hear what was hidden by the sighing trees. Then he dragged the bag off a ways into the woods, as if it was something he would eat in private. When he had untied the neck he reached his arm inside and took out whatever his fist closed around. These wads he placed inside his underpants. He did not rush but neither did he count, and he packed the slippery cutting bills against his waist and bottom and tried to arrange them where they would not hurt his penis no matter how far he had to walk.

He had not been there for more than four minutes before he was stuffing the blue bag back inside the tree. As he came out in the clearing by the cars, the crows were crying to one another in the spreading shade, and the kookaburras were flying from tree to tree, marking out the boundaries of their world. He walked beneath their notice.

41

Dial finished burying Buck. She squished up her face and bashed the dirt hard down on top of him. Parrots flittered in the last wash of light, the size of circus fleas up on the tattered ridge. The boy was up there with Trevor, lost to her, that is what she imagined.

Down in the valley the mosquitoes were already rising. They could smell her body gases a hundred feet away.

Which gases, Dial?

Lactic acid. Carbon dioxide.

Except there was no one there to ask her. No one who gave a damn about what she thought.

Her papa was dead. The boy was gone. She had buried Buck. She walked across the rotting-leaf floor of rain forest, finding the shower in the deepening shadow beneath the bedroom hut. She thought, I purchased a slum but at least I have hot water I can waste.

The shower water was like an easy promise, running down the long trunk of her lonely white body, cooling in a puddle around her ugly feet. That is what she thought. Once she had been beloved. She had met the boy's father in safe houses in four different cities. She had bathed in rose oil. She had been delivered to him like a princess to her groom, trusted servants in Volkswagens, back stairs to a warehouse tower. He kissed her calves, the arches of her feet. Even when she contracted a disease from him, she allowed that he was a man, a soldier in a war, the king.

She had been a goddess, six feet tall, a fool. Who could imagine her made so small and worthless, heartsick for a little boy.

Not till she turned off the shower did she notice anything but her own spaghetti boil of pain. The first cat's cry was drowned. But the second time she heard it clearly and it thumped her heart, a great electric whack that left goose bumps across her scalp.

She stood naked in the pooled-up soapy water. Something rustled. The water dripped. She hadn't even lit the lantern in the big hut but when she heard Buck again she ran down into the forest. There was only just sufficient light to see the grave was as she had left it. It was too shallow, she knew it. If it was Massachusetts there would be raccoons or dogs to dig him up and drag him through the night. What was there here? No bears, that's all she knew. Mosquitoes jabbed their hollow noses through her skin. She dragged the blocky gray carving from in front of the abandoned hut and laid it on top of the loose black dirt.

Lady Macbeth. Exactly.

She ran up to the hut, muddy feet, dead leaves sticking, but no more thought of cleaning up than if she was six years old and scared. Buck cried again. She whimpered. She found the Redhead matches and the propane roared white illuminating her naked skin in all its fright and weakness. There was a pair of overalls by the shower but she was too creeped out to go back down there, to feel banana fronds brushing against her shoulder.

She pulled on Adam's prickly army coat. Not his war, not hers either. She turned the light down and she sat out on the shadow of the front deck where she could keep watch to see whatever blurry black things the night would bring toward her.

She had killed the cat, taken his life to make a point, win an argument. It was Wash your hands, put on your nightgown; look not so pale. She listened to the ghost until it stopped which was pretty quickly, but still she had no chance of sleep.

She climbed up into the loft bed and settled in the nest of quilts and shawls. It smelled of boy. She could not sleep for thinking of him, but it was not until just before dawn, when she heard that cat meow again, that it occurred to her that there must be other cats and she had murdered her sleek lovely mischievous Buck in vain.

She tossed and turned until she heard the car descending Trevor's hill.

Scratchy eyed and heavy headed, she clambered down the ladder and ran to fetch her dew-damp overalls and then, hearing the thump and slam of the car as it bottomed on the track, she sprinted down the hill toward the road, straight through the uncut feathery grass. She heard the bang as its engine slammed the yellow rock, and then she leaped off the cutting and she was in its deadly path.

No headlights.

She cast her hands high in the air and watched the car slide toward her, the front wheels barely missing her, the steaming nose pushed in among the blackberries.

It was Rebecca who was driving, Trevor she saw first, but she did not care about either of them. She wrenched open the back door.

Where is he?

There was nothing there but an unreal shining darkness, black plastic bags. She touched them, immediately imagined they were taking hedge clippings to the dump.

Where is he?

Slap her, said Rebecca. She's a fucking spy.

Where is he?

Where is who?

Where is my son, she bellowed, and her voice echoed along the valley floor, across the shallow rills.

Shut up, said Trevor. He took her shoulders. Be quiet.

They were both looking at her weirdly.

Where is he? she demanded.

He's with you, said Trevor.

He's with you.

She began to howl then properly. It was beyond her, beyond any preparation or understanding.

She's fucked this, said Rebecca, and went back into the car. She turned on the headlights and began to cautiously back up and turn around.

Don't go anywhere, Trevor said to Dial. He had his two meaty hands around her upper arms. Stay here.

He got back into the car and he slammed the door so hard it hurt, and Rebecca, with her big tits and hairy legs, took Trevor back up the hill leaving Dial no comfort but the white clay dust which rose from the road and settled like wiggy talcum in her hair. The cat called. The empty day began.

42

The boy had seen two of Trevor's secrets but he knew Trevor had boxes inside boxes inside boxes. Trevor did not trust banks but he had accounts, in Sydney, Lismore, Tweed Heads. His right hand could not find his left hand. His lungs did not know his heart. There were all sorts of secret stashes—Canadian money in railway lockers, out-of-date Australian pounds, a pack of gelignite strapped inside a concrete pipe buried in his road. The explosive had hung there for two wet seasons so the electrical tape was curling and the pack was dangling, but there were still wires leading up the red clay cutting, lying doggo in the bush like two death adders beneath the fallen leaves. Trevor had a plunger hidden in the rafters of the compound. He was a secret man but so pleased by his secret he had to tell the boy.

Trevor was audiovisual, he said so. He had the Book of Revelation on cassette. He could not read or write but he could imagine the end of the world better than a university professor, also the destruction of Noosa Heads by cyclone, also a police four-wheel drive thrown six feet into the air by gelignite. He would puff out his cheeks and blow his hands apart. He gave the boy bad dreams—fire, sharp black weapons, tree trunks burning like fuse cord in the night.

Rebecca was Trevor's girlfriend, sometimes.

Was Rebecca also afraid of Trevor? Maybe, the boy thought, must have been, for sure. Who would want to know what Rebecca knew, i.e., the trails, huts, shacks, the individual marijuana plants hidden like buried bodies in the bush. Rebecca and Trevor walked the unmarked bush together, Trevor said so, backpack straps cutting into their naked shoulders. The boy had seen them load up with stinky fertilizer, blood and bone. He knew Trevor was an orphan, invisible to infrared. Not even the spies in outer space could see his true occupation.

Rebecca's house was at the bottom of the hill, across from the concrete drain and the explosive charge. Trevor had built her a bed. He had put guttering on her roof.

She lay in wait, near the bottom of their driveway, hating Buck, hating Che, hating Dial for being American.

43

Trevor, in a breathless fury, found Dial, lying like roadkill beside her drive.

Get up, he said, all arrows and orders, pointing at her car.

Drive, he said. Not there, he said. There, he said.

The roads laced through the bush.

The day would soon be hot and sultry but for now the light was cold and sad. Dial stayed behind the wheel while Trevor called up to the hippies in their homes. The best of these were like cocoons made from glued-together sticks, the worst of them like Buckminster Fuller, fired from Harvard, far away.

The Peugeot engine was running rough, pumping out white poison. The hippies descended from their perches, sleepy birds with trailing blankets, egrets in the exhaust smoke mist. She thought, Some of them are graduates. They peered at her. Yesterday she had killed the cat. Now she had lost her son.

She drove Trevor some more.

The starved-chest girl emerged from an ugly A-frame, came right up to the car and tapped on the glass. Dial slowly rolled the window down. When the girl hugged Dial she was all bones, warm from sleep, perfumed with patchouli and poverty.

A chain saw started with a raw hard cough. The two women waited while the saw did its work. Soon they saw five men walk out of the bush, each one carrying a fresh cut pole. They walked in single file down the track, not looking at the car.

She asked the girl what they were doing.

They're going to check out the creek.

In her confusion Dial wondered were they fishing. The starved-chest girl lay her raw-knuckled hand on Dial's arm.

They're going to find your little boy, she said.

What are the poles for?

Dial saw the transparent freckled terror—dumb fear that the girl would be forced to name the dreadful thing that would be done with the poles.

They'll go to the swimming hole too, she said.

Oh. She wanted to throw herself back on the ground, lie in the dust until she was squashed or killed. The men were calling out.

What are they calling?

Coo-ee.

No, his name is Che.

Yes, the girl said, we know his name.

Dial recognized this dreadful sympathy. She gazed distractedly at the signs of hippie industry, beehives, potted rain forest plants beneath shade cloth. When Trevor came back to the car she expected they would go to the swimming hole but instead he told her to wind down her windows and drive very slowly along the road. She could hear the tiny grains of gravel sticking in the tires, a soft rolling noise, and the echoing foreign cry, as sharp as knives: Coo-ee.

At the ford she stopped, looking with dread at the wash of water which flowed around the tires and washed toward the swimming hole.

Up the hill, said Trevor. He was leaning out the window, staring into the bush. For fuck's sake, aren't you looking on your side?

She did now, as she drove on up the steep hill, and then again as they bounced along the logging tracks. Trevor, his head out the window, cried Coo-ee. There was so much bush, beyond acres, beyond hope or forgiveness.

They arrived at a high spot above the creek, almost the end of the track, when Trevor said, Stop. Turn off the engine.

He called, Coo-ee.

A call came back to them.

Of course it was not Che. It was nothing like a boy, but she still insisted that he reply.

Trevor left the car without so much as looking at her. He ran across the flat barefoot, jumping fallen timber, Coo-ee.

Coo-ee, there was an answer.

It's not him, Dial thought, but she left the car. They were parked on a kind of bluff above the creek. On another day she would have found it beautiful, but today it was a horror and when they came upon a man with a blue car and trailer she was angry that they had wasted time.

Let's go, she said.

Trevor lay his hand on her arm and spoke to the man who had glasses thick as soda bottles and hair oiled flat on his little shrunken head. Trevor stroked her shoulder, so gently she could have cried. The man's neck was thin and did not fill his collar and he poked his nose forward, sniffing. Dial's arm, in the palm of Trevor's warm hand, was chicken skin.

The old man was a retired schoolteacher who had been cutting loads of firewood to sell in town. He had seen Che. Oh yes, indeed, he said. He saw him very well. Little fellow, a good set to his shoulders.

Dial tried not to be frightened by his hands, about one inch wide at the knuckles.

Don't you worry, Mum, he said. She let him take possession of her hand, it was like being inside a big warm bag, or being in touch with God or aliens.

He'll be back, he said.

He had been dead. Now he was alive. No one was going to prod his bloated white sausage body with a pole. She ran back to the Peugeot so quickly that by the time Trevor arrived she had turned the car around.

Trevor took his seat, but left the door open, one bare foot resting on clay.

Let's go, she said.

He looked at her wearily, his eyes squinted. What's the plan?

Furious, she drove down the track and he had no choice but to close his door.

So what's the plan?

There was no damn plan except she could not go into the valley and be stared at. She was beyond the pale. She killed her cat. She killed her boy. When she came back on the road she swung left toward Yandina, looking out the window at the wiry scratching undergrowth, and when they came to the Cooloolabin fork she swung away from town. She could not bear to be looked at. She drove past the house where the boy had drunk the milk. She did not know she had come down this road, so short a time before, hundred-dollar bills sewn inside her hem.

Turn here, he said. She did not recognize Bog Onion, but she obeyed, her stomach churning at the steepness of the track, the precipitous drop along its edge.

Suddenly Trevor was like a dog with its ears pricked.

What is it?

He leaned forward, resting his forehead against the dusty sun visor, peering ahead and to each side.

Stop, he called.

She slammed on the brake and the Peugeot locked and sledded. Oh God, she said. What is it?

But Trevor was already out and stumbling, running up the hill. She pulled on the hand brake, but it would not hold. In the spit-smeared mirror she saw Trevor pick up something—

candy wrapper, that's what she thought. He jumped back in the moving car and handed it to her.

Ben Franklin. One hundred dollars U.S.

His eyes were slitted.

Drive, he said.

Brake light all the way.

44

Dial pulled up beside a burned-out shell of a Volkswagen, bullet holes along its door, a ruin consistent with her stomach, knotted in a tangle of dread. She watched in the mirror as Trevor got out and circled behind her back. Would he be her benefactor or her assassin?

Arriving at her open window, he turned off the engine and snatched the keys.

Oh please, she said. I wasn't going to run away. But why did she even say that? What was she thinking—that she had crossed the Mafia? And was it like that? She tried to read his eyes but he held the door open, a match between his teeth.

I should stay here, she said, in case.

He escorted her to the path, the one he had forbidden her the first time. His hand on her arm was not rough, or brutal, but really rather soft, as if he thought kindly of her and might protect her, but she thought of how gently cats hold prey inside their mouths.

Was his anger just about his one hundred dollars? She followed him like a lamb, through the scratchy lantana, the whispering ferns, boneless, without the will to run. He was a pissed-off criminal, clambering out along the horizontal trunk of fallen tree and then doubling back inside like a possum, a ferret, an animal unexpectedly supple and sleek, its muscles and tendons showing through the skin. He dragged out the blue banana bag, showing her his teeth before letting it fall, like trash into a compactor chute, rushed and violent, raising dust. He tore out a paint-splattered plastic sheet and a fistful of sandwich Baggies each big enough to hold two ounces. He shoved the Baggies in his shoplifter's pockets and lay the sheet in the blue shadow of the fallen tree. The wind was gusty from the west. The plastic rose and fell until he subdued it with rocks and logs.

He held her gaze a moment. She did not know how to look at him. His pupils were keyholes. The wind blew and schools of eucalypt leaves turned like silver knives above her head.

Kneeling before his bag, he removed a fistful of currency and tucked it beneath the plastic sheet. She thought this was a good sign—but how could she know what to hope or fear in the awful nothing of this day.

As he defended his stash from the thieving wind, he was shiny and fast, really lovely in his wild and muscled way. He gave a final wad to Dial and pointed at the bone, a cow bone big enough to brain him with.

Put Australian money under that.

Cool, she said, her heart racing.

American, he pointed to two broken yellow rocks. U.S. dollars under there.

She sat cross-legged on the plastic, her skin sweating like processed cheese. He held up a single crumpled hundred-dollar bill, the one he found up the road. There was a violent gust of wind and the plastic rose and brown leaves tumbled past their knees. Something fell or thudded somewhere.

What?

Ssh.

He held his finger to his lips and turned back toward the track.

She stood too.

Stay, he hissed.

He clambered up the muddy bank, so fast that clumps of dirt sprayed on the sheet. She waited, aware mostly of the sky, its storybook blue, its invisible violent life.

He returned quickly.

Was it him?

She watched him pack the rest of the money.

That's yours, he said, OK.

His eyes held hers so tightly that it took a while to see that he was holding two Baggies filled with money. If you needed it, he said, you could come here yourself. His voice was very level. You wouldn't need to send a child.

She was slow to understand him.

It's yours, he insisted. I'm keeping it for you. This is too far for him to come without a grown-up.

You really think I would do that to him?

He shrugged.

She had to stand so he could take the plastic sheet. When he climbed back up the bank to hide the bag she waited.

He said, You going to wash?

I wouldn't do that to him, she said. What sort of monster do you think I am? You want to make this all my fault?

He walked off ahead of her drying his hands on what passed for his backside. She stood by the Peugeot while he searched inside both the burned-out wrecks and under one of them. She could not stand the accusation.

But then he exclaimed and her heart was suddenly in her mouth and she was right beside him, willingly his ally, squatting on the gravel when he emerged from beneath the Volkswagen, all that dull ashy anger washed from his eyes.

In his hand was a second hundred-dollar bill, and a green avocado.

He pushed the avocado at her—it had been gnawed, was still quite fresh, a pale creamy green. He showed his own teeth.

Get in the car, he said.

She obeyed, starting up the engine when he gave the silent signal.

She put the car in gear and heard the cry, the thump against her seat, and she turned to see Trevor dragging up a squirming boy-life from the backseat. It was a puppy-boy held by the neck, slimy, muddy, white, its arms wide, spreading its fingers, and all its boy face swelled up with grief or bites, left eye closed, mouth open.

The car shuddered and jerked. Dial jumped out while it was rolling, ran around the lethal front, opened the back door, tugged the stowaway, violently, as if pulling a rabbit from a hole, held the shivering bawling thing against her breast.

When Trevor charged at them she had nothing to protect herself against the tumult of his fatty orphan's heart, the saline, mucous, the awful sac of grief so big it burst itself wide open.

So they gathered, three of them, joined messily—it was not like anything Dial had envisaged in her life.

45

Dial drove back up Bog Onion, stalling twice. Obviously, the boy thought, she never drove to Montana with anyone. She never had a gun, a wound, a son. Weren't you cold last night? she called to him.

I'm cool, he said, and listened as she tried to make a joke of cool and cold. He did not laugh.

From the plateau they traveled through the pine forest and he did not tell them that he had been inside that old lady's house in the middle of the night. That house. Right there. Dial was peering at him in the rearview mirror but the boy held his secret hard against him. In the pitch dark he had crept in the back door. He could, therefore he did. He expected to get nice and warm but once inside he was so creeped out he could not even move his toe. He stood in the blue-black shiny kitchen and listened to the old lady snoring. Was that what he came for? If so it was a big mistake, for when she stopped, he thought she had died. He knew that feeling from Kenoza Lake, waiting for the breath to start. Let her not die now. He often thought what would he do with Grandma when he found her dead. He was frightened of it, how she would look. The old Australian lady coughed. He imagined her big eyes staring and all her gray hair spread out around her pillow. She moved something, perhaps a tumbler. He grabbed the avocado from the countertop thinking it was something else. There was no time for blankets. He got ahold of the rug on the kitchen floor and rushed out the back. A chair fell. The rug got caught. The door slammed. The yard lights turned on and he almost left the rug behind. Finally he dragged it into the woods like the body of a stinky bear. Then he was inside the belly of the night staring out its burning throat. He was doggo. No one could see or hear him. Soon enough a car arrived. It had no flashing light but a loud radio. He retreated from the flashlight stabbing at the pines. Maybe they would hit him like the priests hit Trevor, with a cane or strap. He dragged the heavy rug down into the dark and out of the pines and into the bush and when he was sick of falling over and cutting his head and arms he rolled himself up in the rug and finally he slept.

The carpet smelled of rancid fat. He should have gotten arrested, but he did not want to go to jail for stealing money.

He made green vomit.

When there was enough light to see, he rolled up the rug and stuffed it in the drainpipe beneath Bog Onion. His stomach tasted of lead sinker, and he knew he had to put the money back for now. The avocado would not be eaten. He returned the money to the blue bag and crawled under the burned-out Volkswagen and stayed there, mostly sleeping. He woke when he heard the Peugeot coming down the hill.

He was captured, but no one knew what he had done. Trevor took the front seat without asking and the boy lay along the length of the broken backseat with his nose pressed against the hot leather and the car shook above the corrugations of the long straight road to town. They turned back on the hairpin toward the valley and, for a moment, the sun flowed across his legs and neck. The snaking braking road soon blocked the light and he breathed the cracked Peugeot leather which had once been a creature with babies of its own. He was pitched and rolled, until they skidded down the steep road onto the splashing ford where he had, only a day ago, seen a blue-and-orange kingfisher swoop like an angel across his path.

Now the Australian trees closed over him like monkey fingers and the light turned green and the road was smooth and sandy so the tires swooshed. Not even God could see him here, curled up like a lost caterpillar, filled with green stuff to be squashed.

There was a bang against the roof. A second one against the window.

Shit, said Dial.

As the car skidded he stung with fright and he itched as if his skin was pierced by prickly seeds with feather tails. The windows were filled with bodies, crushed velvet, beards and bosoms.

She had made the neighbors hate Americans. Now they were all pushing in around the Peugeot. As he sat up he could see there were maybe ten cars, twenty, some VWs with paintings on them, other junky old station wagons and behind them was the buckled so-called hall and on its platform there were mumbos sitting.

Closer there were slitty-mouthed hippies holding skinned and bleeding lengths of tree. They swarmed the car like bees, erupting like bull ants from a nest. In the Bible they would have stoned him. He thrust his hand into his pocket and folded up the hundred-dollar bill.

Rebecca dragged Dial from the car.

When his own door opened he scampered to the other side where the starving-chested woman pulled him out and before he could say anything she crushed his face against her smelly ribs.

He saw Trevor talking to a man with a pole. There was so

much noise and rush and all the kids—some he had seen once, some he hadn't—were grabbing at him with their warty hippie hands. A snotty little pudding-headed girl was Velcroed to his leg. She could not be bucked away.

He looked for Dial but Rebecca had her arms around Dial's neck and Trevor was walking away into the lantana and the boy was being taken away by the kid named Rufus and the kid named Sam. They had made a stretcher—a brown coat with two poles—and Rufus and Sam said, Get on it.

Why?

Come on, Che, they said.

He thought, You don't know my name.

Che, Che, get on.

They were bigger but he could have fought them. His stomach was filled with old balloon air as he was lifted off the giddy bilious earth and four kids took the shafts including the pudding-headed girl who was maybe four years old and they ran lopsided and stumbled along the road. As they swung into the bush the boy saw Trevor, just ahead. His shoulders were sort of round. He was by himself, beginning his lonely climb up to his fort.

The hippie kids dropped him and he hurt his arm and he burped and vomited inside his mouth.

What would you like first? Bath or eat?

He sat on the coat on the ground. He spat. He rubbed at his arm and they all argued with one another and then they were suddenly off again, directly through the slapping sting-ing bush.

Hey, hey, Che, Che.

Rufus was fourteen maybe. Keep your head down, Che, he said.

They jolted him along too fast and when they dropped him a third time they told the pudding-headed girl she should let go and then Rufus took the front and everything was steadier and the Puddinghead tried to hold his hand while she ran alongside. Soon she ran into a tree and began to cry and then he was put on the ground a fourth time and Rufus asked him would he mind walking. Not one bit.

Rufus had long bright red hair. He put his arm around the boy's shoulder and the kid named Sam dragged the stretcher through the tangling scrub and the pudding-headed girl took the boy's hand and that is how they all arrived at a clearing in which stood a long low hut made from logs and tin and sheets of glass on which was printed TELECOM, over and over.

Inside he found a gloomy kind of candle factory with long narrow benches all around the walls and it was on one of these they sat him and cleared away some candles to make space for a glass of milk.

The Puddinghead asked if he liked it. She had snot on her upper lip but her face was round and pretty and her hair was almost white. In a shaft of sunlight he could see soft down on her brown scratched arms.

It's good, thank you, he said. In fact it tasted hairy.

Say something else, she said.

OK.

Something American.

George Washington, he said. He was pretty sure he would have to vomit.

It's from a goat, said the boy named Sam. That's why you don't like it.

What?

The milk. I don't like it either. This Sam had a thin face and beaky nose like a bush animal, a possum, with big dark eyes and very crooked teeth.

Tastes of bum, he said. His voice was all tight and curled up like wood shavings. It came out of his nose and mouth all at once.

Say something else, demanded Sam. His way of speaking made everything into a puzzle you had to peel and flatten out. Say something else American, he demanded.

Can I have a glass of water?

They had been pressed tight around him and now they all sprang away. The Puddinghead came back with water.

I'm Sara.

He nodded, suddenly very pleased.

The boys brought bread and butter and a bowl of honey. Rufus cut a slice of bread with a knife maybe two feet long.

The boy asked, Is that a dagger?

It's a machete.

Yes, but is it a dagger?

No one knew what he meant. Rufus silently cut a thick slice of bread and covered it with butter and honey.

The boy was not exactly happy, but much better than he had been in a while.

We thought you was dead, mate, said Sam. We reckoned you was a goner.

The boy did not understand.

Rufus asked, Did you sleep in the bush?

Yes.

Was it scary?

No, said the boy. I'm used to it.

You must be tough, said Rufus at last.

The boy said, My dad is pretty tough.

Then he asked for another slice of bread and honey and as he ate it he began to look around, trying to locate where he was and what he really felt. He was eating great bread and thick honey but he was thinking about Trevor, his snotty nose, his rounded shoulders, his heavy trudging walk as he set off up his road alone.

46

When the boy was a man he would be known as someone who took large and reckless actions, and he would often think that he had first been like this at Rebus Creek Road where he had first gone beyond what he was brave enough to do and changed himself because of it.

Coming back to Dial's hut he found it changed as well—made beautiful with flotsam, jetsam, linseed oil. There was a twelve-foot wooden ladder, painted yellow and secured by butcher hooks above the sink. It hung parallel to the floor. Above the sink it held pots and pans, but the ladder went much farther along the golden wall and above the cushions it held no more than a single mustard scarf.

The boy could not know that this was the echo of a room at Vassar, a lost life with a Tabriz rug.

She was nice to him, but careful now, and sometimes playing cards he felt a cloud of sadness settle on them both, like bugs around a lamp. She didn't love him the same as before, that's what it felt like, as if he had stretched or broken something without meaning to. He was sorry for all the mean things he said. He wanted her to lay her hand on his shoulder, not that she didn't, but less often, or not in the same way. She did not yell at him at all, as if she didn't know him well enough for that.

Have you seen Trevor? he asked her.

You should visit him, she said, keeping herself apart from him, beyond his proper grasp.

But he had stolen from Trevor who had been his friend. He had gotten caught as well.

And yet these were also the best days he ever lived so far. Better than Kenoza Lake, better than being sad about his swimming grandma and standing in the blue moonlight listening to her breathe. In Sullivan County he had seen redneck boys through the windshield of his grandma's car, kids throwing stones below the creek or bashing their bikes down through the woods. He had thought he would have to live behind the windshield.

But now he was the kid who had lived in the bush at night; he instructed the hippie kids how to make shelters in the bush, digging down in the black soil of the rain forest. They laid fishbone fern as he ordered, then sticks and branches on the top. He had never done this in his life before but no one knew that. He was a prince of liars. He won two dollars underwater. He could stay on the bottom beneath the waterfall and pick up pebbles in his teeth. The water was cold but it tasted of bracken and something else, maybe gold. He thought so definitely. The hippie kids were wild things with feet as hard as leather. They ran along the lacework trails. He made a divining rod from a wire coat hanger and then a map showing where there was gold and water. The gold he marked red, the water blue. As he drew it, he knew it would come true.

He got the last of the black dye cut off. His hair went curly from the water and was bleached white from the sun, like at Kenoza Lake.

Rufus had red hair. Sam had black. The boy and the Puddinghead were both the same color. The boy announced to them they were a gang.

He and his gang climbed the steep ridge behind Dial's hut

and went north as far as Cowpastures, as it was called. The boy led them back by Trevor's which was pretty much the point of the adventure. That was when the boy discovered everyone was scared of Trevor. All the boy thought was how Trevor had been beat and broken and had no mother of his own.

But Rufus said, He has a gun, man, and would not go inside.

The boy entered on his own, recognizing all those smells of rotting and growing and the rich awful smell of blood and bone and Wappa weed. He discovered Trevor lying naked in his hammock listening to the war.

Can we have some carrots, Trevor?

Trevor cast his eyes at him, like a dog, embarrassed. How's Dial, he asked.

She's good. Can we have some carrots.

Help yourself, he said, closing his eyes.

The boy washed the carrots under the green hose. Trevor never told him not to.

I've got a gang, he said, to make Trevor look at him. Trevor kept his eyes closed.

That's good. Who's in it.

Sam and Rufus. As the cold water washed across his feet he missed the days when Trevor was his friend, and when he threw the green tops in the compost it was like doing something precious he would never be allowed to do again.

Who's the other carrot for?

His eyes seemed closed.

Sara, he said. Where's that ol' horse? he asked.

I'm the bloody horse, said Trevor.

The boy stood in front of him begging to be seen. In his pocket he had the hundred dollars and all the other money he'd stolen from him. He could not carry it any longer.

I've got some money of yours, he said at last.

Trevor's eyes stayed shut. I know.

I brought it back, he said, surprising himself.

That's good, said Trevor.

Where will I put it?

On the table.

And that was all. The boy put one hundred and twenty-one dollars on the folding table with the melon rinds and took the carrots out to Rufus and Sam and the Puddinghead.

Squatting, eating carrots, in a state of indignation and relief, he heard that Trevor was a former sanitation worker, had a gelignite bomb below the road. He knew that anyway. He learned how Detective Dolce led a raid on him one Easter morning, and he learned the names of casuarinas, turpentine, flooded gum, ironbark, wattle, jacaranda, flame tree, lemon-grass, bluetop, lantana and groundsel where the bees harvested their honey for Sara's father. He ate lentils for lunch, got to put his head inside the steel boiler where Rufus's father dried pawpaw to sell at the health food shop. It did not taste too good with all its water gone.

No one told him all this had been vacation and that Sam and Rufus would soon go back to school. Suddenly, there was no one left but the little Puddinghead.

Why can't I go to school? the boy asked Dial.

Dial stood on a big metal drum painting the end wall with another coat of linseed oil. She splashed a lot of it around, on her shorts, her long strong legs, frowning very deep, squinting crooked. She did not even look at him until he came out with his question.

Then she jumped off the drum and did that crouching-down thing.

What, he demanded nervously.

She brushed his hair with her oily hand.

It's the law, he said. I have to go to school.

She gave him a lopsided smile that made her nose look big and rubbery. It's the law, she said, to lock me up for kidnapping.

She was a Turk, she said so. A bitzer. He stared at her, into her strange eyes, not knowing who she was. He wished she would love him again, but when she reached for him, he stepped away.

Where is Buck? he asked.

She did that smile again.

I'm a teacher, she said. I can teach you better than anyone in that town.

He stayed staring at her until she looked away and went back to painting. He stood on the back steps awhile and looked up the hill into the gray tangle of the bush. Flies buzzed around his face and knees as well. He was suddenly, all at once, bored by everything. There was nothing to do but go to the candle factory where he found the little Puddinghead playing with a doll in the dirt beneath the kitchen. Together they walked along the creek, not saying anything, and when they ended up back near Dial's house, the Puddinghead said, Let's make a hole.

The boy had invented digging holes and now he was sick to death of it, but he took her sticky little hand and went into the rain forest and began to mess around, pulling rocks out of the tangled web of roots and dirt. It must have been a river once. He didn't bother telling her. She took off her clothes so they would not get dirty and found a piece of shale to chop at the roots.

While they were digging the boy heard Buck meow. The Puddinghead looked at him but he did not want to talk about Buck. He had been told bad things already. Maybe they were true, or maybe not. Now he heard his meow and he had the idea then that they could make something called a blind. Grandpa Selkirk made blinds to shoot waterfowl.

The Puddinghead thought she would find a dinosaur bone and kept on talking about it. He did not listen but she worked very hard and before too long they started to collect sticks for the roof, going into the lantana to cut flexible pieces you could weave. That is where they were, not six feet from the Peugeot, when a white Land Rover arrived, a blue light on its roof.

47

Queensland was a police state run by men who never finished high school. They raided the hippies in Cedar Bay with helicopters and burned down their houses. They parked out on Remus Creek Road at night and searched the hippie cars without permission from a judge. So if you thought you came to Remus Creek Road to get away from being illegal, that was just a joke. The boy knew this. Dial must have learned it when the police arrived to add her to what they called their little map.

When the boy saw their Land Rover, he abandoned the Puddinghead without a word. There was no point in warning Dial. He cut across the rain forest to the yellow track. He was a good runner but the hill was steep and the sun was hot and by the time he got as far as the Volvo and the turkey he had a stitch.

It did not take the police long to threaten Dial and get her name and date of birth. Now the boy could hear the Land Rover rumbling and rolling over the rocks and potholes not so far behind him. He had no choice but to slip off the scary steep side of the road and hang on to a wattle root. He heard a voice above the engine saying, *Egg bloody sandwich.*

If they got to Trevor first the boy thought he could still start the engine on the ice-blue car and have it running. That's why Trevor had taught him, obviously. He pulled his scratched and bleeding limbs onto the road, and followed the police through a settling cloud of dust. He could only walk by twisting sideways, pressing his hand into his stitch, but when he understood that the police had headed down toward the left he hurled himself into that blurred piece of nothing which was made by camouflage nets and trees. Trevor was chopping up tomato stakes but he let the boy take him by his muddy hand, lifting a fat rucksack off a rusty hook, slinging it across one shoulder, as he followed him through the garden up onto the saddle until the boy tripped and fell. Then Trevor carried him. They breathed together, the boy's purple eyelids drooping, feasted on exhaustion. They traveled with one mind through the sharp cutting shale and into the paddock with the purple seeds, skirting around the fence line where no satellites could see. Here Trevor lifted the barbed wire and the boy rolled under and then held up the wire in turn. Then they both walked, hand in hand together, down toward the hidden car, ice blue, cyan blue, turquoise—Trevor called it all these things.

The boy expected they would drive now. Trevor pushed him behind the steering wheel. Che touched his fingers against the silver horn ring which held the tiny reflection of his frightened face.

Trevor opened the rucksack and found a bag of dried pawpaw and a khaki water canteen like the one Cameron took to camp.

The cops were at your place?

All the boy could think was, Drive.

Did they ask for me? Trevor was studying the pawpaw, turning it this way and that. Did they say my name?

I only saw their truck.

They saw you!

No! he cried.

Jeez, calm down.

But the boy's own father stopped loving him when he led the FBI to his door. No, he said. He held out his hands to show Trevor all his wounds.

I know what they did, Trevor. They got Dial's date and place of birth.

Did you hear them?

It's what they do, Trevor.

Is it?

Yes, then they turned down the track by the big drums, Trevor.

Trevor poured water into the palm of his hand and spilled it on the boy's head, patting him. That's the Rabbitoh's place, he said. They'll have a nice long chat with him.

Are we going on the lamb, Trevor?

Trevor sprinkled more water on the boy's hot skin.

We should get started, Trevor. He opened his door, to let Trevor slide over and take the wheel. He was thinking they could get money for his ticket from the stash. They were together now.

Trevor clicked the door shut. There's a path all the way through from my place to Eumundi.

That's what I was thinking too.

It isn't on the maps. It's on the old maps, not the new maps.

That's what I thought.

They'll go to my place. They'll steal some vegetables to take home to their wives. They won't come over here.

But we have to go.

Trevor was chewing on his smile. Don't panic, Tex. Remember Pearl Harbor.

The boy heard *paddy tax*. He would have asked but Trevor was slowly lowering the window.

What is it?

Shut up.

Then he heard the Land Rover lumbering toward them

and Trevor slipped away like a shadow through a net. When he did not return the boy spilled more water on his face and made his pants wet. He waited a good long time, but no one came back. Then he pushed through the dry brambles to get a proper view. The Land Rover was really close—a man's hairy leg sticking out the passenger window.

His heart was walloping and whaling as he got back behind the wheel, ready to turn the key when ordered.

He touched the key. He turned it one click, just to have it set up. It was like a .22 trigger, first pressure, then second. He learned that from his grandpa.

He heard a magpie, flies buzzing inside the car. Then voices.

Once more he pushed through the dried brush and kneeled down behind the dead wattles. A policeman was kicking at the grass.

He returned to the car and sat with the glistening horn in front of him. He traced his finger around it and he could see his thumb reflected bigger than his nose. He guessed it had two positions like the key, like the trigger. He pressed to find the first position. The horn blared.

A hand clamped around his mouth.

The boy would have shrieked but there was no air.

I'll fucking wring your fucking rabbit neck, hissed Trevor from behind.

Even when the hand was taken away, he could not move, was poisoned, paralyzed, stinging in his shame. He waited to get caught and even after the police engine started and drove away and after the light had gone and everything inside the car was black and sick with dry papaya, he stayed in the same place.

OK, get out.

He got out. He could hardly see. Trevor's hand was dry and hard. It took his own and led him through the scratchy dark.

Did you want me to get arrested?

I didn't mean to, Trevor.

Jesus!

He began to say I'm sorry but the word opened up its guts into a howl. He cried and cried and Trevor picked him up and carried him, heaving and bawling, back up to the compound and then down the road past Rebecca's to the bottom of his own place and here he set him down and, in the darkness, the boy felt him kiss his head.

Good night, mate.

Good night, Trevor.

He stayed in the dark of the driveway and rubbed his eyes. After a while he heard Trevor calling outside Rebecca's window and then he went back home to Dial.

48

It is a law of childhood that you are seldom punished immediately but must wait in a state of agony for your crime to be known. That's how it worked for the boy after he sounded the horn at the police. He was ashamed of himself already but he knew the real upset would only arrive when Dial was told, and as he skulked down in the valley and Trevor remained on the hill, this time of torment went on and on. He didn't see Trevor, although he must have visited during those long hours when the boy slept, the dusty crocheted hippie rugs pulled over his head to hide him from the light.

It was in the middle of the fourth night that Che came down the ladder from the loft, each rung so square and hard it hurt his toes, and went outside to pee. If Dial had been asleep he could have gone out on the deck and made the stinky earth smell even worse. But Dial was out there smoking so he crept out the back door and found that the season had turned, not cold by the standards of Sullivan County, but cold enough. There was dew, and when he came back inside he made perfect wet footprints on the perpetually dusty floor.

He got almost as far as the ladder when she called to him.

Come and tell your secrets.

He stayed between the workbench and the ladder, hugging himself, wishing he could hide his ugly self.

Come here, baby.

The slats on the deck were also wet with dew. They were colder even than the earth. He saw the valley was filled with mist and blue moonlight, wet leaves, black pawpaws, dark icy sky above the distant ridge. He waited.

You've been keeping secrets, she said. He looked down at her and she looked straight back at him with her black brows pushing down onto her eyes.

He has a car hidden in the bush, she said. Don't walk away.

I'm getting a blanket.

He climbed up the ladder and threw down one of Adam's quilts.

You knew that, she said. You kept it secret.

He spread the blanket on the floor inside the doorway and then he wrapped himself inside it.

Baby, don't close your eyes.

I'm sleepy.

Look at me. Were you trying to get Trevor caught?

I warned him, he cried.

Were you trying to get me caught?

What!

Were you trying to get me caught?

No, he cried so loud it echoed around the valley.

Shush.

You shush! The police were here. I ran up to Trevor's. I warned him. Let me alone. I'm sleepy.

Now she was kneeling, looking down at him as if he was some poor moth she'd tangled in a string. She tried to peel back the blanket.

You honked.

It was a *mistake,* he said, grabbing the blanket back.

How could it be a mistake, baby? She lay her hand on his shoulder and he felt tears rising.

I thought it had two points to it, he said, sitting up.

What?

The horn, Dial. Two points on it.

I don't get it.

Well she would not get it, he thought. She never would get it. She was not mechanical but he couldn't say that or she would get all pissed.

A first and second, he said. That's all.

He could see her not listening to him and he thought that his grandma would have known—there are the two pressure points on the trigger of the .22 and the car had two points on the key and he had just thought there were two points on the horn but the more he tried to make it clear the more she thought he was lying.

You want me to get caught, she said.

He dropped his blanket enough to hit her, shush her, to make her love him. She held his hand. It's OK, she said. It's natural.

He tugged himself free. I'm not like that.

We're all like that, she said.

But he was not like that at all. He stole some money, that was all. Dial, he said, I don't want you caught. What would happen to me then?

She brushed his hair back from his eyes as if what he said was nothing. You can't know what you feel, she said.

I *can* know what I feel, Dial. You can't, that's all. You can't know.

It's not your fault.

I *do* know how I feel.

You want to go home, baby. Of course you do. She held out her arms to him and he crawled onto her lap, his head between her breasts, and she reached across and wound the quilt around them both up tight around his shoulders, swaddling him tight against her.

If you were grown up you'd know you honked that horn for a reason.

It was a mistake, he said, but he was soothed now, not wanting anything more than to be loved.

Because you're angry with Trevor, or with me. If you were grown up, that would be clear to you. It *feels* like a mistake, but it wasn't. You needed someone to take you home. Shush. It's not wrong. You've been stolen from your grandma. It's no one's fault.

She could not know—it was so much worse than that. He wished she would just be quiet and stroke him till he fell asleep.

We've got to figure this out. She rubbed his head. What's best for all of us.

You do it. He yawned. You decide what's best.

All your life depends on it, she said. I can't do this on my own. You have to help me. The thing is, she said, you're rich.

I guess. I don't know.

You must be. Your mother doesn't have sisters or brothers. Your grandma is a Daschle and Daschle Kent is a private company.

I don't know what that is. Dial, I don't care about money.

There are millions of dollars of artworks in the apartment.

He did not care.

On Park Avenue. Baby, you will have a really nice life, baby, with a nice apartment, lovely paintings most of all. And Kenoza Lake.

He blocked his ears.

Nice things, OK.

Only years later would he understand; she was a socialist. What could she have been thinking?

You don't know, he said. You don't know anything about me.

That's why you have to help me decide for you.

I don't know what you mean, he said.

We have to get you back to Grandma, she said. That's it. That's all there is. We've been so stupid, but we love you, baby, do you understand?

He understood enough to fall asleep. In the morning he woke up in the other hut with his nose pressed against her shoulder.

49

Trevor had iris-blue and yellow bruises on his back but now that there was a plan to save the boy he came visiting with vegetables, in daylight. Avoiding the track which would have taken him past Rebecca's, he forced his way through the sweaty tangle of the rain forest, emerging with drops of water on his brown skin, twigs in his hair, displaying a sleek ruddy animal health. He looked quite wonderful. He had always been like this of course but Dial now saw that he loved the boy, not in a temperate adult way, but in a good way nonetheless. He was not an enemy, so she let herself notice his skin, the limpid rather lovely pale blue eyes. She permitted him to turn off the propane light so they could not be seen from outer space and this, somehow, no longer seemed like a retreat from the Enlightenment. Also, it must be said, the candlelight was golden on her walls and the smoke rose into the shadows of the rafters and the little wishful shadow-bats flew in the back door and did a circle before flitting out the front. The boy seemed to settle, and a peace came on them all. They had done something decent and there would be a brief reward for it, not much, but more than she deserved, more probably than she would have had at Vassar.

In the long mopoke nights when the boy was properly asleep she and Trevor Dobbs sat out on the deck and talked, and marijuana alone could not explain how a body that had previously seemed so strange and feral could now be both foreign and alluring, smelling of bark, the holes he dug, the dark green chard in his square muddy hands. She had wild hair but she was not wild and no matter what *Time* magazine said about her so-called generation she had only made love to one man in her life. She had been a loyal, lingering fool and she had no intention of involving herself with any more criminals, no matter how kind and principled they were. But she did kiss Trevor, more than once, and on one night fell asleep breathing that fragrant well of air between his neck and shoulder. There was a charge of violence around him but—the truth?—she did not mind it. Indeed she was familiar with this particular frisson, a little touch of fugu to the lips, not enough to kill her dead. And if anything surprised her about Trevor Dobbs, it was that he did not jump her—she might not know his heart exactly but there were few secrets between sarongs.

She was a little achy, pleasantly aroused, it was enough. Even if it was a moment, she would take it.

It was Trevor who suggested that they talk to Phil Warriner about how they might return the boy without endangering Dial.

That she agreed was not because her precious Harvard standards had slipped—but there was no other choice.

So Phil was summoned by whatever method Trevor used—it did not seem to involve telephones—and the lawyer finally arrived at the end of a wet day, a warm evening, still raining softly, little pools of water gathering in the banana leaves, then spilling in a crystal rush you would never tire of. Phil parked his Holden Monaro and Dial came out on the deck and watched him for a moment before she understood he was undressing, hanging his shirt and suit on a hanger like a traveling salesman before walking toward her up the rain-soft path, barefoot, bare bottomed, carrying nothing but his briefcase and what turned out to be a pack of Drum tobacco.

Hi-yo, he called.

Oh Christ, she thought.

He came rather shyly into the hut, a big man with hairy thighs and shiny calves, and Trevor made no comment on his appearance. She knew the boy was lying up in the smoky loft pretending to nap, or maybe really napping—she could not tell. Phil sat his rain-wet backside on the dusty floor and took out a yellow pad and asked them questions and Dial looked him steadily in the eyes, anything to avoid the penis which was peeking between his crossed legs like a mushroom.

Later she meant to ask Trevor what Phil imagined he was doing, but she never did. She supposed the lawyer, who had a lot of hippie clients, knew his business better than she did.

The boy, of course, was peering down on the three Fates while they figured out his life. They were not Clotho who spins the Thread of Life or Lachesis who allots the length of the yarn, or Atropos who does the final deadly snip. They were, Dial thought, more Karlo and Slothos and Zappa. She could feel the boy's intense attention.

What did she call you? Phil asked. The nana?

The what?

The grandma.

The boy heard this, every word. He saw the gauze of light in front of the jacaranda, white ants getting born with silver wings.

She called me Anna, said Dial, licking the three cigarette papers and joining them together like a hippie quilt.

Anna Xenos?

The boy never heard that name before. He saw Dial look up at him, but he was spying through the crochet rug. She could not see his eyes.

That's the first lesson, Phil said. Rich people don't know the names of their servants.

Not so fast, said Dial.

You worked for her. She had no fucking idea who you were. Did she pay your taxes?

I was off the books.

See, said Phil, and he took the joint Dial gave him. He creased up his face to drag the smoke down into his lungs, curling up his toes. Some of the smoke stayed hanging around his furry sideburns like valley mist. The boy thought, No one will ever know what it is like to be here now.

See, said Phil.

What am I meant to see? asked Dial, laughing.

They don't know who you are.

I don't know who you are, said Dial and then all of them burst out laughing.

The boy saw Trevor pat Dial on the knee. Dial picked something from his hair, a bug perhaps.

You're very sweet, Phil, said Dial. But they can easily find out who I am. I was at Harvard.

It was not the first time the boy saw how that worked. Phil raised an eyebrow and took another toke.

Fair enough, he said. Everyone was serious now.

Also, there is Che.

These guys are not as efficient as you think, said Phil. Really. They have a lot of trouble with their index cards at immigration. Ask Trevor if you want to know.

Trevor looked sharply at Phil, then shrugged at Dial, sucking on his bottom lip.

Phil, I don't want to go to jail.

Why should you go to jail? The boy's mother asks for him. You do what she asks. She's your employer.

Former employer.

Former, OK. But employer, on that day.

It isn't like that, Phil, said Dial. The boy's mother was legally barred from access to her child. I stole the boy from his legal guardian.

With her permission.

Listen, Dial began.

No, said Phil. He drew a line across his pad. Here's what we'll do.

The boy saw this. He saw Dial look at him.

I'll be your lawyer, Phil said.

OK.

I'll go and visit Mrs. Selkirk.

You'll go to New York?

To Park Avenue. I'll explain the situation as your adviser. I'll represent your interests. You were acting on the legal guardian's instructions.

Phil, I went to Philly.

OK, OK, very funny, but she has her, you know, accident. You take the kid to the father, but the father doesn't want to know. By then you are accused of kidnapping. You get frightened. You run away. Dumb, but not criminal.

Phil, you are so sweet, but this won't work.

I'm a lawyer.

A conveyancing lawyer. That's what you said before.

You think I'm a moron, say so.

Of course I don't.

Conveyancing, Phil nodded, wills, trusts. This is an inheritance issue. And even if I am a moron, you tell me someone else who is dumb enough to do this for you?

How would you get there?

You'd buy me a ticket.

OK.

I'd book into a hotel. I'd negotiate your case and check out the Village Vanguard, you know. Max Gordon. Why not? You can't do anything from Remus Creek Road. You've got to move. You can't move. You're stuck.

Phil, have you ever done anything like this before?

Phil beamed. He raised his eyebrows and twisted up his mustache.

This is lovely, he said.

Really? said Dial, and the boy could hear her old sarcastic

voice and he hoped they wouldn't have a fight. He liked it how it was just fine, her picking twigs from Trevor's hair.

I wouldn't be dead for quids, said Phil, exhaling.

And what might that mean?

It means that there is no amount of money you could pay me, said Phil—filling up his lungs again with smoke—no amount of money you could pay me that would persuade me not to be alive.

And then they all laughed, the Fates, rolling around, stoned out of their gourds most likely.

By then the boy was sleeping.

50

The word *conspiracy* was later attached to what happened on Remus Creek Road but in the weeks while Phil "prepared" himself to travel, the only conspiring the boy noticed was on the deck where he once saw Dial kiss Trevor late at night. Maybe also some noises in the dark.

Early every morning Dial climbed up into the loft and they played poker and ate leftover dinner. He knew this was because he would soon go home, but once that had been decided, the weeks or months that followed were like a vacation and he no longer needed to worry that his grandma would die or that his dad would never be able to find him.

He had bad dreams at night, but each new day brought a lot of Dial-type driving between the mountains and the coast, between one red phone box and another. These telephone boxes would finally be revealed as part of the conspiracy, but they hardly mattered to the boy. What he cared about was the beach, eating pearl perch, teaching Trevor how to swim. Why they drove so much, he did not ask, but they traveled the winding throw-up roads to Mapleton, Maleny, then down to the muddy river at Bli Bli, up to dry Pomona, back to Maroochy which was the name of a pretty aboriginal girl long ago. The boy occupied his rightful seat. Trevor lay across the backseat winding up his cyclone radio. He said that the engine block interfered with his reception—a falsehood that the boy would believe for twenty years—and he would not take the front seat if you paid him. He could not read but he knew everything—five men got caught breaking into the Watergate Hotel. B-52s were bombing Vietnam. The boy did not want to think about the war which seemed to have taken everything from him. He preferred to study the line between his chest and swimsuit to see how brown he was. Sometimes he lay on the dusty floor. Dial had a jade anklet. He watched how her foot moved, the stick shift too. He could do it better but was not allowed.

You crazy thing, get out of there.

They parked beside a red telephone box in the middle of the sugarcane on a bend in the road between Coolum and Yandina, and another above the surf at Peregian Beach.

There was also a phone box in Pomona, the tiny rusty town where they first bought swimsuits from the thrift shop. Maybe Trevor used some twenty-cent coins from the phone money jar they carried with them everywhere. These phones had two buttons A and B; he did not try to work them. In Pomona Dial bought a black swimsuit covered with white flowers, some printed and others stitched onto her breasts. Trevor called her Mrs. Flower. Her skin grew dark quickly on account of she was a Greek with Turkish blood.

The boy also got real dark, his hair bleaching white as white, as he persisted teaching Trevor how to breathe in water. No matter how sad you were, swimming always cleaned your soul. The boy said that to Trevor, those words exactly. He showed Trevor the dead man's float, but the surf picked him up and dumped him and soon they were just running at the waves and it did not matter that the London orphan could not swim because he caught the waves, at Marcus, at Sunshine, Peregian, Coolum.

Che, Trevor, Mrs. Flower, got dumped, got their faces

pushed down into the sand and their legs kicked and tangled in the air and that was the point, that plus the feeling of the skin going tight across your back and face, and some days they were almost the only ones between Coolum and Sunshine. It was almost winter but completely perfect—no one else but a single leather-kneed geezer sweeping a bag across the wet sand to gather worms, they guessed; they did not know.

Trevor loved a band called the Saints. He played them over and over: I'm from Brisbane and I'm rather plain. He carried a whole stalk of bananas beside him on the backseat and they ate them all day long, but when the sun in the west touched the low clouds along the eastern horizon they danced and jumped under the cold shower in a trailer park and headed off in search of fish. Pearl perch. Red snapper. Reef fish. They found old codgers with missing fingers selling fish from the back of plywood vans on roads out of Noosa and Alexandra. And after that they drove back to the valley, which always lost its light before the world outside, and there Dial and Trevor cooked while the boy washed and cleaned the labels of the ice-cream cones to keep as souvenirs.

He collected exactly eighteen of these papers, all identical, white and blue, and marked BUDERIM, and when they were washed he laid them flat on the deck and the next day they would dry and he would put them to one side. Other things he saved were shells, stones, dried grasshoppers. Obviously he was getting ready to say good-bye, but that did not occur to him just then and no one tried to tell him what he really felt.

The three of them began to fix up Dial's garden and although time is the element that makes a garden, the boy did not think of it in those terms. They drove to Wappa Dam with rakes and took the rich smelly carpet of weed for mulch. He got drenched in lake slime, hugging the wet bundles as they filled the trunk with them. The Peugeot sagged and water leaked behind them all the way back home.

They borrowed a rotary hoe from the Puddinghead's father, then broke up the clods by hand, their brown skin coated with sweat and mud. They wound string onto a stick and made the rows straight. They planted broccoli, cabbage, cauliflower, parsley, rocket, spinach, silver beets, onions, carrots, radishes.

The boy kept the seed packets, and in each one he placed a single seed and then sealed the packet with masking tape.

It was hard to believe he was not already filled to bursting with regret, and when his brown back began to itch and peel, when he shed his powdered skin onto the Australian floor, Dial watched with her hand across her mouth.

What is it, Dial?

I'm good.

Penny for your thoughts, Dial.

Nothing really, she said. She could not have explained it to anyone, just motes of dust in sunlight, nothing anyone would ever see.

51

A ridiculous number of twenty-cent pieces had been spent by Trevor arguing with Phil about how he was to be transported to Brisbane Airport, every conversation predicated on the notion that even a call from a public phone box in Bli Bli was being listened in on, and sometimes this seemed humorous to Dial, and other times it seemed wise and mostly it just seemed as if it was better to be cautious. Trevor showed a distinct aversion to going anywhere near the airport and she certainly didn't want him harmed on her account. So very early one misty morning, when the valley surprised her by being both damp and cold, she removed her Vassar skirt and twinset from dry cleaner's plastic, and walked carefully down to the filthy Peugeot, carrying her shoes and a T-shirt in her hand. The T-shirt was to wipe the mud off her ankles.

There was dew on the police cars as she passed through Eumundi heading for Tewantin. She crossed the bridge at Gympie Terrace at exactly 6:00 a.m., and for a moment a pelican floated just outside her window, finally descending through white streaks of mist to the Noosa River. She was dry mouthed but could still appreciate the beauty of the place, and marvel that working people could live like this, here, now.

You could be poor, without snow and shit and Whitey Bulger and his boys, without spending all your life trying to escape your destiny. Of course she thought this before she saw Phil.

She cruised up the terrace and turned back at the round-about. Now the Noosa Yacht Club was on her right and she could see, out on the roof deck, a clergyman with two small cases who turned out on closer inspection to be Phil Warriner in a strange suit.

Later she drew the garments for the boy, the trouser buttons above his navel, the jacket long, like a frock coat. She drew very well but she could not illustrate the way the trousers melted and floated like a gown.

What is it, Dial?

It's called a zoot suit.

She thought, My life is entrusted to this fool, God save me.

The extraordinary creature had seen her. He came down the steps, across the grass, paused a second on the median strip. She thought, What on earth am I doing? She should have run away.

Did you, Dial? Run away.

I waited. Like a good girl.

Like a cow, she thought, about to get a hammer between her eyes. This was her lawyer. Her representative. Yet her greatest feeling, watching him cross the empty road, was not fear—which would have been reasonable—but embarrassment. He had white spats, all the fixings. He carried two cases—a fat satchel and a trumpet case, and when he placed them carefully in the back, she made no comment.

Morning, he said, shaking out his trousers as he settled in.

The suit was daffodil yellow.

Hi, she said, but she could not look at him. She thought, He's going to get cigarette ash all over it. They set off back up toward Eumundi from where they would take the Bruce Highway to Brisbane Airport, and all this time Dial could feel her passenger waiting to talk about his suit. She should have told him, Take the freaking thing off. Burn it. Where in all of the Sunshine Coast would you find a zoot suit? American Negroes wore them, Negroes long since dead.

Why did she not tell him? Because she did not want to hurt him? Was that really true? By the time she was dealing with the bullying trucks on the Bruce Highway, she had sunk into depression. The pleasure of the last few weeks turned out to have been the pleasure of very short-lived things, luminous wisteria, precious for being almost gone.

She had watched the boy collecting every moment of his self. He laid out his blocky dogged drawings of the garden and the beach. She did not ask the obvious, Won't you miss all this. Won't you miss me most of all?

For better or for worse she drove Phil to the airport, two hours to Eagle Farm, every minute of which she was tensed against the suit.

He was going down around Greenwich, he told her, and she did not correct him, to look up Max Gordon and maybe sit in at the Vanguard. Every restaurant in New York had huge plates of food. The white people were uptight, he said as if he himself were blue. Americans had no sense of "irony." The spades were cool. He was going to hang out at Brownies where you got toot right on the bar but you got thrown out for swearing.

She passed the wide-verandaed store where they sold mud crabs to the businessmen about to catch a Melbourne flight. Phil told her all about this, the crab that had escaped and almost crashed a 727. She slid in beside the curb at Brisbane Airport, gave him his expenses in an envelope, and kissed his bristly oddly perfumed cheek.

After Dial got back from Eagle Farm she loudly wished that she had never asked Phil to do a thing. The boy wished too. He was not allowed to say how much.

But a week passed and nothing happened, then another, and after a while all that remained of Phil was Dial's rolling eyes, and her drawings of the zoot suit, way better, he thought, than anything he could do.

Dial and Trevor and the boy went to the beach six days in a row. They found the best avocados on the Sunshine Coast, hidden from the road behind a stand of *Pinus radiata* on the Coolum road. Then, the next week, on the road in from Bli Bli, they came across an old foreign guy selling little fish, not sardines, but small. Dial got watery eyed and cooked the fish like she once cooked them for her father who, she said, was exactly five foot four.

Next morning there was rain on the roof and everyone stayed in bed for hours. Then there were a couple of days of steady rain and the boy witnessed the silky pale green stalk of pea unfolding, pushing aside the crumbling soil. In mud and drizzle he mulched the peas with Wappa weed the way he had learned from Trevor long ago, bumping up the paths with his pallet piled high. He patted down the black stuff, leaving a hole so every curling baby could reach the sky—feathery clouds, high and icy in the sci-fi blue.

No word from Phil.

The three of them walked up the hill. Trevor's tanks were getting nice and full. That night they went to a moon dance at the so-called hall and the boy danced with Dial and then with the little Puddinghead. He learned an Irish jig although the moon was covered up by cloud. He wouldn't be dead for quids. That was a fact.

Through all his happiness, the boy still carried the shame of the tooting horn. He could not say that he no longer *wanted* to go back to Kenoza Lake.

If Phil found Grandma he would send a secret telegram to say Dial had been forgiven for her crime. Hamid the postmaster would write down the telegram and put it in a pigeonhole. It would stay there until they asked, Is there a telegram? No one delivered telegrams to hippies.

He stayed in the car when Dial and Trevor went into the post office. When he saw them returning empty-handed his whole body went loose as a puppy's neck.

There was more rain and Trevor's tanks spilled over and

the ford was flooded and they were just at home playing canasta when they heard the little Puddinghead crying Coo-ee and running over the sodden ground, splash, thump, as she landed on the back step of the hut, no Tinker Bell, her legs what you might call solid, scratched, soft white down all over her. The sodden thing balled up in her hand was the nasty thing, the telegram. Her dad had been given it the week before and he had come home to find the goats among the vegetables.

Brian says, the Puddinghead announced, shivering and holding out her dripping arms. He says, she said, it doesn't look too urgent.

It was dark and overcast outside, dark inside too. The boy felt Dial shiver and saw her hold her arms around her breasts. She did not say a word.

Trevor lay down his canasta hand, faceup. Then Dial rose to her feet. She took the telegram from the small blonde girl.

Shit, she cried, and flung it on the floor.

The boy's heart panicked inside its cage.

Dial said, Airhead.

The boy did not know what an airhead was but Dial looked like an earthquake, her wide mouth torn apart. She struck her head against the wall and a plate fell on the floor and broke. What a moron, she cried.

The Puddinghead turned and ran and they heard her splashing down the hill, bawling.

Trevor retied his sarong and walked to where the crumpled telegram lay dying by the doorway. He passed it to the boy to sound it out for him.

MET J. J. JOHNSON.

Yes, what is it?

He has met a trombone player, Dial said, kneeling beside the broken plate.

What does that mean.

It means he is a flake.

The boy thought, Maybe this is good.

52

The boy saw it happen—the telegram changing Dial's mind.

He felt the heat of her blood as she rushed out the door. She came back with pearls over her chest and mud on her calves. Her court shoes were in her hand. She climbed up into his loft and came down with the jar of twenty-cent pieces.

Who is J. J. Johnson?

A trombone player.

Her hair was frizzed and mad looking. She wiped her calves with a dishcloth and asked Trevor where they should call from.

Is he really a trombone player?

Shush. Yes.

Trevor said there was a phone box up in the ranges beyond Maleny and this part the boy understood, or almost understood, i.e., the random pattern is your key to freedom. Do you understand?

Not really.

You scattered your dope plants through the bush. You did nothing that could be seen or heard from space. Do you understand?

It was yes, no, sort of.

Come on, baby, Dial said now, we're going to take a ride. All this alarming activity brought back the bad feeling from the airplanes. He watched her huge long legs, galloping down the hill toward the Peugeot 203.

Trevor took the backseat and was very quiet, not eating, not winding up his radio, leaning forward so his little mouth was near Dial's ear. He was as alert and watchful as he had been when the police crept across the paddock in their truck.

Where are we going?

Shush.

The boy thought, I am being sent back. His stomach got tight as he listened to them.

He can have my fucking money, Dial said.

Who, Dial?

Shush, she said, talking to Trevor quiet and fast. She would send him extra. He could spend all night at the Blue Note. Or the Gate. And get himself beat up on the A train if that is what he chose. He was way too big a flake for this. She always knew.

Who? the boy insisted, trying not to be whiny.

Please, Dial said. I'll explain. Trust me.

Instead of explaining she drove six miles to Nambour, then fifteen miles to Maleny and another five miles south until they could see the weird broken teeth of the Glass House Mountains shoving out of the prickly bush below the velvet sky. The road was thin and bright black along the grassy ridge and when they came to the phone box Dial parked the car as best she could, nervous about tipping over into the valley below. She got out of the car with a piece of paper held between thumb and finger, fluttering in the breeze. In her other hand she carried the jam jar of coins and the boy stayed in the car with the window open, the soft breeze washing across his skin.

Trevor pushed into the phone box too.

The boy was left alone to be half sick. He did not want to go, not yet, later. Maybe Dial could pay Grandma to have a visit so she could see it was really nice. The rain had stopped and the rabbit's fur cloud was high enough to see all the way to the coast. He imagined Lex and Sixty-second, and the deep dark streets, not letting his mind walk very far.

They rushed out of the phone box, Trevor frowning, Dial blowing out her cheeks.

What? he asked when they got in the car. What?

Dial was busy turning the car around. For a moment the back wheels got stuck and then they broke free, tearing away from Maleny, leaving lumps of yellow mud along the center of the road.

We have to go to Brisbane, baby.

Why?

They won't let us make an international call from a public phone.

At the Brisbane GPO there were police everywhere, like ants pouring from a nest. He looked down at his feet so no one would see his face.

Just be quiet, Dial told him. OK?

He took her slippery frightened hand and stayed tight against her as they walked up the steps of the huge building like a church or synagogue. No air-conditioning. Should have been. At a high counter Dial paid money and was given a ticket with a number on it and then they went into a waiting room with long wooden benches and black telephones around the walls, each one set in its own wood-paneled booth.

This is fancy, the boy said. Old style.

Yes.

When their number was finally called, the three of them pushed together into the booth which smelled of whatever gases people make when they are sad or scared.

Hello, Dial said.

He pressed against her as she asked for Mr. Warriner. Phil.

The boy thought, Flake.

He must be home by now, she said to Trevor.

Hello, said Dial. Hello, Phil.

She listened. She said, Is that Phil Warriner's room? Then she listened again.

That's not your business, she said. I want to speak to Phil.

Then, without saying another word, she placed the big black phone back on its hook. The boy did not see Trevor slip away but Dial found him among the crowd out front. Trevor had his hand across his mouth, his eyes flittering like mad, and the boy knew he was scared.

Cop, Dial said. In his room.

Trevor stared into the distance.

He was from Brooklyn, said Dial. The cop. She looked down at the boy.

I bet you know your grandma's number?

Trevor said, I'll meet you at the car at three.

The boy thought, What will happen to me? He watched Trevor's smooth hipless glide, right through a crowd of policemen getting on a bus.

Where is he going?

Do you know your grandma's phone number?

He looked into Dial's glaring speckly eyes. Everything was hidden in the black bit where Grandpa told him not even God could see.

Why?

She took his hand and he let her take him back to near the high counter where she did that crouching-down thing.

Listen, she said, the idiot's in trouble.

Trevor?

Phil. If he's in trouble I'm in trouble too. Just let me explain it to your grandma before Phil makes it worse.

That's what I said, the boy said. I told you ages ago.

He was crying now, not knowing what was right or wrong. They did not have a tissue. She fetched him a telegram form to blow his nose and it was hard and smeary on his skin and he had to use his wrist instead. Dial took a fresh telegram and wrote both numbers, Sixty-second Street, Kenoza Lake. Through tears he watched her paying at the counter.

It was nighttime where Grandma was, her little swimming body must be hardly showing beneath the surface of her bed, the crackling radio playing to keep away bad dreams. When the phone rang she must have got an awful fright.

Hello, Dial said, this is Anna Xenos.

Xenos? The boy could hear an ambulance. That's how he knew Dial called the city first.

I am your daughter's friend, Dial said. Anna Xenos.

The boy was not mentioned. His grandma could not see him or imagine where he was. A policeman was eating a sandwich and leaning against the counter while he talked to the pretty plump girl who handed out the numbers for the calls. Blood oath, the policeman said.

Dial's senses were as alive as cat's whiskers. She noticed how the policeman was staring at the boy. She heard a tumbler being moved across a glass-topped table in New York City.

OK, Anna Xenos, the old lady said. Do you know what time it is?

Dial thought, I'm nuts to have this conversation.

The police have arrested your accomplice, the grandmother said.

The word—*accomplice*—turned in her gut.

He's in The Tombs right now.

She did not know what The Tombs were exactly, but what she imagined was pretty close, and she hated the old lady for how she said *toombs* from a Park Avenue address.

She looked down at the boy and saw with what misery he clung to her. He was wrung-out looking, sweaty nosed, tugging at her skirt. Poor boy. Poor Phil in his zoot suit. She had been embarrassed to talk about it, but her prissy silence had gotten him locked in jail.

He'll be in court in the morning.

For Christ's sake, he's a lawyer. He's my lawyer.

Let me talk to Jay.

No, not yet.

Dial imagined an old-fashioned telephone, its cable frayed like her mother's corset. She waited while it crackled in her ear.

Do you really have to be so cruel, Mrs. Selkirk said.

Dial pushed the greasy telephone to the boy and he took it in both hands.

Darling, is that you?

The boy heard her voice dragged up from the martini deep of sleep.

Yes Grandma.

Jay?

It's me, Grandma. He saw her gray hair brushed out for bedtime.

Did they hurt you, Jay?

No Grandma.

The boy had heard his grandma weep quite often, like wind through fall leaves, but not like this, a storm of lashing and bashing and gulping. Then it stopped real quick.

Phil will tell you, the boy said quickly. I'm OK.

Who?

The lawyer, Grandma. He went to fix it all up. Everything's just fine.

The police have him, darling, don't you worry.

Everyone is kind to me, Grandma. Phil is nice.

Jay, where are you?

Maybe he should have said where he was. He did not know. The policeman had bushy sandy eyebrows pushing down upon his eyes and he stood with his bottom stuck back, so the lettuce in the sandwich would fall on the floor and not on his badge.

Jay, you have to say.

Dial had her ear right next to the phone. She took it from him and he was pleased he did not have to decide.

Listen, Dial said, I've paid for six minutes, so don't waste time.

I'll have you in Sing Sing, said Grandma Selkirk making static in her ear. I can trace your call, you little fool. How much money do you want?

Why don't you just talk to my lawyer and see if you can settle something. I don't want money.

Lawyer, oh please.

In that *oh please* Dial heard only privilege and condescension.

You're not helping yourself, you silly old woman.

Excuse me?

Jay is here. You want him? Or not?

Dial thought, I have become a kidnapper.

I lost a daughter. I can't lose a grandson too.

Listen to me, please, Dial said, we just want to come home.

Do you have any idea what trouble you are in. Put him on, let me speak to him again.

There isn't time.

You'd better not have hurt him.

Listen to me, Dial said. You've only got one chance. Do you want it?

No, you listen to me, the old lady said.

Shut up and listen, Dial said. She was scaring the boy. She could not help herself. She was in a mad place, swinging a length of two-by-four.

Yes, the old lady said very quietly. Go on, I'll listen.

Then she could hear Phoebe Selkirk crying.

Shut up, Dial said. You rich spoiled bitch. You want to see this boy again, you talk to Phil. You get him out of jail.

She put down the phone, and began to take stock of the damage.

53

The boy and Trevor were digging behind the hut. When the hole was finished you would be able to lie in it and see all the way, above the roof of the hut, to the broken yellow strokes of road. That was the plan, being presently executed with great urgency. In the hut Dial could feel the regular thud of Trevor's pick.

Behind the sink there was a thin lead-light window through which she could, depending on where she stood, see the boy with his head down in the hole scratching dirt behind him like a dog. Gravediggers, she thought, and that was pretty much her mood. She, Anna Xenos, had brought all this about. If only she had not done this. If only she had not done that. Everything she touched was broken. As Rebecca had said to Trevor, Why doesn't she just bomb Cambodia?

It was Trevor's conviction that Phil would quickly confess the boy's location to the New York cops. Who wouldn't? he said and in the hard glaze of his eyes she saw sufficient bitterness to trust. By tomorrow morning the Brisbane police will be out here, he said. Just before dawn. Wait and see.

It was already late now and the valley had lost the sun, and although it was worse than gloomy inside the hut, Dial thought it wiser to not light the lamps. Did the Alice May Twitchell Fellow really believe that they were being spied on from outer space, that her alarm clock was her key to freedom, that she needed to crawl into a muddy hole to keep her liberty?

She changed into a tank top and a pair of shorts and walked barefoot up the hill where she found the boy naked, lying on his stomach, digging with his hands. Trevor, wearing underpants out of some perverse politeness, was shoveling, grunting, the muscles on his back shaded with dirt like charcoal on good linen.

There had been sufficient rain to make the path slippery with mud, but all that rain had not penetrated far below the surface of the hill. It was the dry season, and after a few inches of moist earth there was hard yellow clay which had already broken the boy's fingernails.

Are you OK, baby?

I'm OK, he said, but she thought of trapped animals gnawing off their limbs. He had to go, to be released, but first they must survive the night, so the three of them worked awkwardly together until it was necessary to bring hurricane lamps up from the hut. It was still not finished when the boy was dead eyed and droopy and she took him down to wash. Then he sat on the countertop with a towel around his hunched-up shoulders, and they both listened to the scratch and scrape of Trevor's shovel as she made a kind of ratatouille with pumpkins and potatoes, a bastard thing without a name.

While the rice was cooking, they went up hand in hand and found that Trevor had already roofed the hole with a sheet of tin and covered it with dirt and Wappa weed. He had lined the inside with the black plastic from the garden.

Won't the police find us here? she asked.

They're afraid of the bush, he said. Trust me.

They ate their dinner in darkness on the deck of the hut and afterward they showered and dried themselves and put on what clean clothes they had. Finally they carried and dragged blankets and cushions up the hill, bringing with them twigs and leaves and spiders swept up in the dark.

They crawled down into the cushioned dark, the boy between Dial and Trevor, and although their positions suggested some familial protectiveness, Dial could not forget how she had hurt the boy, screaming like a harpy at his grandmother in that sweaty colonial post office. She imagined her own teeth like de Kooning's mama, growing up into the base of her nose, the criminal auntie, rattrap jaws to mince him up. But of course what she wanted was not this desperate criminal last stand but to take him like a poor injured bird and place him in a box of cotton balls and feed him warm milk from an eyedropper. She loved him, loved his smooth brown skin, the leafy smell of his tangled hair, most of all the eyes which were once more open, limpid, filled with trust. He loved her too.

God bless Phil and keep him from harm, the boy said, and in the stunned silence that followed the prayer, he fell asleep, sliding into a whispery almost silent not-quite-snore.

The hole was tight, the blankets tangled and the boy kicked as usual in his sleep, but Dial fell asleep quickly and did not stir until Trevor shook her shoulder, once, very hard. As she woke, he placed his earthy hand across her mouth and she understood the boy was sitting up. All three of them could see through the gap between the roof and the earth: yellow headlights and brighter, whiter quartz lights sweeping over the hut. They heard men's voices, suddenly very loud, as the unlocked door of the hut was broken open and lights brushed everywhere inside, like mad swooping things with sharp glass wings.

The worst was the breaking of the door, the malice of it. She held the boy and covered his small flat ears and he pushed himself against her but he must have heard the true splintering, cursing, stamping boots, the discordant choir of radio instructions. She was her father's daughter as she waited for the men to come. They laid his hands on a pillow before they shot him. She could have burned them all alive.

54

The boy lay between their bodies. He was held more firmly than he had ever been held, by earth, breath, soft Dial, hard Trevor. Dial covered his ears with shuffling hands and kissed his head while the police attacked the hut as if they wished to make it bleed. What made them so angry? Was it him?

He heard the last thing break, and lay on his back and watched the headlights swing across treetops as the police backed and bogged and pushed and finally got away.

Then, just when he thought it was done, he heard them snaking up through other tracks, visiting their neighbors, looking for him there. He woke in full daylight with Trevor shaking him. They came down the hill together, feet wet with dew. The front door was still red but splintered into pieces, a red lightning bolt sticking in the grass.

Stay, Trevor said. Dial held his hand. Trevor went up the steps.

Dial touched his head.

Trevor returned with the shoes they would have to wear to go inside.

When the boy stood at the open door he thought of raccoons ripping at his grandma's trash, bags torn apart, cushions disemboweled, the golden walls busted up like packing cases in the back of Peck's supermarket. Take them home for kindling if you like.

When he saw what he had caused, the boy knew he must go. There was no choice. He knew this before the Puddinghead arrived and the four of them walked through the bush to see what had happened to her daddy's factory, the candles smashed, the walls all broken.

He told the little Puddinghead, I'm going.

As the sun rose in the sky a crowd toured the damage and each place they arrived at he said, I'm going. The sky was so clear. The sounds were so distinct. The cries of the Australian magpie, like nothing else on earth. Who was it who said like an angel gargling in a crystal vase?

No one said he was allowed to stay. He found himself alone, on the edge of a cliff, when everything in him expected to be tugged back, but even Dial could not go with him although she spent all day by his side. They walked through the bush, having a honey sandwich at this place, a glass of milk at that. The hippies were nice to him.

To them he said, I have to go now. He knew what he was saying.

It was too sudden, but it is always too sudden, there is not a sign to tell you that the artery will burst. You walk in the expectation that you will continue to walk and even when you say I have to go you are saying it in the place you are to go from and it is this place, the one that will soon vanish, that inhabits your eyes, your lungs, its earth packed in black moons beneath your nails.

You say things about the future but you have not been there so you do not know.

The boy said, I must go.

Everybody stepped away from him and even when Trevor made him the satchel for his drawings and Dial sat close as breath beside him, and as they lay out the ice-cream wrappers, the leaves, the drawings, the picture of his daddy, the drawing

Dial did of Phil in his zoot suit, and as the case was closed and tied up and Dial wrote his name on both sides, SIXTY-SECOND STREET on one side, KENOZA LAKE on the other, he could feel the lonely air between him and everybody else.

Everything had become so familiar, the kookaburras marking out their territories at dusk, flying in the path of squares and triangles which made a fence, visible to them at least, meaning that this land was theirs.

Only now did they realize the Peugeot had been stolen, towed away. They did not go back inside the hut. It felt as if someone had died in there, as if all the bats and golden light had been suffocated and cut up.

The boy wanted to sleep down in the rain forest, but Trevor said they must sleep in the same place again tonight.

The boy said, Will they come again.

Trevor said they would not come again and Dial began to cry. She said she was sorry. Then Trevor explained how they would get him back to his grandma without Dial getting caught.

There was a ball of ice as big as an egg inside his stomach.

Rebecca will come for you, Trevor said.

He lay rigid, between them, completely alone. Dial cried but he could not even hear her. He did not cry himself. He felt the stone orphan beside him, all of them awake all night. It was ruined, he had ruined it. She should not have cried. He should not have been angry. It was not their fault and that was all he felt all night—I ruined it.

The morning came slow and gray as dirty hands and Dial dressed him and he was polite and so tired, his eyelids gritty. He would not shower but his skin was sour and he held his case of drawings and a hundred dollars in a single bill and Trevor and Dial walked with him down the slippery path past the place where the car had always been and now was nothing but a dark oil stain and down onto the road where it was still too dark to see the red and yellow pebbles in the road. He took two anyway.

Dial held him by his shoulders and kneeled down on the road.

I love you, Che. Every single thing was worth it.

He did not know what to say. He was angry, but he had to go and Trevor tried to say good-bye and then Rebecca's car came hissing on the sandy track, quiet as a shark, and before anything had passed between them all he was in the front seat with his case and he would never see that hut again in all his entire life, or eat the peas or the papaya, and the skin he left behind would turn to powder dust and centuries would pass and that part of him would never leave the valley.

Are you OK?

Yes.

That was all. He did not ask where he was being taken although he could feel his little ball pouch as tough and hard as a chicken gizzard and he watched all the familiar turns in the headlights of Rebecca's car.

Are you taking me to the police?

No, not exactly.

Maybe she thought he knew what was about to happen, but he did not know at all. When they came out on the Bruce Highway she headed north.

Are we going to Canada?

No, not so far, she said. They drove a good while though, much faster than Dial. There was not much traffic on the road and soon she turned in to the left and there was one of those wire gates like Trevor had, and she opened it and closed it, and then they drove up a track and onto a ridge where finally she stopped the car.

It was dawn and the light was lying low across all the paper-bark and cane from Coolum all the way to the great Mount Ninderry. When he got out of the car with his plywood art case, he felt the wind, and the hairs stood up on his bare arms and on his neck and all over his body and he finally looked at Rebecca and understood she did not know what to say.

I didn't know you, she said.

No.

You're a pretty amazing kid.

Thank you.

I'm sorry about your cat, she said.

That's all right.

No, I really am.

And she was crying and hugging him, her big wide face all shining and red, and he was sorry for her but he could not think.

What will happen now?

She blew her nose.

I have to go and tell them where you are.

My grandma.

The police, she said, looking over her shoulder. There was not much to see. A stand of wattles on the distant fence line and a couple of cows.

Is that a bull?

No, she said, as if she knew. I have to get going.

OK.

I'm sorry I bawled.

That's OK, he said.

She held out her hand and he shook it and he watched as the car started and then drove over the hill and down to the right. From the ridge he could see it moving up north, toward some other town. He guessed she would use a call box from far away.

Then there was nothing to do but wait.

They should have given him a sweater. They forgot. He stood and listened to the lonely sad trucks down on the highway and watched what was maybe a hawk circling overhead. He was pretty frightened by then. As if he might be killed or something. When he saw a police car on the road below he lay down. Farther along there was a hole where a rabbit might have lived. He inched along toward it over the short brown grass. He wished he could just lie down with Trevor and Dial and feel the blood and bone and earth around him and never move again.

No one could see him from the road, and he stayed lying down for maybe five minutes and then maybe five minutes more and it must have been at least half an hour before he heard the car and knew that he had finally come to the end.

Always too sudden. He knew that at eight. The end will come like a tree dropping in the night.

He heard the driver riding on the clutch. He turned to look up at the sky and only then, with both ears working, did he understand that the car wasn't coming from the road but from the wattles and the bull, not far away, the ice-blue seven-hundred-miles Vauxhall Cresta moving fast, too fast, across the paddock, lifting and crashing, aiming itself at him, then drifting sideways like a plane about to land, and at the wheel behind the glistening windshield was Anna Xenos, her elbows wide, her head forward, and beside her was Trevor and they were coming so fast that the boy jumped up so as not to get killed and they saw him and opened the passenger door to scoop him up, to hold him tight, to take him now, recklessly, because they would not lose him from their lives.

What happened to the boy in that moment felt as if it could be measured with a twelve-inch ruler, a sharp searing pain that somehow did not hurt. Something stabbed him, he thought. Even as an adult he would believe that something physical had been left inside him—small, smooth, not a pearl, more lustrous, luminous, a sort of seed which he would eventually pretend to believe was simply a memory, nothing more, that he would carry along that littered path which would be his own comic and occasionally disastrous life.

A NOTE ON THE TYPE

This book was set in Caledonia, a typeface designed by W. A. Dwiggins (1880–1956). It belongs to the family of printing types called "modern face" by printers—a term used to mark the change in style of the type letters that occurred around 1800. Caledonia borders on the general design of Scotch Roman but it is more freely drawn than that letter. This version of Caledonia was adapted by David Berlow in 1979.

Composed by North Market Street Graphics,
Lancaster, Pennsylvania
Printed and bound by R. R. Donnelley,
Harrisonburg, Virginia
Designed by Virginia Tan